D1592672

Japanese
Ghost
Stories

This edition is first published in 2023 by Flame Tree 451

FLAME TREE 451
6 Melbray Mews,
Fulham, London SW3 3NS
United Kingdom
www.flametree451.com

Flame Tree 451 is an imprint of Flame Tree Publishing Ltd
www.flametreepublishing.com

A CIP record for this book is available from the British Library

Print ISBN: 978-1-80417-592-7
ebook ISBN: 978-1-80417-596-5

23 25 27 28 26 24
1 3 5 7 8 6 4 2

The stories by Ueda Akinari are used with permission, courtesy of
Monumenta Nipponica, Sophia University, Tokyo.
The stories translated by Marian Ury are used with permission,
courtesy of the University of Michigan Press.
See Biographies & Sources at the back of the book for full citations.

Cover image was created by Flame Tree Studio, based on
elements courtesy Shutterstock.com/Fogey/Joel Askey.

Printed and bound in China

Japanese
Ghost
Stories

With an introduction by
Hiroko Yoda

Contents

Collected by Grace James

Translated by Yei Theodora Ozaki

*Tsuruya Namboku IV, Shunkintei Ryuō et al.,
adapted by James S. De Benneville*

Collected by Richard Gordon Smith

Translated by Marian Ury

Ueda Akinari

Retold by Hiroko Yoda

A Taste for the Fantastic

From mystery to crime, the supernatural and fantasy to science fiction, the terrific range of paperbacks and ebooks from Flame Tree 451 offers a healthy diet of werewolves and mechanicals, vampires and villains, mad scientists, secret worlds, lost civilizations, escapist fantasies and dystopian visions. Discover a storehouse of tales gathered specifically for the reader of the fantastic.

Great works by H.G. Wells and Bram Stoker stand shoulder to shoulder with gripping reads by titans of the gothic novel (Charles Brockden Brown, Nathaniel Hawthorne), and individual novels by literary giants (Jane Austen, Charles Dickens, Emily Brontë) mingle with the intensity of H.P. Lovecraft and the psychological magic of Edgar Allan Poe.

Of course there are classic Conan Doyle adventures, Wilkie Collins mysteries and the pioneering fantasies of Mary Shelley, but there are so many other tales to tell: *The White Worm, Black Magic, The Murder Monster, The Awakening, Darkwater* and more.

Check our website for regular updates and new additions to our curated range of speculative fiction at *flametreepublishing.com*

Introduction

There's no bad time for a good ghost story, of course, but in my homeland of Japan the traditional season for spooks is summer.

There are several reasons for this. One is a very old custom of ours called *obon*, a holiday in August where the spirits of our ancestors are said to visit. Families gather and clean the graves of relatives, offer food and flowers at household altars, and generally welcome the souls of their loved ones for their brief return to the land of the living. It is a time for reminiscence and celebration, for tears and laughter. But the thing about *obon* is that hell goes on holiday, too. The old stories say that when the great hereafter opens up to let our dearly departed pass through, so too does it let all sorts of mischievous spirits and ghouls into our realm. Summer is the perfect time for ghost stories in my country because it's the time when the lines between the living and the dead blur the most.

There is a traditional summer parlour game called *hyaku-monogatari*, literally 'one hundred scary stories,' which was all the rage several centuries ago. People would gather at night and light one hundred candles. They would take turns telling frightening tales, extinguishing a candle after each story was told. As the night went on the light would dim and the shadows grow. There were minor variations on how the game was played, but the goal was always the same: when that last candle snuffed out, something spooky would happen in the inky darkness. The dead of night, indeed.

The Japanese word for ghost is *yurei*, and it is written with characters literally meaning 'intangible spirit.' A yurei is something that manifests in the darkness. The players of *hyaku-monogatari* endeavoured to prepare an environment more suitable for the dead, in hopes that the dead might show themselves to the living. They say the game started as a test of bravery among *samurai* warriors. But whatever its origins, it quickly spread throughout the populace, emerging as a popular form of entertainment during the summer months. For as anyone who has visited Japan in August knows, the doldrums of summer are a terrifically muggy season. We played *hyaku-monogatari* not only for fun, but to conjure up a good shiver or two in hopes of forgetting the heat.

Back then, before the advent of electricity, night descended like a thick curtain. The best one could hope for was the meagre glow of a candle. Today, of course, we have light enough to banish the darkness and illuminate our surroundings twenty-four hours a day. We have air conditioners and dehumidifiers to control our environments so they are always comfortable. And science tells us that ghosts are just superstitions. Yet even in modern Japan, we still love our ghost stories. Why is that?

If you ask me, it's because ghosts remind us of ourselves. The dead cannot speak, but they do have tales. Ghosts aren't a 'something,' they are a 'someone,' just like us. Each of us has our own personal histories and stories. Ghosts are no different. Some of their tales are terrifying, some are brutal, some are bittersweet, and a few are even funny. The huge variety of ghost stories mirrors the ups and downs of our own lives. Because in the end, ghost stories are about people. That is why we feel such an affinity with ghosts and their stories and the myriad ways in which they end. In which we end.

It's safe to say that Lady O-Iwa, the tragic protagonist of *Yotsuya Kaidan* (or *Kwaidan*, as spelt by writers such as Lafcadio Hearn and James S. de Bennevile), is the scariest *yurei* in all of Japan. Tricked into ingesting poison by her philandering husband, the skin sloughs off half her face, her hair falls out in clumps, and she dies in agony, horribly disfigured. But her soul, filled with anger and fuelled by grudge, remains on our mortal plane to take revenge. She looks like a monster, but her story forces us to question the meaning of the term. In life she was a beautiful, dutiful wife and a kind mother. She deserved better than this. We recoil in fear and empathize with her all at once. The conflicting stew of emotions her story evokes in us is what makes *Yotsuya Kaidan* such a classic tale for the ages.

Another classic tale, *Hoichi the Earless*, contains one of the most terrifying images in all of Japanese literature: the *yurei* of a fallen *samurai* tearing the ears off of a young monk. But this story evokes complicated feelings in us as well. That *samurai* was a member of an ancient clan called the Heike, which really existed almost a millennium ago. The Heike were cunning and ruthless and successful. At the peak of their power they ruled all of Japan, arrogantly leading them to declare anyone not of their bloodline less than human. But we have a saying in Japanese. *Shogyo-mujo*: nothing lasts for ever. In the epic sea-battle of Dan-no-Ura in 1185, the Heike were wiped out to a man, woman, and child. Their bodies sank deep into the waters. In the centuries thereafter, and even occasionally today, local fishermen caught crabs with patterns resembling angry human faces on their shells. We call these the Crabs of Heike. It is tradition to release them back into the sea, in hope the souls of that once powerful clan continue to rest in peace. Today Japanese see the Heike as a symbol of the impermanence of things. Because of this, even when fearsome *yurei* such as Heike warriors or O-Iwa manifest, it is difficult for us to see them as pure monsters. They were humans just like us, after all, and so we feel their pain even as they frighten us.

Medical science tells us that death is the inevitable cessation of life. And while we understand this as modern people, at some level we continue to wonder if death truly represents the end. We can't help thinking that maybe, just maybe, our souls might continue to wander even after they leave our corporeal bodies behind. In Japan, the afterlife takes many different forms for different groups and individuals. When I was a little girl, a teacher told us that she thought our souls went back to wherever they came from before we were born. One Buddhist sect holds that the world of the departed lies far to the West; in the lore of our tropical islands, far beyond the horizon to the East. In times of old, some monks set sail in hopes they might reach their school's promised land in the distant South. Shinto locates its underworld deep underground, in caverns far beneath our feet. The point is, nobody knows. The only thing linking these disparate worldviews is the fact that once people die, they are no longer part of our living world.

Ghost stories provide us with another point of view. But unlike religious teachings, they are not doctrine or dogma. They exist to entertain, but also to comfort and even empower us to confront the terrifying concept of death. *Yurei* make us feel that perhaps the world of the dead may not be so very far away as it seems. That the souls of the departed, fearful or beloved, might well sit right beside us. Maybe they're here right now, watching over our shoulders, as I write these words and you read them, perhaps many years hence. That's the power of the *yurei*, to bridge realms: of living and dead, Japan and the world, and all of us, wherever and whenever we may be.

Hiroko Yoda

Japanese
Ghost
Stories

Furisodé
Collected by Lafcadio Hearn

Recently, while passing through a little street tenanted chiefly by dealers in old wares, I noticed a *furisodé*, or long-sleeved robe, of the rich purple tint called *murasaki*, hanging before one of the shops. It was a robe such as might have been worn by a lady of rank in the time of the Tokugawa. I stopped to look at the five crests upon it; and in the same moment there came to my recollection this legend of a similar robe said to have once caused the destruction of Yedo.

Nearly two hundred and fifty years ago, the daughter of a rich merchant of the city of the Shōguns, while attending some temple-festival, perceived in the crowd a young *samurai* of remarkable beauty, and immediately fell in love with him. Unhappily for her, he disappeared in the press before she could learn through her attendants who he was or whence he had come. But his image remained vivid in her memory – even to the least detail of his costume. The holiday attire then worn by *samurai* youths was scarcely less brilliant than that of young girls; and the upper dress of this handsome stranger had seemed wonderfully beautiful to the enamoured maiden. She fancied that by wearing a robe of like quality and colour, bearing the same crest, she might be able to attract his notice on some future occasion.

Accordingly she had such a robe made, with very long sleeves, according to the fashion of the period; and she prized it greatly. She wore it whenever she went out; and when at home she would suspend it in her room, and try to imagine the form of her unknown beloved within it. Sometimes she would pass hours before it – dreaming and weeping by turns. And she would pray to the gods and the Buddhas that she might win the young man's affection – often repeating the invocation of the Nichiren sect: *Namu myō hō rengé kyō!*

But she never saw the youth again; and she pined with longing for him, and sickened, and died, and was buried. After her burial, the long-sleeved robe that she had so much prized was given to the Buddhist temple of which her family were parishioners. It is an old custom to thus dispose of the garments of the dead.

The priest was able to sell the robe at a good price; for it was a costly silk, and bore no trace of the tears that had fallen upon it. It was bought by a girl of about the same age as the dead lady. She wore it only one day. Then she fell sick, and began to act strangely – crying out that she was haunted by the vision of a beautiful young man, and that for love of him she was going to die. And within a little while she died; and the long-sleeved robe was a second time presented to the temple.

Again the priest sold it; and again it became the property of a young girl, who wore it only once. Then she also sickened, and talked of a beautiful shadow, and died, and was buried. And the robe was given a third time to the temple; and the priest wondered and doubted.

Nevertheless he ventured to sell the luckless garment once more. Once more it was purchased by a girl and once more worn; and the wearer pined and died. And the robe was given a fourth time to the temple.

Then the priest felt sure that there was some evil influence at work; and he told his acolytes to make a fire in the temple-court, and to burn the robe.

So they made a fire, into which the robe was thrown. But as the silk began to burn, there suddenly appeared upon it dazzling characters of flame – the characters of the invocation, *Namu myō hō rengé kyō* – and these, one by one, leaped like great sparks to the temple roof; and the temple took fire.

Embers from the burning temple presently dropped upon neighbouring roofs; and the whole street was soon ablaze. Then a sea-wind, rising, blew destruction into further streets; and the conflagration spread from street to street, and from district into district, till nearly the whole of the city was consumed. And this calamity, which occurred upon the eighteenth day of the first month of the first year of Meiréki (1655), is still remembered in Tokyo as the *Furisodé-Kwaji* – the Great Fire of the Long-sleeved Robe.

According to a story-book called *Kibun-Daijin*, the name of the girl who caused the robe to be made was O-Samé; and she was the daughter of Hikoyemon, a wine-merchant of Hyakushō-machi, in the district of Azabu. Because of her beauty she was also called Azabu-Komachi, or the Komachi of Azabu. The same book says that the temple of the tradition was a Nichiren temple called Hon-myoji, in the district of Hongo; and that the crest upon the robe was a *kikyō*-flower. But there are many different versions of the story; and I distrust the *Kibun-Daijin* because it asserts that the beautiful *samurai* was not really a man, but a transformed dragon, or water-serpent, that used to inhabit the lake at Uyéno – Shinobazu-no-Iké.

A Passional Karma
(The Peony Lantern)
Collected by Lafcadio Hearn

I

There once lived in the district of Ushigomé, in Yedo, a *hatamoto* called Iijima Heizayémon, whose only daughter, Tsuyu, was beautiful as her name, which signifies 'Morning Dew'. Iijima took a second wife when his daughter was about sixteen; and, finding that O-Tsuyu could not be happy with her mother-in-law, he had a pretty villa built for the girl at Yanagijima, as a separate residence, and gave her an excellent maidservant, called O-Yoné, to wait upon her.

O-Tsuyu lived happily enough in her new home until one day when the family physician, Yamamoto Shijō, paid her a visit in company with a young *samurai* named Hagiwara Shinzaburō, who resided in the Nedzu quarter. Shinzaburō was an unusually handsome lad, and very gentle; and the two young people fell in love with each other at sight. Even before the brief visit was over, they contrived, – unheard by the old doctor, – to pledge themselves to each other for life. And, at parting, O-Tsuyu whispered to the youth, – *"Remember! If you do not come to see me again, I shall certainly die!"*

Shinzaburō never forgot those words; and he was only too eager to see more of O-Tsuyu. But etiquette forbade him to make the visit alone: he was obliged to wait for some other chance to accompany the doctor, who had promised to take him to the villa a second time. Unfortunately the old man did not keep this promise. He had perceived the sudden affection of O-Tsuyu; and he feared that her father would hold him responsible for any serious results. Iijima Heizayémon had a reputation for cutting off heads. And the more Shijō thought about the possible consequences of his introduction of Shinzaburō at the Iijima villa, the more he became afraid. Therefore he purposely abstained from calling upon his young friend.

Months passed; and O-Tsuyu, little imagining the true cause of Shinzaburō's neglect, believed that her love had been scorned. Then she pined away, and died. Soon afterwards, the faithful servant O-Yoné also died, through grief at the loss of her mistress; and the two were buried side by side in the cemetery of Shin-Banzui-In, – a temple which still stands in the neighbourhood of Dango-Zaka, where the famous chrysanthemum-shows are yearly held.

II

Shinzaburō knew nothing of what had happened; but his disappointment and his anxiety had resulted in a prolonged illness. He was slowly recovering, but still very weak, when he unexpectedly received another visit from Yamamoto Shijō. The old man made a number of plausible excuses for his apparent neglect. Shinzaburō said to him: "I have been sick ever since the beginning of spring; – even now I cannot eat anything.... Was it not rather unkind of you never to call? I thought that we were to make another visit together to the house of the Lady Iijima; and I wanted to take to her some little present as a return for our kind reception. Of course I could not go by myself."

Shijō gravely responded, – "I am very sorry to tell you that the young lady is dead!"

"Dead!" repeated Shinzaburō, turning white, – "did you say that she is dead?"

The doctor remained silent for a moment, as if collecting himself: then he resumed, in the quick light tone of a man resolved not to take trouble seriously:

"My great mistake was in having introduced you to her; for it seems that she fell in love with you at once. I am afraid that you must have said something to encourage this affection – when you were in that little room together. At all events, I saw how she felt towards you; and then I became uneasy, – fearing that her father might come to hear of the matter, and lay the whole blame upon me. So – to be quite frank with you, – I decided that it would be better not to call upon you; and I purposely stayed away for a long time. But, only a few days ago, happening to visit Iijima's house, I heard, to my great surprise, that his daughter had died, and that her servant O-Yoné had also died. Then, remembering all that had taken place, I knew that the young lady must have died of love for you.... [*Laughing*] Ah, you are really a sinful fellow! Yes, you are! [*Laughing*] Isn't it a sin to have been born so handsome that the girls die for love of you? [*Seriously*] Well, we must leave the dead to the dead. It is no use to talk further about the matter; – all that you now can do for her is to repeat the Nembutsu.... Good-bye."

And the old man retired hastily, – anxious to avoid further converse about the painful event for which he felt himself to have been unwittingly responsible.

III

Shinzaburō long remained stupefied with grief by the news of O-Tsuyu's death. But as soon as he found himself again able to think clearly, he inscribed the dead girl's name upon a mortuary tablet, and placed the tablet in the Buddhist shrine of his house, and set offerings before it, and recited prayers. Every day thereafter he presented offerings, and repeated the *Nembutsu*; and the memory of O-Tsuyu was never absent from his thought.

Nothing occurred to change the monotony of his solitude before the time of the Bon, – the great Festival of the Dead, – which begins upon the thirteenth day of the seventh month. Then he decorated his house, and prepared everything for the festival; – hanging out the lanterns that guide the returning spirits, and setting the food of ghosts on the *shōryōdana*, or Shelf of Souls. And on the first evening of the Bon, after sun-down, he kindled a small lamp before the tablet of O-Tsuyu, and lighted the lanterns.

The night was clear, with a great moon, – and windless, and very warm. Shinzaburō sought the coolness of his verandah. Clad only in a light summer-robe, he sat there thinking, dreaming, sorrowing; – sometimes fanning himself; sometimes making a little smoke to drive the mosquitoes away. Everything was quiet. It was a lonesome neighbourhood, and there were few passers-by. He could hear only the soft rushing of a neighbouring stream, and the shrilling of night-insects.

But all at once this stillness was broken by a sound of women's *geta* approaching – *kara-kon, kara-kon;* – and the sound drew nearer and nearer, quickly, till it reached the live-hedge surrounding the garden. Then Shinzaburō, feeling curious, stood on tiptoe, so as to look over the hedge; and he saw two women passing. One, who was carrying a beautiful lantern decorated with peony-flowers, appeared to be a servant; – the other was a slender girl of about seventeen, wearing a long-sleeved robe embroidered with designs of autumn-blossoms. Almost at the same instant both women turned their faces toward Shinzaburō; – and to his utter astonishment, he recognized O-Tsuyu and her servant O-Yoné.

They stopped immediately; and the girl cried out, – "Oh, how strange!... Hagiwara Sama!"

Shinzaburō simultaneously called to the maid: "O-Yoné! Ah, you are O-Yoné! – I remember you very well."

"Hagiwara Sama!" exclaimed O-Yoné in a tone of supreme amazement. "Never could I have believed it possible!... Sir, we were told that you had died."

"How extraordinary!" cried Shinzaburō. "Why, I was told that both of you were dead!"

"Ah, what a hateful story!" returned O-Yoné. "Why repeat such unlucky words?... Who told you?"

"Please to come in," said Shinzaburō; – "here we can talk better. The garden-gate is open."

So they entered, and exchanged greeting; and when Shinzaburō had made them comfortable, he said:

"I trust that you will pardon my discourtesy in not having called upon you for so long a time. But Shijō, the doctor, about a month ago, told me that you had both died."

"So it was he who told you?" exclaimed O-Yoné. "It was very wicked of him to say such a thing. Well, it was also Shijō who told us that *you* were dead. I think that he wanted to deceive you, – which was not a difficult thing to do, because you are so confiding and trustful. Possibly my mistress betrayed her liking for you in some words which found their way to her father's ears; and, in that case, O-Kuni – the new wife – might have planned to make the doctor tell you that we were dead, so as to bring about a separation. Anyhow, when my mistress heard that you had died, she wanted to cut off her hair immediately, and to become a nun. But I was able to prevent her from cutting off her hair; and I persuaded her at last to become a nun only in her heart. Afterwards her father wished her to marry a certain young man; and she refused. Then there was a great deal of trouble, – chiefly caused by O-Kuni; – and we went away from the villa, and found a very small house in Yanaka-no-Sasaki. There we are now just barely able to live, by doing a little private work.... My mistress has been constantly repeating the *Nembutsu* for your sake. Today, being the first day of the Bon, we went to visit the temples; and we were on our way home – thus late – when this strange meeting happened."

"Oh, how extraordinary!" cried Shinzaburō. "Can it be true? – or is it only a dream? Here I, too, have been constantly reciting the *Nembutsu* before a tablet with her name upon it! Look!" And he showed them O-Tsuyu's tablet in its place upon the Shelf of Souls.

"We are more than grateful for your kind remembrance," returned O-Yoné, smiling.... "Now as for my mistress," – she continued, turning towards O-Tsuyu, who had all the while remained demure and silent, half-hiding her face with her sleeve,

– "as for my mistress, she actually says that she would not mind being disowned by her father for the time of seven existences, or even being killed by him, for your sake! Come! will you not allow her to stay here tonight?"

Shinzaburō turned pale for joy. He answered in a voice trembling with emotion:

"Please remain; but do not speak loud – because there is a troublesome fellow living close by, – a *ninsomi* called Hakuōdō Yusai, who tells peoples fortunes by looking at their faces. He is inclined to be curious; and it is better that he should not know."

The two women remained that night in the house of the young *samurai*, and returned to their own home a little before daybreak. And after that night they came every night for seven nights, – whether the weather were foul or fair – always at the same hour. And Shinzaburō became more and more attached to the girl; and the twain were fettered, each to each, by that bond of illusion which is stronger than bands of iron.

IV

Now there was a man called Tomozō, who lived in a small cottage adjoining Shinzaburō's residence. Tomozō and his wife O-Miné were both employed by Shinzaburō as servants. Both seemed to be devoted to their young master; and by his help they were able to live in comparative comfort.

One night, at a very late hour, Tomozō heard the voice of a woman in his master's apartment; and this made him uneasy. He feared that Shinzaburō, being very gentle and affectionate, might be made the dupe of some cunning wanton, – in which event the domestics would be the first to suffer. He therefore resolved to watch; and on the following night he stole on tiptoe to Shinzaburō's dwelling, and looked through a chink in one of the sliding shutters. By the glow of a night-lantern within the sleeping-room, he was able to perceive that his master and a strange woman were talking together under the mosquito-net. At first he could not see the woman distinctly. Her back was turned to him; – he only observed that she was very slim, and that she appeared to be very young, – judging from the fashion of her dress and hair. Putting his ear to the chink, he could hear the conversation plainly. The woman said:

"And if I should be disowned by my father, would you then let me come and live with you?"

Shinzaburō answered:

"Most assuredly I would – nay, I should be glad of the chance. But there is no reason to fear that you will ever be disowned by your father; for you are his only daughter, and he loves you very much. What I do fear is that some day we shall be cruelly separated."

She responded softly:

"Never, never could I even think of accepting any other man for my husband. Even if our secret were to become known, and my father were to kill me for what I have done, still – after death itself – I could never cease to think of you. And I am now quite sure that you yourself would not be able to live very long without me." … Then clinging closely to him, with her lips at his neck, she caressed him; and he returned her caresses.

Tomozō wondered as he listened, – because the language of the woman was not the language of a common woman, but the language of a lady of rank. Then he determined at all hazards to get one glimpse of her face; and he crept round the house, backwards and forwards, peering through every crack and chink. And at last he was able to see; – but therewith an icy trembling seized him; and the hair of his head stood up.

For the face was the face of a woman long dead, – and the fingers caressing were fingers of naked bone, – and of the body below the waist there was not anything: it melted off into thinnest trailing shadow. Where the eyes of the lover deluded saw youth and grace and beauty, there appeared to the eyes of the watcher horror only, and the emptiness of death. Simultaneously another woman's figure, and a weirder, rose up from within the chamber, and swiftly made toward the watcher, as if discerning his presence. Then, in uttermost terror, he fled to the dwelling of Hakuōdō Yusai, and, knocking frantically at the doors, succeeded in arousing him.

V

Hakuōdō Yusai, the *ninsomi*, was a very old man; but in his time he had travelled much, and he had heard and seen so many things that he could not be easily surprised. Yet the story of the terrified Tomozō both alarmed and amazed him. He had read in ancient Chinese books of love between the living and the dead; but he had never believed it possible. Now, however, he felt convinced that the statement of Tomozō was not a falsehood, and that something very strange was really going on in the house of Hagiwara. Should the truth prove to be what Tomozō imagined, then the young *samurai* was a doomed man.

"If the woman be a ghost," – said Yusai to the frightened servant, "—if the woman be a ghost, your master must die very soon, – unless something extraordinary can be done to save him. And if the woman be a ghost, the signs of death will appear upon his face. For the spirit of the living is *yōki*, and pure; – the spirit of the dead is *inki*, and unclean: the one is Positive, the other Negative. He whose bride is a ghost cannot live. Even though in his blood there existed the force of a life of one hundred years, that force must quickly perish.... Still, I shall do all that I can to save Hagiwara Sama. And in the meantime, Tomozō, say nothing to any other person, – not even to your wife, – about this matter. At sunrise I shall call upon your master."

VI

When questioned next morning by Yusai, Shinzaburō at first attempted to deny that any women had been visiting the house; but finding this artless policy of no avail, and perceiving that the old man's purpose was altogether unselfish, he was finally persuaded to acknowledge what had really occurred, and to give his reasons for wishing to keep the matter a secret. As for the lady Iijima, he intended, he said, to make her his wife as soon as possible.

"Oh, madness!" cried Yusai, – losing all patience in the intensity of his alarm. "Know, sir, that the people who have been coming here, night after night, are dead! Some frightful delusion is upon you!... Why, the simple fact that you long supposed O-Tsuyu to be dead, and repeated the *Nembutsu* for her, and made offerings before her tablet, is itself the proof!... The lips of the dead have touched you! – the hands of the dead have caressed you!... Even at this moment I

28

see in your face the signs of death – and you will not believe!… Listen to me now, sir, – I beg of you, – if you wish to save yourself: otherwise you have less than twenty days to live. They told you – those people – that they were residing in the district of Shitaya, in Yanaka-no-Sasaki. Did you ever visit them at that place? No! – of course you did not! Then go today, – as soon as you can, – to Yanaka-no-Sasaki, and try to find their home!…"

And having uttered this counsel with the most vehement earnestness, Hakuōdō Yusai abruptly took his departure.

Shinzaburō, startled though not convinced, resolved after a moment's reflection to follow the advice of the *ninsomi*, and to go to Shitaya. It was yet early in the morning when he reached the quarter of Yanaka-no-Sasaki, and began his search for the dwelling of O-Tsuyu. He went through every street and side-street, read all the names inscribed at the various entrances, and made inquiries whenever an opportunity presented itself. But he could not find anything resembling the little house mentioned by O-Yoné; and none of the people whom he questioned knew of any house in the quarter inhabited by two single women. Feeling at last certain that further research would be useless, he turned homeward by the shortest way, which happened to lead through the grounds of the temple Shin-Banzui-In.

Suddenly his attention was attracted by two new tombs, placed side by side, at the rear of the temple. One was a common tomb, such as might have been erected for a person of humble rank: the other was a large and handsome monument; and hanging before it was a beautiful peony-lantern, which had probably been left there at the time of the Festival of the Dead. Shinzaburō remembered that the peony-lantern carried by O-Yoné was exactly similar; and the coincidence impressed him as strange. He looked again at the tombs; but the tombs explained nothing. Neither bore any personal name, – only the Buddhist *kaimyō*, or posthumous appellation. Then he determined to seek information at the temple. An acolyte stated, in reply to his questions, that the large tomb had been recently erected for the daughter of Iijima Heizayémon, the *hatamoto* of Ushigomé; and that the small tomb next to it was that of her servant O-Yoné, who had died of grief soon after the young lady's funeral.

Immediately to Shinzaburō's memory there recurred, with another and sinister meaning, the words of O-Yoné: "*We went away, and found a very small house in Yanaka-no-Sasaki. There we are now just barely able to live – by doing a little private work….*" Here was indeed the very small house, – and in Yanaka-no-Sasaki. But the little *private work*…?

Terror-stricken, the *samurai* hastened with all speed to the house of Yusai, and begged for his counsel and assistance. But Yusai declared himself unable to be of any aid in such a case. All that he could do was to send Shinzaburō to the high-priest Ryōseki, of Shin-Banzui-In, with a letter praying for immediate religious help.

VII

The high-priest Ryōseki was a learned and a holy man. By spiritual vision he was able to know the secret of any sorrow, and the nature of the karma that had caused it. He heard unmoved the story of Shinzaburō, and said to him:

"A very great danger now threatens you, because of an error committed in one of your former states of existence. The karma that binds you to the dead is very strong; but if I tried to explain its character, you would not be able to understand. I shall therefore tell you only this, – that the dead person has no desire to injure you out of hate, feels no enmity towards you: she is influenced, on the contrary, by the most passionate affection for you. Probably the girl has been in love with you from a time long preceding your present life, – from a time of not less than three or four past existences; and it would seem that, although necessarily changing her form and condition at each succeeding birth, she has not been able to cease from following after you. Therefore it will not be an easy thing to escape from her influence.... But now I am going to lend you this powerful *mamori*. It is a pure gold image of that Buddha called the Sea-Sounding Tathâgata – *Kai-On-Nyōrai*, – because his preaching of the Law sounds through the world like the sound of the sea. And this little image is especially a *shiryō-yoké*, – which protects the living from the dead. This you must wear, in its covering, next to your body – under the girdle.... Besides, I shall presently perform in the temple, a segaki-service for the repose of the troubled spirit.... And here is a holy sutra, called *Ubō-Darani-Kyō*, or 'Treasure-Raining Sûtra' you must be careful to recite it every night in your house – without fail.... Furthermore I shall give you this package of *o-fuda*; – you must paste one of them over every opening of your house, – no matter how small. If you do this, the power of the holy texts will prevent the dead from entering. But – whatever may happen – do not fail to recite the sutra."

Shinzaburō humbly thanked the high-priest; and then, taking with him the image, the sutra, and the bundle of sacred texts, he made all haste to reach his home before the hour of sunset.

VIII

With Yusai's advice and help, Shinzaburō was able before dark to fix the holy texts over all the apertures of his dwelling. Then the *ninsomi* returned to his own house – leaving the youth alone.

Night came, warm and clear. Shinzaburō made fast the doors, bound the precious amulet about his waist, entered his mosquito-net, and by the glow of a night-lantern began to recite the *Ubō-Darani-Kyō*. For a long time he chanted the words, comprehending little of their meaning; – then he tried to obtain some rest. But his mind was still too much disturbed by the strange events of the day. Midnight passed; and no sleep came to him. At last he heard the boom of the great temple-bell of Dentsu-In announcing the eighth hour.

It ceased; and Shinzaburō suddenly heard the sound of *geta* approaching from the old direction, – but this time more slowly: *karan-koron, karan-koron*! At once a cold sweat broke over his forehead. Opening the sutra hastily, with trembling hand, he began again to recite it aloud. The steps came nearer and nearer, – reached the live hedge, – stopped! Then, strange to say, Shinzaburō felt unable to remain under his mosquito-net: something stronger even than his fear impelled him to look; and, instead of continuing to recite the *Ubō-Darani-Kyō*, he foolishly approached the shutters, and through a chink peered out into the night. Before the house he saw O-Tsuyu standing, and O-Yoné with the peony-lantern; and both of them were gazing at the Buddhist texts pasted above the entrance. Never before – not even in what time she lived – had O-Tsuyu appeared so beautiful; and Shinzaburō felt his heart drawn towards her with a power almost resistless. But the terror of death and the terror of the unknown restrained; and there went on within him such a struggle between his love and his fear that he became as one suffering in the body the pains of the Shō-netsu hell.

Presently he heard the voice of the maid-servant, saying:

"My dear mistress, there is no way to enter. The heart of Hagiwara Sama must have changed. For the promise that he made last night has been broken; and the doors have been made fast to keep us out.... We cannot go in tonight.... It will be wiser for you to make up your mind not to think any more about him, because his feeling towards you has certainly changed. It is evident that he does not want to see you. So it will be better not to give yourself any more trouble for the sake of a man whose heart is so unkind."

But the girl answered, weeping:

"Oh, to think that this could happen after the pledges which we made to each other!... Often I was told that the heart of a man changes as quickly as the sky of autumn; – yet surely the heart of Hagiwara Sama cannot be so cruel that he should really intend to exclude me in this way!... Dear Yone, please find some means of taking me to him.... Unless you do, I will never, never go home again."

Thus she continued to plead, veiling her face with her long sleeves, – and very beautiful she looked, and very touching; but the fear of death was strong upon her lover.

O-Yoné at last made answer, – "My dear young lady, why will you trouble your mind about a man who seems to be so cruel?... Well, let us see if there be no way to enter at the back of the house: come with me!"

And taking O-Tsuyu by the hand, she led her away toward the rear of the dwelling; and there the two disappeared as suddenly as the light disappears when the flame of a lamp is blown out.

IX

Night after night the shadows came at the Hour of the Ox; and nightly Shinzaburō heard the weeping of O-Tsuyu. Yet he believed himself saved, – little imagining that his doom had already been decided by the character of his dependents.

Tomozō had promised Yusai never to speak to any other person – not even to O-Miné – of the strange events that were taking place. But Tomozō was not long suffered by the haunters to rest in peace. Night after night O-Yoné entered into his dwelling, and roused him from his sleep, and asked him to remove the *o-fuda* placed over one very small window at the back of his master's house. And Tomozō, out of fear, as often promised her to take away the *o-fuda* before the next sundown; but never by day could he make up his mind to remove it, – believing that evil was intended to Shinzaburō. At last, in a night of storm, O-Yoné startled him from slumber with a cry of reproach, and stooped above his pillow, and said to him: "Have a care how you trifle with us! If, by tomorrow night, you do not take away that text, you shall learn how I can hate!" And she made her face so frightful as she spoke that Tomozō nearly died of terror.

O-Miné, the wife of Tomozō, had never till then known of these visits: even to her husband they had seemed like bad dreams. But on this particular night it chanced that, waking suddenly, she heard the voice of a woman talking to Tomozō. Almost in the same moment the talk-ing ceased; and when O-Miné looked about her, she saw, by the light of the night-lamp, only her husband, – shuddering and white with fear. The stranger was gone; the doors were fast: it seemed impossible that anybody could have entered. Nevertheless the jealousy of the wife had been aroused; and she began to chide

34

and to question Tomozō in such a manner that he thought himself obliged to betray the secret, and to explain the terrible dilemma in which he had been placed.

Then the passion of O-Miné yielded to wonder and alarm; but she was a subtle woman, and she devised immediately a plan to save her husband by the sacrifice of her master. And she gave Tomozō a cunning counsel, – telling him to make conditions with the dead.

They came again on the following night at the Hour of the Ox; and O-Miné hid herself on hearing the sound of their coming, – *karan-koron, karan-koron*! But Tomozō went out to meet them in the dark, and even found courage to say to them what his wife had told him to say:

"It is true that I deserve your blame; – but I had no wish to cause you anger. The reason that the *o-fuda* has not been taken away is that my wife and I are able to live only by the help of Hagiwara Sama, and that we cannot expose him to any danger without bringing misfortune upon ourselves. But if we could obtain the sum of a hundred *ryō* in gold, we should be able to please you, because we should then need no help from anybody. Therefore if you will give us a hundred *ryō*, I can take the *o-fuda* away without being afraid of losing our only means of support."

When he had uttered these words, O-Yoné and O-Tsuyu looked at each other in silence for a moment. Then O-Yoné said:

"Mistress, I told you that it was not right to trouble this man, – as we have no just cause of ill will against him. But it is certainly useless to fret yourself about Hagiwara Sama, because his heart has changed towards you. Now once again, my dear young lady, let me beg you not to think any more about him!"

But O-Tsuyu, weeping, made answer:

"Dear Yone, whatever may happen, I cannot possibly keep myself from thinking about him! You know that you can get a hundred *ryō* to have the *o-fuda* taken off.... Only once more, I pray, dear Yone! – only once more bring me face to face with Hagiwara Sama, – I beseech you!" And hiding her face with her sleeve, she thus continued to plead.

"Oh! why will you ask me to do these things?" responded O-Yoné. "You know very well that I have no money. But since you will persist in this whim of yours, in spite of all that I can say, I suppose that I must try to find the money somehow, and to bring it here tomorrow night...." Then, turning to the faithless Tomozō, she said: "Tomozō, I must tell you that Hagiwara Sama now wears upon his body a *mamori* called by the name of *Kai-On-Nyōrai*, and that so long as he wears it we cannot approach him. So you will have to get that *mamori* away from him, by some means or other, as well as to remove the *o-fuda*."

Tomozō feebly made answer:

"That also I can do, if you will promise to bring me the hundred *ryō*."

"Well, mistress," said O-Yoné, "you will wait, – will you not, – until tomorrow night?"

"Oh, dear Yoné!" sobbed the other, – "have we to go back tonight again without seeing Hagiwara Sama? Ah! it is cruel!"

And the shadow of the mistress, weeping, was led away by the shadow of the maid.

X

Another day went, and another night came, and the dead came with it. But this time no lamentation was heard without the house of

Hagiwara; for the faithless servant found his reward at the Hour of the Ox, and removed the *o-fuda*. Moreover he had been able, while his master was at the bath, to steal from its case the golden *mamori*, and to substitute for it an image of copper; and he had buried the *Kai-On-Nyōrai* in a desolate field. So the visitants found nothing to oppose their entering. Veiling their faces with their sleeves they rose and passed, like a streaming of vapour, into the little window from over which the holy text had been torn away. But what happened thereafter within the house Tomozō never knew.

The sun was high before he ventured again to approach his master's dwelling, and to knock upon the sliding-doors. For the first time in years he obtained no response; and the silence made him afraid. Repeatedly he called, and received no answer. Then, aided by O-Miné, he succeeded in effecting an entrance and making his way alone to the sleeping-room, where he called again in vain. He rolled back the rumbling shutters to admit the light; but still within the house there was no stir. At last he dared to lift a corner of the mosquito-net. But no sooner had he looked beneath than he fled from the house, with a cry of horror.

Shinzaburō was dead – hideously dead; – and his face was the face of a man who had died in the uttermost agony of fear; – and lying beside him in the bed were the bones of a woman! And the bones of the arms, and the bones of the hands, clung fast about his neck.

XI

Hakuōdō Yusai, the fortune-teller, went to view the corpse at the prayer of the faithless Tomozō. The old man was terrified and astonished at the spectacle, but looked about him with a keen eye. He soon perceived that the *o-fuda* had been taken from the little window at the back of the house; and on searching the body of Shinzaburō, he discovered that the golden *mamori* had been taken from its wrapping, and a copper image of Fudō put in place of it. He suspected Tomozō of the theft; but the whole occurrence was so very extraordinary that he thought it prudent to consult with the priest Ryōseki before taking further action. Therefore, after having made a careful examination of the premises, he betook himself to the temple Shin-Banzui-In, as quickly as his aged limbs could bear him.

Ryōseki, without waiting to hear the purpose of the old man's visit, at once invited him into a private apartment.

"You know that you are always welcome here," said Ryōseki. "Please seat yourself at ease.... Well, I am sorry to tell you that Hagiwara Sama is dead."

Yusai wonderingly exclaimed: "Yes, he is dead; – but how did you learn of it?"

The priest responded:

"Hagiwara Sama was suffering from the results of an evil karma; and his attendant was a bad man. What happened to Hagiwara Sama was unavoidable; – his destiny had been determined from a time long before his last birth. It will be better for you not to let your mind be troubled by this event."

Yusai said:

"I have heard that a priest of pure life may gain power to see into the future for a hundred years; but truly this is the first time in my existence that I have had proof of such power.... Still, there is another matter about which I am very anxious...."

"You mean," interrupted Ryōseki, "the stealing of the holy *mamori*, the *Kai-On-Nyōrai*. But you must not give yourself any concern about that. The image has been buried in a field; and it will be found there and returned to me during the eighth month of the coming year. So please do not be anxious about it."

More and more amazed, the old *ninsomi* ventured to observe:

"I have studied the *In-Yō*, and the science of divination; and I make my living by telling peoples' fortunes; – but I cannot possibly understand how you know these things."

Ryōseki answered gravely:

"Never mind how I happen to know them.... I now want to speak to you about Hagiwara's funeral. The House of Hagiwara has its own family-cemetery, of course; but to bury him there would not be proper. He must be buried beside O-Tsuyu, the Lady Iijima; for his karma-relation to her was a very deep one. And it is but right that you should erect a tomb for him at your own cost, because you have been indebted to him for many favours."

Thus it came to pass that Shinzaburō was buried beside O-Tsuyu, in the cemetery of Shin-Banzui-In, in Yanaka-no-Sasaki.

Ingwa-banashi
Collected by Lafcadio Hearn

The daimyo's wife was dying, and knew that she was dying. She had not been able to leave her bed since the early autumn of the tenth Bunsei. It was now the fourth month of the twelfth Bunsei, – the year 1829 by Western counting; and the cherry-trees were blossoming. She thought of the cherry-trees in her garden, and of the gladness of spring. She thought of her children. She thought of her husband's various concubines, – especially the Lady Yukiko, nineteen years old.

"My dear wife," said the *daimyo*, "you have suffered very much for three long years. We have done all that we could to get you well, – watching beside you night and day, praying for you, and often fasting for your sake, But in spite of our loving care, and in spite of the skill of our best physicians, it would now seem that the end of your life is not far off. Probably we shall sorrow more than you will sorrow because of your having to leave what the Buddha so truly termed 'this burning-house of the world'. I shall order to be performed – no matter what the cost – every religious rite that can serve you in regard to your next rebirth; and all of us will pray without ceasing for you, that you may not have to wander in the Black Space, but may quickly enter Paradise, and attain to Buddha-hood."

He spoke with the utmost tenderness, pressing her the while. Then, with eyelids closed, she answered him in a voice thin as the voice of in insect:

"I am grateful – most grateful – for your kind words.... Yes, it is true, as you say, that I have been sick for three long years, and that I have been treated with all possible care and affection.... Why, indeed, should I turn away from the one true Path at the very moment of my death?... Perhaps to think of worldly matters at such a time is not right; – but I have one last request to make, – only one.... Call here to me the Lady Yukiko; – you know that I love her like a sister. I want to speak to her about the affairs of this household."

Yukiko came at the summons of the lord, and, in obedience to a sign from him, knelt down beside the couch. The *daimyo*'s wife opened her eyes, and looked at Yukiko, and spoke: "Ah, here is Yukiko!... I am so pleased to see you, Yukiko!... Come a little closer, – so that you can hear me well: I am not able to speak loud.... Yukiko, I am going to die. I hope that you will be faithful in all things to our dear lord; – for I want you to take my place when I am gone.... I hope that you will always be loved by him, – yes, even a hundred times more than I have been, – and that you will very soon be promoted to a higher rank, and become his honoured wife.... And I beg of you always to cherish our dear lord: never allow another woman to rob you of his affection.... This is what I wanted to say to you, dear Yukiko.... Have you been able to understand?"

"Oh, my dear Lady," protested Yukiko, "do not, I entreat you, say such strange things to me! You well know that I am of poor and mean condition: how could I ever dare to aspire to become the wife of our lord!"

"Nay, nay!" returned the wife, huskily, – "this is not a time for words of ceremony: let us speak only the truth to each other. After my death, you will certainly be promoted to a higher place; and I now assure you again that I wish you to become the wife of our lord – yes, I wish this, Yukiko, even more than I wish to become a Buddha!... Ah, I had almost forgotten! – I want you to do something for me, Yukiko. You know that in the garden there is a *yaë-zakura*, which was brought here, the year before last, from Mount Yoshino in Yamato. I have been told that it is now in full bloom; – and I wanted so much to see it in flower! In a little while I shall be dead; – I must see that tree before I die. Now I wish you to carry me into the garden – at once, Yukiko, – so that I can see it.... Yes, upon your back, Yukiko; – take me upon your back...."

While thus asking, her voice had gradually become clear and strong, – as if the intensity of the wish had given her new force: then she suddenly burst into tears. Yukiko knelt motionless, not knowing what to do; but the lord nodded assent.

"It is her last wish in this world," he said. "She always loved cherry-flowers; and I know that she wanted very much to see that Yamato-tree in blossom. Come, my dear Yukiko, let her have her will."

As a nurse turns her back to a child, that the child may cling to it, Yukiko offered her shoulders to the wife, and said:

"Lady, I am ready: please tell me how I best can help you."

"Why, this way!" – responded the dying woman, lifting herself with an almost superhuman effort by clinging to Yukiko's shoulders. But as she stood erect, she quickly slipped her thin hands down over the shoulders, under the robe, and clutched the breasts of the girl, and burst into a wicked laugh.

"I have my wish!" she cried – "I have my wish for the cherry-bloom, – but not the cherry-bloom of the garden!… I could not die before I got my wish. Now I have it! – oh, what a delight!"

And with these words she fell forward upon the crouching girl, and died.

The attendants at once attempted to lift the body from Yukiko's shoulders, and to lay it upon the bed. But – strange to say! – this seemingly easy thing could not be done. The cold hands had attached themselves in some unaccountable way to the breasts of the girl, – appeared to have grown into the quick flesh. Yukiko became senseless with fear and pain.

Physicians were called. They could not understand what had taken place. By no ordinary methods could the hands of the dead woman be unfastened from the body of her victim; – they so clung that any effort to remove them brought blood. This was not because the fingers held: it was because the flesh of the palms had united itself in some inexplicable manner to the flesh of the breasts!

At that time the most skilful physician in Yedo was a foreigner, – a Dutch surgeon. It was decided to summon him. After a careful examination he said that he could not understand the case, and that for the immediate relief of Yukiko there was nothing to be done except to cut the hands from the corpse. He declared that it would be dangerous to attempt to detach them from the breasts. His advice was accepted; and the hands' were amputated at the wrists. But they remained clinging to the breasts; and there they soon darkened and dried up, – like the hands of a person long dead.

Yet this was only the beginning of the horror.

Withered and bloodless though they seemed, those hands were not dead. At intervals they would stir – stealthily, like great grey spiders. And nightly thereafter, – beginning always at the Hour of the Ox, – they would clutch and compress and torture. Only at the Hour of the Tiger the pain would cease.

Yukiko cut off her hair, and became a mendicant-nun, – taking the religious name of Dassetsu. She had an *ihai* (mortuary tablet) made, bearing the *kaimyō* of her dead mistress, – '*Myō-Kō-In-Den Chizan-Ryō-Fu Daishi*'; – and this she carried about with her in all her wanderings; and every day before it she humbly besought the dead for pardon, and performed a Buddhist service in order that the jealous spirit might find rest. But the evil karma that had rendered such an affliction possible could not soon be exhausted. Every night at the Hour of the Ox, the hands never failed to torture her, during more than seventeen years, – according to the testimony of those persons to whom she last told her story, when she stopped for one evening at the house of Noguchi Dengozayémon, in the village of Tanaka in the district of Kawachi in the province of Shimotsuké. This was in the third year of Kōkwa (1846). Thereafter nothing more was ever heard of her.

Jiu-roku-zakura
Collected by Lafcadio Hearn

In Wakegori, a district of the province of Iyo, there is a very ancient and famous cherry-tree, called Jiu-roku-zakura, or 'the Cherry-tree of the Sixteenth Day', because it blooms every year upon the sixteenth day of the first month (by the old lunar calendar), – and only upon that day. Thus the time of its flowering is the Period of Great Cold, – though the natural habit of a cherry-tree is to wait for the spring season before venturing to blossom. But the Jiu-roku-zakura blossoms with a life that is not – or, at least, that was not originally – its own. There is the ghost of a man in that tree.

He was a *samurai* of Iyo; and the tree grew in his garden; and it used to flower at the usual time, – that is to say, about the end of March or the beginning of April. He had played under that tree when he was a child; and his parents and grandparents and ancestors had hung to its blossoming branches, season after season for more than a hundred years, bright strips of coloured paper inscribed with poems of praise. He himself became very old, – outliving all his children; and there was nothing in the world left for him to live except that tree. And lo! in the summer of a certain year, the tree withered and died!

45

Exceedingly the old man sorrowed for his tree. Then kind neighbours found for him a young and beautiful cherry-tree, and planted it in his garden, – hoping thus to comfort him. And he thanked them, and pretended to be glad. But really his heart was full of pain; for he had loved the old tree so well that nothing could have consoled him for the loss of it.

At last there came to him a happy thought: he remembered a way by which the perishing tree might be saved. (It was the sixteenth day of the first month.) Along he went into his garden, and bowed down before the withered tree, and spoke to it, saying: "Now deign, I beseech you, once more to bloom, – because I am going to die in your stead." (For it is believed that one can really give away one's life to another person, or to a creature or even to a tree, by the favour of the gods; – and thus to transfer one's life is expressed by the term *migawari ni tatsu*, 'to act as a substitute'.) Then under that tree he spread a white cloth, and divers coverings, and sat down upon the coverings, and performed hara-kiri after the fashion of a *samurai*. And the ghost of him went into the tree, and made it blossom in that same hour.

And every year it still blooms on the sixteenth day of the first month, in the season of snow.

Yuki-Onna

Collected by Lafcadio Hearn

In a village of Musashi Province, there lived two woodcutters: Mosaku and Minokichi. At the time of which I am speaking, Mosaku was an old man; and Minokichi, his apprentice, was a lad of eighteen years. Every day they went together to a forest situated about five miles from their village. On the way to that forest there is a wide river to cross; and there is a ferry-boat. Several times a bridge was built where the ferry is; but the bridge was each time carried away by a flood. No common bridge can resist the current there when the river rises.

Mosaku and Minokichi were on their way home, one very cold evening, when a great snowstorm overtook them. They reached the ferry; and they found that the boatman had gone away, leaving his boat on the other side of the river. It was no day for swimming; and the woodcutters took shelter in the ferryman's hut, – thinking themselves lucky to find any shelter at all. There was no brazier in the hut, nor any place in which to make a fire: it was only a two-mat hut, with a single door, but no window. Mosaku and Minokichi fastened the door, and lay down to rest, with their straw rain-coats over them. At first they did not feel very cold; and they thought that the storm would soon be over.

The old man almost immediately fell asleep; but the boy, Minokichi, lay awake a long time, listening to the awful wind, and the continual slashing of the snow against the door. The river was roaring; and the hut swayed and creaked like a junk at sea. It was a terrible storm; and the air was every moment becoming colder; and Minokichi shivered under his rain-coat. But at last, in spite of the cold, he too fell asleep.

He was awakened by a showering of snow in his face. The door of the hut had been forced open; and, by the snow-light (*yuki-akari*), he saw a woman in the room, – a woman all in white. She was bending above Mosaku, and blowing her breath upon him; – and her breath was like a bright white smoke. Almost in the same moment she turned to Minokichi, and stooped over him. He tried to cry out, but found that he could not utter any sound. The white woman bent down over him, lower and lower, until her face almost touched him; and he saw that she was very beautiful, – though her eyes made him afraid. For a little time she continued to look at him; – then she smiled, and she whispered: "I intended to treat you like the other man. But I cannot help feeling some pity for you, – because you are so young.... You are a pretty boy, Minokichi; and I will not hurt you now. But, if you ever tell anybody – even your own mother – about what you have seen this night, I shall know it; and then I will kill you.... Remember what I say!"

With these words, she turned from him, and passed through the doorway. Then he found himself able to move; and he sprang up, and looked out. But the woman was nowhere to be seen; and the snow was driving furiously into the hut. Minokichi closed the door, and secured it by fixing several billets of wood against it. He wondered if the wind had blown it open; – he thought that he might have been only dreaming, and might have mistaken the gleam of the snow-light in the doorway for the figure of a white woman: but he could not be sure. He called to Mosaku, and was frightened because the old man did not answer. He put out his hand in the dark, and touched Mosaku's face, and found that it was ice! Mosaku was stark and dead...

By dawn the storm was over; and when the ferryman returned to his station, a little after sunrise, he found Minokichi lying senseless beside the frozen body of Mosaku. Minokichi was promptly cared for, and soon came to himself; but he remained a long time ill from the effects of the cold of that terrible night. He had been greatly frightened also by the old man's death; but he said nothing about the vision of the woman in white. As soon as he got well again, he returned to his calling, – going alone every morning to the forest, and coming back at nightfall with his bundles of wood, which his mother helped him to sell.

One evening, in the winter of the following year, as he was on his way home, he overtook a girl who happened to be travelling by the same road. She was a tall, slim girl, very good-looking; and she answered Minokichi's greeting in a voice as pleasant to the ear as the voice of a song-bird. Then he walked beside her; and they began to talk. The girl said that her name was O-Yuki; that she had lately lost both of her parents; and that she was going to Yedo, where she happened to have some poor relations, who might help her to find a situation as a servant. Minokichi soon felt charmed by this strange girl; and the more that he looked at her, the handsomer she appeared to be. He asked her whether she was yet betrothed; and she answered, laughingly, that she was free. Then, in her turn, she asked Minokichi whether he was married, or pledged to marry; and he told her that, although he had only a widowed mother to support, the question of an 'honourable daughter-in-law' had not yet been considered, as he was very young.… After these confidences, they walked on for a long while without speaking; but, as the proverb declares, *Ki ga areba, me mo kuchi hodo ni mono wo iu*: "When the wish is there, the eyes can say as much as the mouth." By the time they reached the village, they had become very much pleased with each other; and then Minokichi asked O-Yuki to rest awhile at his house. After some shy hesitation, she went there with him; and his mother made her welcome, and prepared a warm meal for her. O-Yuki behaved so nicely that Minokichi's mother took a sudden fancy to her, and persuaded her to delay her journey to Yedo. And the natural end of the matter was that Yuki never went to Yedo at all. She remained in the house, as an 'honourable daughter-in-law'.

O-Yuki proved a very good daughter-in-law. When Minokichi's mother came to die, – some five years later, – her last words were words of affection and praise for the wife of her son. And O-Yuki bore Minokichi ten children, boys and girls, – handsome children all of them, and very fair of skin.

The country-folk thought O-Yuki a wonderful person, by nature different from themselves. Most of the peasant-women age early; but O-Yuki, even after having become the mother of ten children, looked as young and fresh as on the day when she had first come to the village.

One night, after the children had gone to sleep, O-Yuki was sewing by the light of a paper lamp; and Minokichi, watching her, said:

"To see you sewing there, with the light on your face, makes me think of a strange thing that happened when I was a lad of eighteen.

I then saw somebody as beautiful and white as you are now – indeed, she was very like you...."

Without lifting her eyes from her work, O-Yuki responded:

"Tell me about her.... Where did you see her?"

Then Minokichi told her about the terrible night in the ferryman's hut, – and about the White Woman that had stooped above him, smiling and whispering, – and about the silent death of old Mosaku. And he said:

"Asleep or awake, that was the only time that I saw a being as beautiful as you. Of course, she was not a human being; and I was afraid of her, – very much afraid, – but she was so white!... Indeed, I have never been sure whether it was a dream that I saw, or the Woman of the Snow...."

O-Yuki flung down her sewing, and arose, and bowed above Minokichi where he sat, and shrieked into his face:

"It was I – I – I! Yuki it was! And I told you then that I would kill you if you ever said one word about it!... But for those children asleep there, I would kill you this moment! And now you had better take very, very good care of them; for if ever they have reason to complain of you, I will treat you as you deserve!..."

Even as she screamed, her voice became thin, like a crying of wind; – then she melted into a bright white mist that spired to the roof-beams, and shuddered away through the smoke-hole.... Never again was she seen.

Hoichi the Earless
(Mimi-nashi Hōichi no Hanashi)
Collected by Lafcadio Hearn

More than seven hundred years ago, at Dan-no-ura, in the Straits of Shimonoseki, was fought the last battle of the long contest between the Heiké, or Taira clan, and the Genji, or Minamoto clan. There the Heiké perished utterly, with their women and children, and their infant emperor likewise – now remembered as Antoku Tenno. And that sea and shore have been haunted for seven hundred years.... Elsewhere I told you about the strange crabs found there, called Heiké crabs, which have human faces on their backs, and are said to be the spirits of the Heiké warriors. But there are many strange things to be seen and heard along that coast. On dark nights thousands of ghostly fires hover about the beach, or flit above the waves, – pale lights which the fishermen call *Oni-bi*, or demon-fires; and, whenever the winds are up, a sound of great shouting comes from that sea, like a clamour of battle.

In former years the Heiké were much more restless than they now are. They would rise about ships passing in the night, and try to sink them; and at all times they would watch for swimmers, to pull them down. It was in order to appease those dead that the

Buddhist temple, Amidaji, was built at Akamagaseki. A cemetery also was made close by, near the beach; and within it were set up monuments inscribed with the names of the drowned emperor and of his great vassals; and Buddhist services were regularly performed there, on behalf of the spirits of them. After the temple had been built, and the tombs erected, the Heiké gave less trouble than before; but they continued to do queer things at intervals, – proving that they had not found the perfect peace.

Some centuries ago there lived at Akamagaseki a blind man named Hoichi, who was famed for his skill in recitation and in playing upon the *biwa*. From childhood he had been trained to recite and to play; and while yet a lad he had surpassed his teachers. As a professional *biwa-hoshi* he became famous chiefly by his recitations of the history of the Heiké and the Genji; and it is said that when he sang the song of the battle of Dan-no-ura "even the goblins [kijin] could not refrain from tears."

At the outset of his career, Hoichi was very poor; but he found a good friend to help him. The priest of the Amidaji was fond of poetry and music; and he often invited Hoichi to the temple, to play and recite. Afterwards, being much impressed by the wonderful skill of the lad, the priest proposed that Hoichi should make the temple his home; and this offer was gratefully accepted. Hoichi was given a room in the temple-building; and, in return for food and lodging, he was required only to gratify the priest with a musical performance on certain evenings, when otherwise disengaged.

One summer night the priest was called away, to perform a Buddhist service at the house of a dead parishioner; and he went there with his acolyte, leaving Hoichi alone in the temple. It was a hot night; and the blind man sought to cool himself on the verandah before his sleeping-room. The verandah overlooked a small garden in the rear of the Amidaji. There Hoichi waited for the priest's return, and tried to relieve his solitude by practicing upon his *biwa*. Midnight passed; and the priest did not appear. But the atmosphere was still too warm for comfort within doors; and Hoichi remained outside. At last he heard steps approaching from the back gate. Somebody crossed the garden, advanced to the verandah, and halted directly in front of him – but it was not the priest. A deep voice called the blind man's name – abruptly and unceremoniously, in the manner of a *samurai* summoning an inferior:

"Hoichi!"

Hoichi was too much startled, for the moment, to respond; and the voice called again, in a tone of harsh command, –

"Hoichi!"

"*Hai*!" answered the blind man, frightened by the menace in the voice, – "I am blind! – I cannot know who calls!"

"There is nothing to fear," the stranger exclaimed, speaking more gently. "I am stopping near this temple, and have been sent to you with a message. My present lord, a person of exceedingly high rank, is now staying in Akamagaseki, with many noble attendants. He wished to view the scene of the battle of Dan-no-ura; and today he visited that place. Having heard of your skill in reciting the story of the battle, he now desires to hear your performance: so you will take your *biwa* and come with me at once to the house where the august assembly is waiting."

In those times, the order of a *samurai* was not to be lightly disobeyed. Hoichi donned his sandals, took his *biwa*, and went away with the stranger, who guided him deftly, but obliged him to walk very fast. The hand that guided was iron; and the clank of the warrior's stride proved him fully armed, – probably some palace-guard on duty. Hoichi's first alarm was over: he began to imagine himself in good luck; – for, remembering the retainer's assurance about a "person of exceedingly high rank," he thought that the lord who wished to hear the recitation could not be less than a *daimyo* of the first class. Presently the *samurai* halted; and Hoichi became aware that they had arrived at a large gateway; – and he wondered, for he could not remember any large gate in that part of the town, except the main gate of the Amidaji. "*Kaimon!*" the *samurai* called, – and there was a sound of unbarring; and the twain passed on. They traversed a space of garden, and halted again before some entrance; and the retainer cried in a loud voice, "Within there! I have brought Hoichi." Then came sounds of feet hurrying, and screens sliding, and rain-doors opening, and voices of women in converse. By the language of the women Hoichi knew them to be domestics in some noble household; but he could not imagine to what place he had been conducted. Little time was allowed him for conjecture. After he had been helped to mount several stone steps, upon the last of which he was told to leave his sandals, a woman's hand guided him along interminable reaches of polished planking, and round pillared angles too many to remember, and over widths amazing of matted floor, – into the middle of some vast apartment. There he thought that many great people were assembled: the sound of the rustling of silk was like the sound of leaves in a forest. He heard also a great humming of voices, – talking in undertones; and the speech was the speech of courts.

Hoichi was told to put himself at ease, and he found a kneeling-cushion ready for him. After having taken his place upon it, and tuned his instrument, the voice of a woman – whom he divined to be the *Rojo*, or matron in charge of the female service – addressed him, saying, –

"It is now required that the history of the Heiké be recited, to the accompaniment of the *biwa*."

Now the entire recital would have required a time of many nights: therefore Hoichi ventured a question:

"As the whole of the story is not soon told, what portion is it augustly desired that I now recite?"

The woman's voice made answer:

"Recite the story of the battle at Dan-no-ura, – for the pity of it is the most deep."

Then Hoichi lifted up his voice, and chanted the chant of the fight on the bitter sea, – wonderfully making his *biwa* to sound like the straining of oars and the rushing of ships, the whirr and the hissing of arrows, the shouting and trampling of men, the crashing of steel upon helmets, the plunging of slain in the flood. And to left and right of him, in the pauses of his playing, he could hear voices murmuring praise: "How marvellous an artist!" – "Never in our own province was playing heard like this!" – "Not in all the empire is there another singer like Hoichi!" Then fresh courage came to him, and he played and sang yet better than before; and a hush of wonder deepened about him. But when at last he came to tell the fate of the fair and helpless, – the piteous perishing of the women and children, – and the death-leap of Nii-no-Ama, with the imperial infant in her arms, – then all the listeners uttered together one long, long shuddering cry of anguish; and thereafter they wept and wailed so loudly and so wildly that the blind man was frightened by the violence and grief that he had made. For much time the sobbing and the wailing continued. But gradually the sounds of lamentation died away; and again, in the great stillness that followed, Hoichi heard the voice of the woman whom he supposed to be the *Rojo*.

She said:

"Although we had been assured that you were a very skillful player upon the *biwa*, and without an equal in recitative, we did not know that any one could be so skillful as you have proved yourself tonight. Our lord has been pleased to say that he intends to bestow upon you a fitting reward. But he desires that you shall perform before him once every night for the next six nights – after which time he will probably make his august return-journey. Tomorrow night, therefore, you are to come here at the same hour. The retainer who tonight conducted you will be sent for you.... There is another matter about which I have been ordered to inform you. It is required that you shall speak to no one of your visits here, during the time of our lord's august sojourn at Akamagaseki. As he is travelling incognito, he commands that no mention of these things be made.... You are now free to go back to your temple."

After Hoichi had duly expressed his thanks, a woman's hand conducted him to the entrance of the house, where the same retainer, who had before guided him, was waiting to take him home. The retainer led him to the verandah at the rear of the temple, and there bade him farewell.

It was almost dawn when Hoichi returned; but his absence from the temple had not been observed, – as the priest, coming back at a very late hour, had supposed him asleep. During the day Hoichi was able to take some rest; and he said nothing about his strange adventure. In the middle of the following night the *samurai* again came for him, and led him to the august assembly, where he gave another recitation with the same success that had attended his previous performance. But during this second visit his absence from the temple was accidentally discovered; and after his return in the morning he was summoned to the presence of the priest, who said to him, in a tone of kindly reproach:

"We have been very anxious about you, friend Hoichi. To go out, blind and alone, at so late an hour, is dangerous. Why did you go without telling us? I could have ordered a servant to accompany you. And where have you been?"

Hoichi answered, evasively, –

"Pardon me kind friend! I had to attend to some private business; and I could not arrange the matter at any other hour."

The priest was surprised, rather than pained, by Hoichi's reticence: he felt it to be unnatural, and suspected something wrong. He feared that the blind lad had been bewitched or deluded by some evil spirits. He did not ask any more questions; but he privately instructed the men-servants of the temple to keep watch upon Hoichi's movements, and to follow him in case that he should again leave the temple after dark.

On the very next night, Hoichi was seen to leave the temple; and the servants immediately lighted their lanterns, and followed after him. But it was a rainy night, and very dark; and before the temple-folks could get to the roadway, Hoichi had disappeared. Evidently he had walked very fast, – a strange thing, considering his blindness; for the road was in a bad condition. The men hurried through the streets, making inquiries at every house which Hoichi was accustomed to visit; but nobody could give them any news of him. At last, as they were returning to the temple by way of the shore, they were startled by the sound of a *biwa*, furiously played, in the cemetery of the Amidaji. Except for some ghostly fires – such as usually flitted there on dark nights – all was blackness in that direction. But the men at once hastened to the cemetery; and there, by the help of their lanterns, they discovered Hoichi, – sitting alone in the rain before the memorial tomb of Antoku Tenno, making his *biwa* resound, and loudly chanting the chant of the battle of Dan-no-ura. And behind him, and about him, and everywhere above the tombs, the fires of the dead were burning, like candles. Never before had so great a host of *Oni-bi* appeared in the sight of mortal man....

"Hoichi San! – Hoichi San!" the servants cried, – "you are bewitched!... Hoichi San!"

But the blind man did not seem to hear. Strenuously he made his *biwa* to rattle and ring and clang; – more and more wildly he chanted the chant of the battle of Dan-no-ura. They caught hold of him; – they shouted into his ear, –

"Hoichi San! – Hoichi San! – come home with us at once!"

Reprovingly he spoke to them:

"To interrupt me in such a manner, before this august assembly, will not be tolerated."

Whereat, in spite of the weirdness of the thing, the servants could not help laughing. Sure that he had been bewitched, they now seized him, and pulled him up on his feet, and by main force hurried him back to the temple, – where he was immediately relieved of his wet clothes, by order of the priest. Then the priest insisted upon a full explanation of his friend's astonishing behaviour.

Hoichi long hesitated to speak. But at last, finding that his conduct had really alarmed and angered the good priest, he decided to abandon his reserve; and he related everything that had happened from the time of first visit of the *samurai*.

The priest said:

"Hoichi, my poor friend, you are now in great danger! How unfortunate that you did not tell me all this before! Your wonderful skill in music has indeed brought you into strange trouble. By this time you must be aware that you have not been visiting any house whatever, but have been passing your nights in the cemetery, among the tombs of the Heiké; – and it was before the memorial-tomb of Antoku Tenno that our people tonight found you, sitting in the rain. All that you have been imagining was illusion – except the calling of the dead. By once obeying them, you have put yourself in their power. If you obey them again, after what has already occurred, they will tear you in pieces. But they would have destroyed you, sooner or later, in any event…. Now I shall not be able to remain with you tonight: I am called away to perform another service. But, before I go, it will be necessary to protect your body by writing holy texts upon it."

Before sundown the priest and his acolyte stripped Hoichi: then, with their writing-brushes, they traced upon his breast and back, head and face and neck, limbs and hands and feet, – even upon the soles of his feet, and upon all parts of his body, – the text of the holy sutra called *Hannya-Shin-Kyo*. When this had been done, the priest instructed Hoichi, saying:

"Tonight, as soon as I go away, you must seat yourself on the verandah, and wait. You will be called. But, whatever may happen, do not answer, and do not move. Say nothing and sit still – as if meditating. If you stir, or make any noise, you will be torn asunder. Do not get frightened; and do not think of calling for help – because no help could save you. If you do exactly as I tell you, the danger will pass, and you will have nothing more to fear."

After dark the priest and the acolyte went away; and Hoichi seated himself on the verandah, according to the instructions given him. He laid his *biwa* on the planking beside him, and, assuming the attitude of meditation, remained quite still, – taking care not to cough, or to breathe audibly. For hours he stayed thus.

Then, from the roadway, he heard the steps coming. They passed the gate, crossed the garden, approached the verandah, stopped – directly in front of him.

"Hoichi!" the deep voice called. But the blind man held his breath, and sat motionless.

"Hoichi!" grimly called the voice a second time. Then a third time – savagely:

"Hoichi!"

Hoichi remained as still as a stone, – and the voice grumbled:

"No answer! – that won't do!... Must see where the fellow is...."

There was a noise of heavy feet mounting upon the verandah. The feet approached deliberately, – halted beside him. Then, for long minutes, – during which Hoichi felt his whole body shake to the beating of his heart, – there was dead silence.

At last the gruff voice muttered close to him:

"Here is the *biwa*; but of the *biwa*-player I see – only two ears!... So that explains why he did not answer: he had no mouth to answer with – there is nothing left of him but his ears.... Now to my lord those ears I will take – in proof that the august commands have been obeyed, so far as was possible...."

At that instant Hoichi felt his ears gripped by fingers of iron, and torn off! Great as the pain was, he gave no cry. The heavy footfalls receded along the verandah, – descended into the garden, – passed out to the roadway, – ceased. From either side of his head, the blind man felt a thick warm trickling; but he dared not lift his hands...

Before sunrise the priest came back. He hastened at once to the verandah in the rear, stepped and slipped upon something clammy, and uttered a cry of horror; – for he saw, by the light of his lantern, that the clamminess was blood. But he perceived Hoichi sitting there, in the attitude of meditation – with the blood still oozing from his wounds.

"My poor Hoichi!" cried the startled priest, – "what is this?... You have been hurt?"

At the sound of his friend's voice, the blind man felt safe. He burst out sobbing, and tearfully told his adventure of the night.

"Poor, poor Hoichi!" the priest exclaimed, – "all my fault! – my very grievous fault!... Everywhere upon your body the holy texts had been written – except upon your ears! I trusted my acolyte to do that part of the work; and it was very, very wrong of me not to have made sure that he had done it!... Well, the matter cannot now be helped; – we can only try to heal your hurts as soon as possible.... Cheer up, friend! – the danger is now well over. You will never again be troubled by those visitors."

With the aid of a good doctor, Hoichi soon recovered from his injuries. The story of his strange adventure spread far and wide, and soon made him famous. Many noble persons went to Akamagaseki to hear him recite; and large presents of money were given to him, – so that he became a wealthy man.... But from the time of his adventure, he was known only by the appellation of Mimi-nashi-Hoichi: 'Hoichi-the-Earless'.

In a Cup of Tea
Collected by Lafcadio Hearn

Have you ever attempted to mount some old tower stairway, spiring up through darkness, and in the heart of that darkness found yourself at the cobwebbed edge of nothing? Or have you followed some coast path, cut along the face of a cliff, only to discover yourself, at a turn, on the jagged verge of a break? The emotional worth of such experience – from a literary point of view – is proved by the force of the sensations aroused, and by the vividness with which they are remembered.

Now there have been curiously preserved, in old Japanese story-books, certain fragments of fiction that produce an almost similar emotional experience…. Perhaps the writer was lazy; perhaps he had a quarrel with the publisher; perhaps he was suddenly called away from his little table, and never came back; perhaps death stopped the writing-brush in the very middle of a sentence. But no mortal man can ever tell us exactly why these things were left unfinished…. I select a typical example.

On the fourth day of the first month of the third *Tenwa*, – that is to say, about two hundred and twenty years ago, – the lord Nakagawa Sado, while on his way to make a New Year's visit, halted with his train at a tea-house in Hakusan, in the Hongō district of Yedo. While the party were resting there, one of the lord's attendants, – a *wakatō* named Sekinai, – feeling very thirsty, filled for himself a large water-cup with tea. He was raising the cup to his lips when he suddenly perceived, in the transparent yellow infusion, the image or reflection of a face that was not his own. Startled, he looked around, but could see no one near him. The face in the tea appeared, from the coiffure, to be the face of a young *samurai*: it was strangely distinct, and very handsome, – delicate as the face of a girl. And it seemed the reflection of a living face; for the eyes and the lips were moving. Bewildered by this mysterious apparition, Sekinai threw away the tea, and carefully examined the cup. It proved to be a very cheap water-cup, with no artistic devices of any sort. He found and filled another cup; and again the face appeared in the tea. He then ordered fresh tea, and refilled the cup; and once more the strange face appeared, – this time with a mocking smile. But Sekinai did not allow himself to be frightened. "Whoever you are," he muttered, "you shall delude me no further!" – then he swallowed the tea, face and all, and went his way, wondering whether he had swallowed a ghost.

Late in the evening of the same day, while on watch in the palace of the lord Nakagawa, Sekinai was surprised by the soundless coming of a stranger into the apartment. This stranger, a richly dressed young *samurai*, seated himself directly in front of Sekinai, and, saluting the *wakatō* with a slight bow, observed:

"I am Shikibu Heinai – met you today for the first time.... You do not seem to recognize me."

He spoke in a very low, but penetrating voice. And Sekinai was astonished to find before him the same sinister, handsome face

64

of which he had seen, and swallowed, the apparition in a cup of tea. It was smiling now, as the phantom had smiled; but the steady gaze of the eyes, above the smiling lips, was at once a challenge and an insult.

"No, I do not recognize you," returned Sekinai, angry but cool; – "and perhaps you will now be good enough to inform me how you obtained admission to this house?"

[In feudal times the residence of a lord was strictly guarded at all hours; and no one could enter unannounced, except through some unpardonable negligence on the part of the armed watch.]

"Ah, you do not recognize me!" exclaimed the visitor, in a tone of irony, drawing a little nearer as he spoke. "No, you do not recognize me! Yet you took upon yourself this morning to do me a deadly injury!..."

Sekinai instantly seized the *tantō* at his girdle, and made a fierce thrust at the throat of the man. But the blade seemed to touch no substance. Simultaneously and soundlessly the intruder leaped sideward to the chamber-wall, and through it! ... The wall showed no trace of his exit. He had traversed it only as the light of a candle passes through lantern-paper.

When Sekinai made report of the incident, his recital astonished and puzzled the retainers. No stranger had been seen either to enter or to leave the palace at the hour of the occurrence; and no one in the service of the lord Nakagawa had ever heard of the name 'Shikibu Heinai'.

On the following night Sekinai was off duty, and remained at home with his parents. At a rather late hour he was informed that some strangers had called at the house, and desired to speak with him for a moment. Taking his sword, he went to the entrance, and there found three armed men, – apparently retainers, – waiting in front of the doorstep. The three bowed respectfully to Sekinai; and one of them said:

"Our names are Matsuoka Bungō, Tsuchibashi Bungō, and Okamura Heiroku. We are retainers of the noble Shikibu Heinai. When our master last night deigned to pay you a visit, you struck him with a sword. He was much hurt, and has been obliged to go to the hot springs, where his wound is now being treated. But on the sixteenth day of the coming month he will return; and he will then fitly repay you for the injury done him...."

Without waiting to hear more, Sekinai leaped out, sword in hand, and slashed right and left, at the strangers. But the three men sprang to the wall of the adjoining building, and flitted up the wall like shadows, and...

Here the old narrative breaks off; the rest of the story existed only in some brain that has been dust for a century.

I am able to imagine several possible endings; but none of them would satisfy an Occidental imagination. I prefer to let the reader attempt to decide for himself the probable consequence of swallowing a Soul.

The Ghost of O-Kiku
from Banchō Sarayashiki,
or The Lady of the Plates
Excerpt from 'In a Japanese Garden'
Collected by Lafcadio Hearn

There is one place in Japan where it is thought unlucky to cultivate chrysanthemums, for reasons which shall presently appear; and that place is in the pretty little city of Himeji, in the province of Harima. Himeji contains the ruins of a great castle of thirty turrets; and a *daimyo* used to dwell therein whose revenue was one hundred and fifty-six thousand *koku* of rice. Now, in the house of one of that *daimyo*'s chief retainers there was a maid-servant, of good family, whose name was O-Kiku; and the name 'Kiku' signifies a chrysanthemum flower. Many precious things were intrusted to her charge, and among others ten costly dishes of gold. One of these was suddenly missed, and could not be found; and the girl, being responsible therefor, and knowing not how otherwise to prove her innocence, drowned herself in a well. But ever thereafter her ghost, returning nightly, could be heard counting the dishes slowly, with sobs:

Ichi-mai, Yo-mai, Shichi-mai,
Ni-mai, Go-mai, Hachi-mai,
San-mai, Roku-mai, Ku-mai—

Then would be heard a despairing cry and a loud burst of weeping; and again the girl's voice counting the dishes plaintively: "One – two – three – four – five – six – seven – eight – nine—"

Her spirit passed into the body of a strange little insect, whose head faintly resembles that of a ghost with long dishevelled hair; and it is called O-Kiku-mushi, or 'the fly of O-Kiku'; and it is found, they say, nowhere save in Himeji. A famous play was written about O-Kiku, which is still acted in all the popular theatres, entitled *Banshu-O-Kiku-no-Sara-yashiki*; or, 'The Manor of the Dish of O-Kiku of Banshu'.

Some declare that Banshu is only the corruption of the name of an ancient quarter of Tokyo (*Yedo*), where the story should have been laid. But the people of Himeji say that part of their city now called Go-Ken-Yashiki is identical with the site of the ancient manor. What is certainly true is that to cultivate chrysanthemum flowers in the part of Himeji called Go-Ken-Yashiki is deemed unlucky, because the name of O-Kiku signifies 'Chrysanthemum'. Therefore, nobody, I am told, ever cultivates chrysanthemums there.

The Reconciliation
Collected by Lafcadio Hearn

There was a young *Samurai* of Kyoto who had been reduced to poverty by the ruin of his lord, and found himself obliged to leave his home, and to take service with the Governor of a distant province. Before quitting the capital, this *Samurai* divorced his wife, – a good and beautiful woman, – under the belief that he could better obtain promotion by another alliance. He then married the daughter of a family of some distinction, and took her with him to the district whither he had been called.

But it was in the time of the thoughtlessness of youth, and the sharp experience of want, that the *Samurai* could not understand the worth of the affection so lightly cast away. His second marriage did not prove a happy one; the character of his new wife was hard and selfish; and he soon found every cause to think with regret of Kyoto days. Then he discovered that he still loved his first wife – loved her more than he could ever love the second; and he began to feel how unjust and how thankless he had been. Gradually his repentance deepened into a remorse that left him no peace of mind. Memories of the woman he had wronged – her gentle speech, her smiles, her dainty, pretty ways, her faultless patience – continually haunted him. Sometimes in dreams he saw her at her loom, weaving as when she toiled night and day to help him during the years of their distress: more often he saw her kneeling alone in the desolate little room where he had left her, veiling her tears with her poor worn sleeve. Even in the hours of official duty, his thoughts would wander back to her: then he would ask himself how she was living, what she was doing. Something in his heart assured him that she could not accept another husband, and that she never would refuse to pardon him. And he secretly resolved to seek her out as soon as he could return to Kyoto, – then to beg her forgiveness, to take her back, to do everything that a man could do to make atonement. But the years went by.

At last the Governor's official term expired, and the *Samurai* was free. "Now I will go back to my dear one," he vowed to himself. "Ah, what a cruelty, – what a folly to have divorced her!" He sent his second wife to her own people (she had given him no children); and hurrying to Kyoto, he went at once to seek his former companion, – not allowing himself even the time to change his travelling-garb.

When he reached the street where she used to live, it was late in the night, – the night of the tenth day of the ninth month; – and the city was silent as a cemetery. But a bright moon made everything visible; and he found the house without difficulty. It had a deserted look: tall weeds were growing on the roof. He knocked at the sliding-doors, and no one answered. Then, finding that the doors had not been fastened from within, he pushed them open, and entered. The front room was matless and empty: a chilly wind was blowing through crevices in the planking; and the moon shone through a ragged break in the wall of the alcove. Other rooms presented a like forlorn condition. The house, to all seeming, was unoccupied. Nevertheless, the *Samurai* determined to visit one other apartment at the further end of the dwelling, – a very small room that had been his wife's favourite resting-place. Approaching the sliding-screen that closed it, he was startled to perceive a glow within. He pushed the screen aside, and uttered a cry of joy; for he saw her there, – sewing by the light of a paper-lamp. Her eyes at the same instant met his own; and with a happy smile she greeted him, – asking only: "When did you come back to Kyoto? How did you find your way here to me, through all those black rooms?" The years had not changed her. Still she seemed as fair and young as in his fondest memory of her; – but sweeter than any memory there came to him the music of her voice, with its trembling of pleased wonder.

Then joyfully he took his place beside her, and told her all: how deeply he repented his selfishness, – how wretched he had been without her, – how constantly he had regretted her, – how long he had hoped and planned to make amends; – caressing her the while, and asking her forgiveness over and over again. She answered him, with loving gentleness, according to his heart's desire, – entreating him to cease all self-reproach. It was wrong, she said, that he should have allowed himself to suffer on her account: she had always felt that she was not worthy to be his wife. She knew that he had separated from her, notwithstanding, only because of poverty; and while he lived with her, he had always been kind; and she had never ceased to pray for his happiness. But even if there had been a reason for speaking of amends, this honourable visit would be ample amends; – what greater happiness than thus to see him again, though it were only for a moment? "Only for a moment!" he answered, with a glad laugh, – "say, rather, for the time of seven existences! My loved one, unless you forbid, I am coming back to live with you always – always – always! Nothing shall ever separate us again. Now I have means and friends: we need not fear poverty. Tomorrow my goods will be brought here; and my servants will come to wait upon you; and we shall make this house beautiful.... Tonight," he added, apologetically, "I came thus late – without even changing my dress – only because of the longing I had to see you, and to tell you this." She seemed greatly pleased by these words; and in her turn she told him about all that had happened in Kyoto since the time of his departure, – excepting her own sorrows, of which she sweetly refused to speak. They chatted far into the night: then she conducted him to a warmer room, facing south, – a room that had been their bridal chamber in former time. "Have you no one in the house to help you?" he asked, as she began to prepare the couch for him. "No," she answered, laughing cheerfully: "I could not afford a servant; – so I have been living all alone."

"You will have plenty of servants tomorrow," he said, – "good servants, – and everything else that you need." They lay down to rest, – not to sleep: they had too much to tell each other; – and they talked of the past and the present and the future, until the dawn was grey. Then, involuntarily, the *Samurai* closed his eyes, and slept.

When he awoke, the daylight was streaming through the chinks of the sliding-shutters; and he found himself, to his utter amazement, lying upon the naked boards of a mouldering floor.... Had he only dreamed a dream? No: she was there; – she slept.... He bent above her, – and looked, – and shrieked; – for the sleeper had no face!... Before him, wrapped in its grave-sheet only, lay the corpse of a woman, – a corpse so wasted that little remained save the bones, and the long black tangled hair.

Slowly, – as he stood shuddering and sickening in the sun, – the icy horror yielded to a despair so intolerable, a pain so atrocious, that he clutched at the mocking shadow of a doubt. Feigning ignorance of the neighbourhood, he ventured to ask his way to the house in which his wife had lived.

"There is no one in that house," said the person questioned. "It used to belong to the wife of a *Samurai* who left the city several years ago. He divorced her in order to marry another woman before he went away; and she fretted a great deal, and so became sick. She had no relatives in Kyoto, and nobody to care for her; and she died in the autumn of the same year, – on the tenth day of the ninth month...."

The Corpse-Rider
Collected by Lafcadio Hearn

The body was cold as ice; the heart had long ceased to beat: yet there were no other signs of death. Nobody even spoke of burying the woman. She had died of grief and anger at having been divorced. It would have been useless to bury her, – because the last undying wish of a dying person for vengeance can burst asunder any tomb and rift the heaviest graveyard stone. People who lived near the house in which she was lying fled from their homes. They knew that she was only waiting for the return of the man who had divorced her.

At the time of her death he was on a journey. When he came back and was told what had happened, terror seized him. "If I can find no help before dark," he thought to himself, "she will tear me to pieces." It was yet only the Hour of the Dragon; but he knew that he had no time to lose.

He went at once to an *inyōshi* and begged for succour. The *inyōshi* knew the story of the dead woman; and he had seen the body. He said to the supplicant: "A very great danger threatens you. I will try to save you. But you must promise to do whatever I shall tell you to do. There is only one way by which you can be saved. It is a fearful way. But unless you find the courage to attempt it, she will tear you limb from limb. If you can be brave, come to me again in the evening before sunset." The man shuddered; but he promised to do whatever should be required of him.

At sunset the *inyōshi* went with him to the house where the body was lying. The *inyōshi* pushed open the sliding-doors, and told his client to enter. It was rapidly growing dark. "I dare not!" gasped the man, quaking from head to foot; – "I dare not even look at her!"

"You will have to do much more than look at her," declared the *inyōshi*; – "and you promised to obey. Go in!" He forced the trembler into the house and led him to the side of the corpse.

The dead woman was lying on her face. "Now you must get astride upon her," said the *inyōshi*, "and sit firmly on her back, as if you were riding a horse.... Come! – you must do it!" The man shivered so that the *inyōshi* had to support him – shivered horribly; but he obeyed. "Now take her hair in your hands," commanded the *inyōshi*, – "half in the right hand, half in the left.... So!... You must grip it like a bridle. Twist your hands in it – both hands – tightly. That is the way!... Listen to me! You must stay like that till morning. You will have reason to be afraid in the night – plenty of reason. But whatever may happen, never let go of her hair. If you let go – even for one second – she will tear you into gobbets!"

The *inyōshi* then whispered some mysterious words into the ear of the body, and said to its rider: "Now, for my own sake, I must leave you alone with her.... Remain as you are!... Above all things, remember that you must not let go of her hair." And he went away, closing the doors behind him.

Hour after hour the man sat upon the corpse in black fear; – and the hush of the night deepened and deepened about him till he screamed to break it. Instantly the body sprang beneath him, as to cast him off; and the dead woman cried out loudly, "Oh, how heavy it is! Yet I shall bring that fellow here now!"

Then tall she rose, and leaped to the doors, and flung them open, and rushed into the night – always bearing the weight of the man. But he, shutting his eyes, kept his hands twisted in her long hair – tightly, tightly – though fearing with such a fear that he could not even moan. How far she went, he never knew. He saw nothing: he heard only the sound of her naked feet in the dark – *picha-picha, picha-picha* – and the hiss of her breathing as she ran.

At last she turned, and ran back into the house, and lay down upon the floor exactly as at first. Under the man she panted and moaned till the cocks began to crow. Thereafter she lay still.

But the man, with chattering teeth, sat upon her until the *inyōshi* came at sunrise. "So you did not let go of her hair!" – observed the *inyōshi*, greatly pleased. "That is well … Now you can stand up." He whispered again into the ear of the corpse, and then said to the man: "You must have passed a fearful night; but nothing else could have saved you. Hereafter you may feel secure from her vengeance."

A Dead Secret

Collected by Lafcadio Hearn

A long time ago, in the province of Tamba, there lived a rich merchant named Inamuraya Gensuké. He had a daughter called O-Sono. As she was very clever and pretty, he thought it would be a pity to let her grow up with only such teaching as the country-teachers could give her: so he sent her, in care of some trusty attendants, to Kyoto, that she might be trained in the polite accomplishments taught to the ladies of the capital. After she had thus been educated, she was married to a friend of her father's family – a merchant named Nagaraya; – and she lived happily with him for nearly four years. They had one child, – a boy. But O-Sono fell ill and died, in the fourth year after her marriage.

On the night after the funeral of O-Sono, her little son said that his mamma had come back, and was in the room upstairs. She had smiled at him, but would not talk to him: so he became afraid, and ran away. Then some of the family went upstairs to the room which had been O-Sono's; and they were startled to see, by the light of a small lamp which had been kindled before a shrine in that room, the figure of the dead mother. She

77

appeared as if standing in front of a *tansu*, or chest of drawers, that still contained her ornaments and her wearing-apparel. Her head and shoulders could be very distinctly seen; but from the waist downwards the figure thinned into invisibility; – it was like an imperfect reflection of her, and transparent as a shadow on water.

Then the folk were afraid, and left the room. Below they consulted together; and the mother of O-Sono's husband said: "A woman is fond of her small things; and O-Sono was much attached to her belongings. Perhaps she has come back to look at them. Many dead persons will do that, – unless the things be given to the parish temple. If we present O-Sono's robes and girdles to the temple, her spirit will probably find rest."

It was agreed that this should be done as soon as possible. So on the following morning the drawers were emptied; and all of O-Sono's ornaments and dresses were taken to the temple. But she came back the next night, and looked at the *tansu* as before. And she came back also on the night following, and the night after that, and every night; – and the house became a house of fear.

The mother of O-Sono's husband then went to the parish temple, and told the chief priest all that had happened, and asked for ghostly counsel. The temple was a Zen temple; and the head priest was a learned old man, known as Daigen Oshō. He said: "There must be something about which she is anxious, in or near that *tansu*." – "But we emptied all the drawers," replied the woman; – "there is nothing in the *tansu*." – "Well," said Daigen Oshō, "tonight I shall go to your house, and keep watch in that room, and see what can be done. You must give orders that no person shall enter the room while I am watching, unless I call."

After sundown, Daigen Oshō went to the house, and found the room made ready for him. He remained there alone, reading the sûtras; and nothing appeared until after the Hour of the Rat. Then the figure of O-Sono suddenly outlined itself in front of the *tansu*. Her face had a wistful look; and she kept her eyes fixed upon the *tansu*.

The priest uttered the holy formula prescribed in such cases, and then, addressing the figure by the *kaimyō* of O-Sono, said: – "I have come here in order to help you. Perhaps in that *tansu* there is something about which you have reason to feel anxious. Shall I try to find it for you?" The shadow appeared to give assent by a slight motion of the head; and the priest, rising, opened the top drawer. It was empty. Successively he opened the second, the third, and the fourth drawer; – he searched carefully behind them and beneath them; – he carefully examined the interior of the chest. He found nothing. But the figure remained gazing as wistfully as before. "What can she want?" thought the priest. Suddenly it occurred to him that there might be something hidden under the paper with which the drawers were lined. He removed the lining of the first drawer: – nothing! He removed the lining of the second and third drawers: – still nothing. But under the lining of the lowermost drawer he found – a letter. "Is this the thing about which you have been troubled?" he asked. The shadow of the woman turned toward him, – her faint gaze fixed upon the letter. "Shall I burn it for you?" he asked. She bowed before him. "It shall be burned in the temple this very morning," he promised; – "and no one shall read it, except myself." The figure smiled and vanished.

Dawn was breaking as the priest descended the stairs, to find the family waiting anxiously below. "Do not be anxious," he said to them: "She will not appear again." And she never did.

The letter was burned. It was a love-letter written to O-Sono in the time of her studies at Kyoto. But the priest alone knew what was in it; and the secret died with him.

Mujina

Collected by Lafcadio Hearn

On the Akasaka Road, in Tokyo, there is a slope called Kii-no-kuni-zaka, – which means the Slope of the Province of Kii. I do not know why it is called the Slope of the Province of Kii. On one side of this slope you see an ancient moat, deep and very wide, with high green banks rising up to some place of gardens; – and on the other side of the road extend the long and lofty walls of an imperial palace. Before the era of street-lamps and jinrikishas, this neighbourhood was very lonesome after dark; and belated pedestrians would go miles out of their way rather than mount the Kii-no-kuni-zaka, alone, after sunset.

All because of a Mujina that used to walk there.

The last man who saw the Mujina was an old merchant of the Kyōbashi quarter, who died about thirty years ago. This is the story, as he told it: –

One night, at a late hour, he was hurrying up the Kii-no-kuni-zaka, when he perceived a woman crouching by the moat, all alone, and weeping bitterly. Fearing that she intended to drown herself, he stopped to offer her any assistance or consolation in his power. She appeared to be a slight and graceful person, handsomely dressed;

and her hair was arranged like that of a young girl of good family. "O-jochū," he exclaimed, approaching her, – "O-jochū, do not cry like that!… Tell me what the trouble is; and if there be any way to help you, I shall be glad to help you." (He really meant what he said; for he was a very kind man.) But she continued to weep, – hiding her face from him with one of her long sleeves. "O-jochū," he said again, as gently as he could, – "please, please listen to me!… This is no place for a young lady at night! Do not cry, I implore you! – only tell me how I may be of some help to you!" Slowly she rose up, but turned her back to him, and continued to moan and sob behind her sleeve. He laid his hand lightly upon her shoulder, and pleaded: –"O-jochū! – O-jochū! – O-jochū!… Listen to me, just for one little moment!… O-jochū! –O-jochū!"… Then that O-jochū turned around, and dropped her sleeve, and stroked her face with her hand; – and the man saw that she had no eyes or nose or mouth, – and he screamed and ran away.

Up Kii-no-kuni-zaka he ran and ran; and all was black and empty before him. On and on he ran, never daring to look back; and at last he saw a lantern, so far away that it looked like the gleam of a firefly; and he made for it. It proved to be only the lantern of an itinerant soba seller, who had set down his stand by the roadside; but any light and any human companionship was good after that experience; and he flung himself down at the feet of the soba seller, crying out, "Ah! – aa!! – *aa*!!!"…

"*Koré! koré!*" roughly exclaimed the soba-man. "Here! What is the matter with you? Anybody hurt you?"

"No – nobody hurt me," panted the other, – "only… *Ah! – aa!*"

"—Only   scared   you?"   queried   the   peddler, unsympathetically. "Robbers?"

"Not robbers, – not robbers," gasped the terrified man... "I saw ... I saw a woman – by the moat; – and she showed me ... *Ah*! I cannot tell you what she showed me!"...

"*Hé*! Was it anything like THIS that she showed you?" cried the soba-man, stroking his own face – which therewith became like unto an Egg... And, simultaneously, the light went out.

The Strange Story of the Golden Comb

Collected by Grace James

In ancient days two *samurai* dwelt in Sendai of the North. They were friends and brothers in arms.

Hasunuma one was named, and the other Saito. Now it happened that a daughter was born to the house of Hasunuma, and upon the selfsame day, and in the selfsame hour, there was born to the house of Saito a son. The boy child they called Konojo, and the girl they called Aiko, which means the Child of Love.

Or ever a year had passed over their innocent heads the children were betrothed to one another. And as a token the wife of Saito gave a golden comb to the wife of Hasunuma, saying: "For the child's hair when she shall be old enough." Aiko's mother wrapped the comb in a handkerchief, and laid it away in her chest. It was of gold lacquer, very fine work, adorned with golden dragon-flies.

This was very well; but before long misfortune came upon Saito and his house, for, by sad mischance, he aroused the ire of his feudal lord, and he was fain to fly from Sendai by night, and his wife was with him, and the child. No man knew where they went, or had any news of them, nor of how they fared, and for long, long years Hasunuma heard not one word of them.

The child Aiko grew to be the loveliest lady in Sendai. She had longer hair than any maiden in the city, and she was the most graceful dancer ever seen. She moved as a wave of the sea, or a cloud of the sky, or the wild bamboo grass in the wind. She had a sister eleven moons younger than she, who was called Aiyamé, or the Water Iris; and she was the second loveliest lady in Sendai. Aiko was white, but Aiyamé was brown, quick, and light, and laughing. When they went abroad in the streets of Sendai, folk said, "There go the moon and the south wind."

Upon an idle summer day when all the air was languid, and the cicala sang ceaselessly as he swung on the pomegranate bough, the maidens rested on the cool white mats of their lady mother's bower. Their dark locks were loose, and their slender feet were bare. They had between them an ancient chest of red lacquer, a Bride Box of their lady mother's, and in the chest they searched and rummaged for treasure.

"See, sister," said Aiyamé, "here are scarlet thongs, the very thing for my sandals ... and what is this? A crystal rosary, I declare! How beautiful!"

Aiko said, "My mother, I pray you give me this length of violet silk, it will make me very fine undersleeves to my new grey gown; and, mother, let me have the crimson for a petticoat; and surely, mother, you do not need this little bit of brocade?"

"And what an *obi*," cried Aiyamé, as she dragged it from the chest, "grass green and silver!" Springing lightly up, she wound the length about her slender body. "Now behold me for the finest lady in all Sendai. Very envious shall be the daughter of the rich Hachiman, when she sees this wonder *obi*; but I shall be calm and careless, and say, looking down thus humbly, 'Your pardon, noble lady, that I wear this foolish trifling *obi*, unmeet for your great presence!' Mother, mother, give me the *obi*."

"Arah! Arah! Little pirates!" said the mother, and smiled.

Aiko thrust her hand to the bottom of the chest. "Here is something hard," she murmured, "a little casket wrapped in a silken handkerchief. How it smells of orris and ancient spices! – now what may it be?" So saying, she unwound the kerchief and opened the casket. "A golden comb!" she said, and laid it on her knee.

"Give it here, child," cried the mother quickly; "it is not for your eyes."

But the maiden sat quite still, her eyes upon the golden comb. It was of gold lacquer, very fine work, adorned with golden dragon-flies.

For a time the maiden said not a word, nor did her mother, though she was troubled; and even the light Lady of the South Wind seemed stricken into silence, and drew the scarlet sandal thongs through and through her fingers.

"Mother, what of this golden comb?" said Aiko at last.

"My sweet, it is the love-token between you and Konojo, the son of Saito, for you two were betrothed in your cradles. But now it is full fifteen years since Saito went from Sendai in the night, he and all his house, and left no trace behind."

"Is my love dead?" said Aiko.

"Nay, that I know not – but he will never come; so, I beseech you, think no more of him, my pretty bird. There, get you your fan, and dance for me and for your sister."

Aiko first set the golden comb in her hair. Then she flung open her fan to dance. She moved like a wave of the sea, or a cloud of the sky, or the wild bamboo grass in the wind. She had not danced long before she dropped the fan, with a long cry, and she herself fell her length upon the ground. From that hour she was in a piteous way, and lay in her bed sighing, like a maid lovelorn and forsaken. She could not eat nor sleep; she had no pleasure in life. The sunrise and the sound of rain at night were nothing to her any more. Not her father, nor her mother, nor her sister, the Lady of the South Wind, were able to give her any ease.

Presently she turned her face to the wall. "It is more than I can understand," she said, and so died.

When they had prepared the poor young maid for her grave, her mother came, crying, to look at her for the last time. And she set the golden comb in the maid's hair, saying:

"My own dear little child, I pray that in other lives you may know happiness. Therefore take your golden token with you; you will have need of it when you meet the wraith of your lover." For she believed that Konojo was dead.

But, alas, for Karma that is so pitiless, one short moon had the maid been in her grave when the brave young man, her betrothed, came to claim her at her father's house.

"Alas and alack, Konojo, the son of Saito, alas, my brave young man, too late you have come! Your joy is turned to mourning, for your bride lies under the green grass, and her sister goes weeping in the moonlight to pour the water of the dead." Thus spoke Hasunuma the *samurai*.

"Lord," said the brave young man, "there are three ways left, the sword, the strong girdle, and the river. These are the short roads to Yomi. Farewell."

But Hasunuma held the young man by the arm. "Nay, then, thou son of Saito," he said, "but hear the fourth way, which is far better.

The road to Yomi is short, but it is very dark; moreover, from the confines of that country few return. Therefore stay with me, Konojo, and comfort me in my old age, for I have no sons."

So Konojo entered the household of Hasunuma the *samurai*, and dwelt in the garden house by the gate. Now in the third month Hasunuma and his wife and the daughter that was left them arose early and dressed them in garments of ceremony, and presently were borne away in *kago*, for to the temple they were bound, and to their ancestral tombs, where they offered prayers and incense the live-long day.

It was bright starlight when they returned, and cold the night was, still and frosty. Konojo stood and waited at the garden gate. He waited for their home-coming, as was meet. He drew his cloak about him and gave ear to the noises of the evening. He heard the sound of the blind man's whistle, and the blind man's staff upon the stones. Far off he heard a child laugh twice; then he heard men singing in chorus, as men who sing to cheer themselves in their labour, and in the pauses of song he heard the creak, creak of swinging *kago* that the men bore upon their shoulders, and he said, "They come."

> "I go to the house of the Beloved,
> Her plum tree stands by the eaves;
> It is full of blossom.
> The dew lies in the heart of the flowers,
> So they are the drinking-cups of the sparrows.
> How do you go to your love's house?
> Even upon the wings of the night wind.
> Which road leads to your love's house?
> All the roads in the world."

This was the song of the *kago* men. First the *kago* of Hasunuma the *samurai* turned in at the garden gate, then followed his lady; last came Aiyamé of the South Wind. Upon the roof of her *kago* there lay a blossoming bough.

"Rest well, lady," said Konojo, as she passed, and had no answer back. Howbeit it seemed that some light thing dropped from the *kago*, and fell with a little noise to the ground. He stooped and picked up a woman's comb. It was of gold lacquer, very fine work, adorned with golden dragon-flies. Smooth and warm it lay in the hand of Konojo. And he went his way to the garden house. At the hour of the rat the young *samurai* threw down his book of verse, laid himself upon his bed, and blew out his light. And the selfsame moment he heard a wandering step without.

"And who may it be that visits the garden house by night?" said Konojo, and he wondered. About and about went the wandering feet till at length they stayed, and the door was touched with an uncertain hand.

"Konojo! Konojo!"

"What is it?" said the *samurai*.

"Open, open; I am afraid."

"Who are you, and why are you afraid?"

"I am afraid of the night. I am the daughter of Hasunuma the *samurai*.... Open to me for the love of the gods."

Konojo undid the latch and slid back the door of the garden house to find a slender and drooping lady upon the threshold. He could not see her face, for she held her long sleeve so as to hide it from him; but she swayed and trembled, and her frail shoulders shook with sobbing.

"Let me in," she moaned, and forthwith entered the garden house.
Half smiling and much perplexed, Konojo asked her:

"Are you Aiyamé, whom they call the Lady of the South Wind?"

"I am she."

"Lady, you do me much honour."

"The comb!" she said, "the golden comb!"

As she said this, she threw the veil from her face, and taking
the robe of Konojo in both her little hands, she looked into his
eyes as though she would draw forth his very soul. The lady was
brown and quick and light. Her eyes and her lips were made for
laughing, and passing strange she looked in the guise that she
wore then.

"The comb!" she said, "the golden comb!"

"I have it here," said Konojo; "only let go my robe, and I will fetch
it you."

At this the lady cast herself down upon the white mats in a
passion of bitter tears, and Konojo, poor unfortunate, pressed his
hands together, quite beside himself.

"What to do?" he said; "what to do?"

At last he raised the lady in his arms, and stroked her little hand
to comfort her.

"Lord," she said, as simply as a child, "lord, do you love me?"

And he answered her in a moment, "I love you more than many
lives, O Lady of the South Wind."

"Lord," she said, "will you come with me then?"

He answered her, "Even to the land of Yomi," and took her hand.

Forth they went into the night, and they took the road together.
By river-side they went, and over plains of flowers; they went by
rocky ways, or through the whispering pines, and when they had

wandered far enough, of the green bamboos they built them a little house to dwell in. And they were there for a year of happy days and nights.

Now upon a morning of the third month Konojo beheld men with *kago* come swinging through the bamboo grove. And he said:

"What have they to do with us, these men and their *kago*?"

"Lord," said Aiyamé, "they come to bear us to my father's house."

He cried, "What is this foolishness? We will not go."

"Indeed, and we must go," said the lady.

"Go you, then," said Konojo; "as for me, I stay here where I am happy."

"Ah, lord," she said, "ah, my dear, do you then love me less, who vowed to go with me, even to the Land of Yomi?"

Then he did all that she would. And he broke a blossoming bough from a tree that grew near by and laid it upon the roof of her *kago*.

Swiftly, swiftly they were borne, and the *kago* men sang as they went, a song to make labour light.

> *"I go to the house of the Beloved,*
> *Her plum tree stands by the eaves;*
> *It is full of blossom.*
> *The dew lies in the heart of the flowers,*
> *So they are the drinking-cups of the sparrows.*
> *How do you go to your love's house?*
> *Even upon the wings of the night wind.*
> *Which road leads to your love's house?*
> *All the roads in the world."*

This was the song of the *kago* men.

About nightfall they came to the house of Hasunuma the *samurai*.

"Go you in, my dear lord," said the Lady of the South Wind. "I will wait without; if my father is very wroth with you, only show him the golden comb." And with that she took it from her hair and gave it him. Smooth and warm it lay in his hand. Then Konojo went into the house.

"Welcome, welcome home, Konojo, son of Saito!" cried Hasunuma. "How has it fared with your knightly adventure?"

"Knightly adventure!" said Konojo, and blushed.

"It is a year since your sudden departure, and we supposed that you had gone upon a quest, or in the expiation of some vow laid upon your soul."

"Alas, my good lord," said Konojo, "I have sinned against you and against your house." And he told Hasunuma what he had done.

When he had made an end of his tale:

"Boy," said the *samurai*, "you jest, but your merry jest is ill-timed. Know that my child lies even as one dead. For a year she has neither risen nor spoken nor smiled. She is visited by a heavy sickness and none can heal her."

"Sir," said Konojo, "your child, the Lady of the South Wind, waits in a *kago* without your garden wall. I will fetch her in presently."

Forth they went together, the young man and the *samurai*, but they found no *kago* without the garden wall, no *kago*-bearers and no lady. Only a broken bough of withered blossom lay upon the ground.

"Indeed, indeed, she was here but now!" cried Konojo. "She gave me her comb – her golden comb. See, my lord, here it is."

"What comb is this, Konojo? Where got you this comb that was set in a dead maid's hair, and buried with her beneath the green grass? Where got you the comb of Aiko, the Lady of the Moon, that died for love? Speak, Konojo, son of Saito. This is a strange thing."

Now whilst Konojo stood amazed, and leaned silent and bewildered against the garden wall, a lady came lightly through the trees. She moved as a wave of the sea, or a cloud of the sky, or the wild bamboo grass in the wind.

"Aiyamé," cried the *samurai*, "how are you able to leave your bed?"

The young man said nothing, but fell on his knees beside the garden wall. There the lady came to him and bent so that her hair and her garments overshadowed him, and her eyes held his.

"Lord," she said, "I am the spirit of Aiko your love. I went with a broken heart to dwell with the shades of Yomi. The very dead took pity on my tears. I was permitted to return, and for one short year to inhabit the sweet body of my sister. And now my time is come. I go my ways to the grey country. I shall be the happiest soul in Yomi – I have known you, beloved. Now take me in your arms, for I grow very faint."

With that she sank to the ground, and Konojo put his arms about her and laid her head against his heart. His tears fell upon her forehead.

"Promise me," she said, "that you will take to wife Aiyamé, my sister, the Lady of the South Wind."

"Ah," he cried, "my lady and my love!"

"Promise, promise," she said.

Then he promised.

After a little she stirred in his arms.

"What is it?" he said.

So soft her voice that it did not break the silence but floated upon it.

"The comb," she murmured, "the golden comb."

And Konojo set it in her hair.

A burden, pale but breathing, Konojo carried into the house of Hasunuma and laid upon the white mats and silken cushions. And after three hours a young maid sat up and rubbed her sleepy eyes. She was brown and quick and light and laughing. Her hair was tumbled about her rosy cheeks, unconfined by any braid or comb. She stared first at her father, and then at the young man that was in her bower. She smiled, then flushed, and put her little hands before her face.

"Greeting, O Lady of the South Wind," said Konojo.

The Spirit of the Lantern
Translated by Yei Theodora Ozaki

Some three hundred years ago, in the province of Kai and the town of Aoyagi, there lived a man named Koharu Tomosaburo, of well-known ancestry. His grandfather had been a retainer of Ota Dokan, the founder of Yedo, and had committed suicide when his lord fell in battle.

This brave clansman's grandson was Tomosaburo, who, when this story begins, had been happily married for many years to a woman of the same province and was the proud father of a son some ten years of age.

At this time it happened, one day, that his wife fell suddenly ill and was unable to leave her bed. Physicians were called in but had to acknowledge themselves baffled by the curious symptoms of the patient: to relieve the paroxysms of pain from which she suffered, *Moxa* was applied and burned in certain spots down her back. But half a month passed by and the anxious household realized that there was no change for the better in the mysterious malady that was consuming her: day by day she seemed to lose ground and waste away.

Tomosaburo was a kind husband and scarcely left her bedside: day and night he tenderly ministered to his stricken wife, and did all in his power to alleviate her condition.

One evening, as he was sitting thus, worn out with the strain of nursing and anxiety, he fell into a doze. Suddenly there came a change in the light of the standing-lantern, it flushed a brilliant red, then flared up into the air to the height of at least three feet, and within the crimson pillar of flame there appeared the figure of a woman.

Tomosaburo gazed in astonishment at the apparition, who thus addressed him:

"Your anxiety concerning your wife's illness is well-known to me, therefore I have come to give you some good advice. The affliction with which she is visited is the punishment for some faults in her character. For this reason she is possessed of a devil. If you will worship me as a god, I will cast out the tormenting demon."

Now Tomosaburo was a brave, strong-minded *samurai*, to whom the sensation of fear was totally unknown.

He glared fiercely at the apparition, and then, half unconsciously, turned for the *samurai's* only safeguard, his sword, and drew it from its sheath. The sword is regarded as sacred by the Japanese knight and was supposed to possess the occult power assigned to the sign of the cross in mediæval Europe – that of exorcising evil.

The spirit laughed superciliously when she saw his action.

"No motive but the kindest of intentions brought me here to proffer you my assistance in your trouble, but without the least appreciation of my goodwill you show this enmity towards me. However, your wife's life shall pay the penalty," and with these malicious words the phantom disappeared.

From that hour the unhappy woman's sufferings increased, and to the distress of all about her, she seemed about to draw her last breath.

Her husband was beside himself with grief. He realized at once what a false move he had made in driving away the friendly spirit in such an uncouth and hostile manner, and, now thoroughly alarmed at his wife's desperate plight, he was willing to comply with any demand, however strange. He thereupon prostrated himself before the family shrine and addressed fervent prayers to the Spirit of the Lantern, humbly imploring her pardon for his thoughtless and discourteous behaviour.

From that very hour the invalid began to mend, and steadily improving day by day, her normal health was soon entirely regained, until it seemed to her as though her long and strange illness had been but an evil dream.

One evening after her recovery, when the husband and wife were sitting together and speaking joyfully of her unexpected and almost miraculous restoration to health, the lantern flared up as before and in the column of brilliant light the form of the spirit again appeared.

"Notwithstanding your unkind reception of me the last time I came, I have driven out the devil and saved your wife's life. In return for this service I have come to ask a favour of you, Tomosaburo San," said the spirit. "I have a daughter who is now of a marriageable age. The reason of my visit is to request you to find a suitable husband for her."

"But I am a human being," remonstrated the perplexed man, "and you are a spirit! We belong to different worlds, and a wide and impassable gulf separates us. How would it be possible for me to do as you wish?"

"It is an easier matter than you imagine," replied the spirit. "All you have to do is to take some blocks of *kiri*-wood and to carve out from them several little figures of men; when they are finished I will bestow upon one of them the hand of my daughter."

"If that is all, then it is not so difficult as I thought, and I will undertake to do as you wish," assented Tomosaburo, and no sooner had the spirit vanished than he opened his tool box and set to work upon the appointed task with such alacrity that in a few days he had fashioned out in miniature several very creditable effigies of the desired bridegroom, and when the wooden dolls were completed he laid them out in a row upon his desk.

The next morning, on awaking, he lost no time in ascertaining what had befallen the quaint little figures, but apparently they had found favour with the spirit, for all had disappeared during the night. He now hoped that the strange and supernatural visitant would trouble them no more, but the next night she again appeared:

"Owing to your kind assistance my daughter's future is settled. As a mark of our gratitude for the trouble you have taken, we earnestly desire the presence of both yourself and your wife at the marriage feast. When the time arrives promise to come without fail."

By this time Tomosaburo was thoroughly wearied of these ghostly visitations and considered it highly obnoxious to be in league with such weird and intangible beings, yet fully aware of their powers of working evil, he dared not offend them. He racked his brains for some way of escape from this uncanny invitation, but before he could frame any reply suitable to the emergency, and while he was hesitating, the spirit vanished.

Long did the perplexed man ponder over the strange situation, but the more he thought the more embarrassed he became: and there seemed no solution of his dilemma.

The next night the spirit again returned.

"As I had the honour to inform you, we have prepared an entertainment at which your presence is desired. All is now in readiness. The wedding ceremony has taken place and the assembled company await your arrival with impatience. Kindly follow me at once!" and the wraith made imperious gestures to Tomosaburo and his wife to accompany her. With a sudden movement she darted from the lantern flame and glided out of the room, now and again looking back with furtive glances to see that they were surely following – and thus they passed, the spirit guiding them, along the passage to the outer porch.

The idea of accepting the spirit's hospitality was highly repugnant to the astonished couple, but remembering the dire consequences of his first refusal to comply with the ghostly visitor's request, Tomosaburo thought it wiser to simulate acquiescence. He was well aware that in some strange and incomprehensible manner his wife owed her sudden recovery to the spirit's agency, and for this boon he felt it would be both unseemly and ungrateful – and possibly dangerous – to refuse. In great embarrassment, and at a loss for any plausible excuse, he felt half dazed, and as though all capacity for voluntary action was deserting him.

What was Tomosaburo's surprise on reaching the entrance to find stationed there a procession, like the train of some great personage, awaiting him. On their appearance the liveried bearers hastened to bring forward two magnificent palanquins of lacquer and gold, and at the same moment a tall man garbed in ceremonial robes advanced and with a deep obeisance requested them not to hesitate, saying:

"Honoured sir, these *kago* are for your august conveyance – deign to enter so that we may proceed to your destination."

At the same time the members of the procession and the bearers bowed low, and in curious high-pitched voices all repeated the invitation in a chorus:

"Please deign to enter the *kago*!"

Both Tomosaburo and his wife were not only amazed at the splendour of the escort which had been provided for them, but they realized that what was happening to them was most mysterious, and might have unexpected consequences. However, it was too late to draw back now, and all they could do was to fall in with the arrangement with as bold a front as they could muster. They both stepped valiantly into the elaborately decorated *kago*; thereupon the attendants surrounded the palanquins, the bearers raised the shafts shoulder high, and the procession formed in line and set out on its ghostly expedition.

The night was still and very dark. Thick masses of sable cloud obscured the heavens, with no friendly gleams of moon or stars to illumine their unknown path, and peering through the bamboo blinds nothing met Tomosaburo's anxious gaze but the impenetrable gloom of the inky sky.

Seated in the palanquins the adventurous couple were undergoing a strange experience. To their mystified senses it did not seem as if the *kago* was being borne along over the ground in the ordinary manner, but the sensation was as though they were being swiftly impelled by some mysterious unseen force, which caused them to skim through the air like the flight of birds. After some time had elapsed the sombre blackness of the night somewhat lifted, and they were dimly able to discern the curved outlines of a large mansion which they were now approaching, and which appeared to be situated in a spacious and thickly wooded park.

The bearers entered the large roofed gate and, crossing an intervening space of garden, carefully lowered their burdens before the main entrance of the house, where a body of servants and retainers were already waiting to welcome the expected guests with assiduous attentions. Tomosaburo and his wife alighted from their conveyances and were ushered into a reception room of great size and splendour, where, as soon as they were seated in the place of honour near the alcove, refreshments were served by a bevy of fair waiting-maids in ceremonial costumes. As soon as they were rested from the fatigues of their journey an usher appeared and bowing profoundly to the bewildered new-comers announced that the marriage feast was about to be celebrated and their presence was requested without delay.

Following this guide they proceeded through the various ante-rooms and along the corridors. The whole interior of the mansion, the sumptuousness of its appointments and the delicate beauty of its finishings, were such as to fill their hearts with wonder and admiration.

The floors of the passages shone like mirrors, so fine was the quality of the satiny woods, and the richly inlaid ceilings showed that no expense or trouble had been spared in the selection of all that was ancient and rare, both in materials and workmanship. Certain of the pillars were formed by the trunks of petrified trees, brought from great distances, and on every side perfect taste and limitless wealth were apparent in every detail of the scheme of decoration.

More and more deeply impressed with his surroundings, Tomosaburo obediently followed in the wake of the ushers. As they neared the stately guest-chamber an eerie and numbing sensation seemed to creep through his veins.

Observing more closely the surrounding figures that flitted to and fro, with a shock of horror he suddenly became aware that their faces were well known to him and of many in that shadowy throng he recognized the features and forms of friends and relatives long since dead. Along the corridors leading to the principal hall numerous attendants were gathered: all their features were familiar to Tomosaburo, but none of them betrayed the slightest sign of recognition. Gradually his dazed brain began to understand that he was visiting in the underworld, that everything about him was unreal – in fact, a dream of the past – and he feebly wondered of what hallucination he could be the victim to be thus abruptly bidden to such an illusory carnival, where all the wedding guests seemed to be denizens of the *Meido*, that dusky kingdom of departed spirits! But no time was left him for conjecture, for on reaching the ante-room they were immediately ushered into a magnificent hall where all preparations for the feast had been set out, and where the Elysian Strand and the symbols of marriage were all duly arranged according to time-honoured custom.

Here the bridegroom and his bride were seated in state, both attired in elegant robes as befitting the occasion. Tomosaburo, who had acted such a strange and important part in providing the farcical groom for this unheard-of marriage, gazed searchingly at the newly wedded husband, whose mien was quite dignified and imposing, and whose thick dark locks were crowned with a nobleman's coronet. He wondered what part the wooden figures he had carved according to the spirit's behest had taken in the composition of the bridegroom he now saw before him. Strangely, indeed, his features bore a striking resemblance to the little puppets that Tomosaburo had fashioned from the *kiri*-wood some days before.

The nuptial couple were receiving the congratulations of the assembled guests, and no sooner had Tomosaburo and his wife entered the room than the wedding party all came forward in a body to greet them and to offer thanks for their condescension in gracing that happy occasion with their presence. They were ceremoniously conducted to seats in a place of honour, and invited with great cordiality to participate in the evening's entertainment.

Servants then entered bearing all sorts of tempting dainties piled on lacquer trays in the form of large shells; the feast was spread before the whole assemblage; wine flowed in abundance, and by degrees conversation, laughter, and merriment became universal and the banquet-hall echoed with the carousal of the ghostly throng.

Under the influence of the good cheer Tomosaburo's apprehension and alarm of his weird environment gradually wore off, he partook freely of the refreshments, and associated himself more and more with the gaiety and joviality of the evening's revel.

* * *

The night wore on and when the hour of midnight struck the banquet was at its height.

In the mirth and glamour of that strange marriage feast Tomosaburo had lost all track of time, when suddenly the clear sound of a cock's crow penetrated his clouded brain and, looking up, the transparency of the *shoji* of the room began to slowly whiten in the grey of dawn. Like a flash of lightning Tomosaburo and his wife found themselves transported back, safe and sound, into their own room.

On reflection he found his better nature more and more troubled by such an uncanny experience, and he spent much time pondering over the matter, which seemed to require such delicate handling. He determined that at all costs communications must be broken off with the importunate spirit.

A few days passed and Tomosaburo began to cherish the hope that he had seen the last of the Spirit of the Lantern, but his congratulations on escaping her unwelcome attentions proved premature. That very night, no sooner had he laid himself down to rest, than lo! and behold, the lantern shot up in the familiar shaft of light, and there in the lurid glow appeared the spirit, looking more than ever bent on mischief. Tomosaburo lost all patience. Glaring savagely at the unwelcome visitant he seized his wooden pillow and, determining to rid himself of her persecutions once and for all, he exerted his whole strength and hurled it straight at the intruder. His aim was true, and the missile struck the goblin squarely on the forehead, overturning the lantern and plunging the room into black darkness. "Wa, Wa!" wailed the spirit in a thin haunting cry, that gradually grew fainter and fainter till she finally disappeared like a luminous trail of vanishing blue smoke.

From that very hour Tomosaburo's wife was again stricken with her former malady, and no remedies being of any avail, within two days it took a turn for the worse and she died.

The sorrow-stricken husband bitterly regretted his impetuous action in giving way to that fatal fit of anger and, moreover, in appearing so forgetful of the past favour he had received from the spirit. He therefore prayed earnestly to the offended apparition, apologizing with humble contrition for his cruelty and ingratitude.

But the Spirit of the Lantern had been too deeply outraged to return, and Tomosaburo's repentance for his rash impulse proved all in vain.

These melancholy events caused the unhappy husband to take a strong aversion to the house, which he felt sure must be haunted, and he decided to leave that neighbourhood with as little delay as possible.

As soon as a suitable dwelling was found and the details of his migration arranged, the carriers were summoned to transport his household goods to the new abode, but to the alarm and consternation of every one, when the servants attempted to move the furniture, the whole contents of the house by some unseen power adhered fast to the floor, and no human power was available to dislodge them.

Then Tomosaburo's little son fell ill and died. Such was the revenge of the Spirit of the Lantern.

The Badger-Haunted Temple
Translated by Yei Theodora Ozaki

Once long ago, in southern Japan, in the town of Kumamoto, there lived a young *samurai*, who had a great devotion to the sport of fishing. Armed with his large basket and tackle, he would often start out in the early morning and pass the whole day at his favourite pastime, returning home only at nightfall.

One fine day he had more than usual luck. In the late afternoon, when he examined his basket, he found it full to overflowing. Highly delighted at his success, he wended his way homewards with a light heart, singing snatches of merry songs as he went along.

It was already dusk when he happened to pass a deserted Buddhist temple. He noticed that the gate stood half open, and hung loosely on its rusty hinges, and the whole place had a dilapidated and tumbledown appearance.

What was the young man's astonishment to see, in striking contrast to such a forlorn environment, a pretty young girl standing just within the gate.

As he approached she came forward, and looking at him with a meaning glance, smiled, as if inviting him to enter into conversation. The *samurai* thought her manner somewhat strange, and at first was on his guard. Some mysterious influence, however, compelled him to stop, and he stood irresolutely admiring the fair young face, blooming like a flower in its sombre setting.

When she noticed his hesitation she made a sign to him to approach. Her charm was so great and the smile with which she accompanied the gesture so irresistible, that half-unconsciously, he went up the stone steps, passed through the semi-open portal, and entered the courtyard where she stood awaiting him.

The maiden bowed courteously, then turned and led the way up the stone-flagged pathway to the temple. The whole place was in the most woeful condition, and looked as if it had been abandoned for many years.

When they reached what had once been the priest's house, the *samurai* saw that the interior of the building was in a better state of preservation than the outside led one to suppose. Passing along the verandah into the front room, he noticed that the *tatami* were still presentable, and that a sixfold screen adorned the chamber.

The girl gracefully motioned her guest to sit down in the place of honour near the alcove.

"Does the priest of the temple live here?" asked the young man, seating himself.

"No," answered the girl, "there is no priest here now. My mother and I only came here yesterday. She has gone to the next village to buy some things and may not be able to come back tonight. But honourably rest awhile, and let me give you some refreshment."

The girl then went into the kitchen apparently to make the tea, but though the guest waited a long time, she never returned.

By this time the moon had risen, and shone so brightly into the room, that it was as light as day. The *samurai* began to wonder at the strange behaviour of the damsel, who had inveigled him into such a place only to disappear and leave him in solitude.

Suddenly he was startled by someone sneezing loudly behind the screen. He turned his head in the direction from whence the sound came. To his utter amazement, not the pretty girl whom he had expected, but a huge, red-faced, bald-headed priest stalked out. He must have been about seven feet in height, for his head towered nearly to the ceiling, and he carried an iron wand, which he raised in a threatening manner.

"How dare you enter my house without my permission?" shouted the fierce-looking giant. "Unless you go away at once I will beat you into dust."

Frightened out of his wits, the young man took to his heels, and rushed with all speed out of the temple.

As he fled across the courtyard he heard peals of loud laughter behind him. Once outside the gate he stopped to listen, and still the strident laugh continued. Suddenly it occurred to him, that in the alarm of his hasty exit, he had forgotten his basket of fish. It was left behind in the temple. Great was his chagrin, for never before had he caught so much fish in a single day; but lacking the courage to go back and demand it, there was no alternative but to return home empty-handed.

The following day he related his strange experience to several of his friends. They were all highly amused at such an adventure, and some of them plainly intimated that the seductive maiden and the aggressive giant were merely hallucinations that owed their origin to the sake flask.

At last one man, who was a good fencer, said:

"Oh, you must have been deluded by a badger who coveted your fish. No one lives in that temple. It has been deserted ever since I can remember. I will go there this evening and put an end to his mischief."

He then went to a fishmonger, purchased a large basket of fish, and borrowed an angling rod. Thus equipped, he waited impatiently for the sun to set. When the dusk began to fall he buckled on his sword and set out for the temple, carefully shouldering his bait that was to lead to the undoing of the badger. He laughed confidently to himself as he said: "I will teach the old fellow a lesson!"

As he approached the ruin what was his surprise to see, not one, but three girls standing there.

"O, ho! that is the way the wind lies, is it, but the crafty old sinner won't find it such an easy matter to make a fool of me."

No sooner was he observed by the pretty trio than by gestures they invited him to enter. Without any hesitation, he followed them into the building, and boldly seated himself upon the mats. They placed the customary tea and cakes before him, and then brought in a flagon of wine and an extraordinarily large cup.

The swordsman partook neither of the tea nor the sake, and shrewdly watched the demeanour of the three maidens.

Noticing his avoidance of the proffered refreshment, the prettiest of them artlessly inquired:

"Why don't you take some sake?"

"I dislike both tea and sake," replied the valiant guest, "but if you have some accomplishment to entertain me with, if you can dance or sing, I shall be delighted to see you perform."

"Oh, what an old-fashioned man of propriety you are! If you don't drink, you surely know nothing of love either. What a dull existence yours must be! But we can dance a little, so if you will condescend to look, we shall be very pleased to try to amuse you with our performance, poor as it is."

The maidens then opened their fans and began to posture and dance. They exhibited so much skill and grace, however, that the swordsman was astonished, for it was unusual that country girls should be so deft and well-trained. As he watched them he became more and more fascinated, and gradually lost sight of the object of his mission.

Lost in admiration, he followed their every step, their every movement, and as the Japanese storyteller says, he forgot himself entirely, entranced at the beauty of their dancing.

Suddenly he saw that the three performers had become *headless*! Utterly bewildered, he gazed at them intently to make sure that he was not dreaming. Lo! and behold! each was holding her own head in her hands. They then threw them up and caught them as they fell. Like children playing a game of ball, they tossed their heads from one to the other. At last the boldest of the three threw her head at the young fencer. It fell on his knees, looked up in his face, and laughed at him. Angered at the girl's impertinence, he cast the head back at her in disgust, and drawing his sword, made several attempts to cut down the goblin dancer as she glided to and fro playfully tossing up her head and catching it.

But she was too quick for him, and like lightning darted out of the reach of his sword.

"Why don't you catch me?" she jeered mockingly. Mortified at his failure, he made another desperate attempt, but once more she adroitly eluded him, and sprang up to the top of the screen.

"I am here! Can you not reach me this time?" and she laughed at him in derision.

Again he made a thrust at her, but she proved far too nimble for him, and again, for the third time, he was foiled.

Then the three girls tossed their heads on their respective necks, shook them at him, and with shouts of weird laughter they vanished from sight.

As the young man came to his senses he vaguely gazed around. Bright moonlight illumined the whole place, and the stillness of the midnight was unbroken save for the thin tinkling chirping of the insects. He shivered as he realized the lateness of the hour and the wild loneliness of that uncanny spot. His basket of fish was nowhere to be seen. He understood, that he, too, had come under the spell of the wizard-badger, and like his friend, at whom he had laughed so heartily the day before, he had been bewitched by the wily creature.

But, although deeply chagrined at having fallen such an easy dupe, he was powerless to take any sort of revenge. The best he could do was to accept his defeat and return home.

Among his friends there was a doctor, who was not only a brave man, but one full of resource. On hearing of the way the mortified swordsman had been bamboozled, he said:

"Now leave this to me. Within three days I will catch that old badger and punish him well for all his diabolical tricks."

The doctor went home and prepared a savoury dish cooked with meat. Into this he mixed some deadly poison. He then cooked a second portion for himself. Taking these separate dishes and a bottle of sake with him, towards evening he set out for the ruined temple.

When he reached the mossy courtyard of the old building he found it solitary and deserted. Following the example of his friends, he made his way into the priest's room, intensely curious to see what might befall him, but, contrary to his expectation, all was empty and still. He knew that goblin-badgers were such crafty animals that it was almost impossible for anyone, however cautious, to be able to cope successfully with their snares and *Fata Morganas*. But he determined to be particularly wide awake and on his guard, so as not to fall a prey to any hallucination that the badger might raise.

The night was beautiful, and calm as the mouldering tombs in the temple graveyard. The full moon shone brightly over the great black sloping roofs, and cast a flood of light into the room where the doctor was patiently awaiting the mysterious foe. The minutes went slowly by, an hour elapsed, and still no ghostly visitant appeared. At last the baffled intruder placed his flask of wine before him and began to make preparations for his evening meal, thinking that possibly the badger might be unable to resist the tempting savour of the food.

"There is nothing like solitude," he mused aloud. "What a perfect night it is! How lucky I am to have found this deserted temple from which to view the silvery glory of the autumn moon."

For some time he continued to eat and drink, smacking his lips like a country gourmet in enjoyment of the meal. He began to think that the badger, knowing that he had found his match at last, Intended to leave him alone. Then to his delight, he heard the sound of footsteps. He watched the entrance to the room, expecting the old wizard to assume his favourite disguise, and that some pretty maiden would come to cast a spell upon him with her fascinations.

But, to his surprise, who should come into sight but an old priest, who dragged himself into the room with faltering steps and sank down upon the mats with a deep long-drawn sigh of weariness.

Apparently between seventy and eighty years of age, his clothes were old and travel-stained, and in his withered hands he carried a rosary. The effort of ascending the steps had evidently been a great trial to him, he breathed heavily and seemed in a state of great exhaustion. His whole appearance was one to arouse pity in the heart of the beholder.

"May I inquire who are you?" asked the doctor.

The old man replied, in a quavering voice, "I am the priest who used to live here many years ago when the temple was in a prosperous condition. As a youth I received my training here under the abbot then in charge, having been dedicated from childhood to the service of the most holy Buddha by my parents. At the time of the great Saigo's rebellion I was sent to another parish. When the castle of Kumamoto was besieged, alas! my own temple was burned to the ground. For years I wandered from place to place and fell on very hard times. In my old age and misfortunes my heart at last yearned to come back to this temple, where I spent so many happy years as an acolyte. It is my hope to spend my last days here. You can imagine my grief when I found it utterly abandoned, sunk in decay, with no priest in charge to offer up the daily prayers to the Lord Buddha, or to keep up the rites for the dead buried here. It is now my sole desire to collect money and to restore the temple. But alas! age and illness and want of food have robbed me of my strength, and I fear that I shall never be able to achieve what I have planned," and here the old man broke down and shed tears – a pitiful sight.

When wiping his eyes with the sleeve of his threadbare robe, he looked hungrily at the food and wine on which the doctor was regaling himself, and added, wistfully:

"Ah, I see you have a delicious meal there and wine withal, which you are enjoying while gazing at the moonlit scenery. I pray you spare me a little, for it is many days since I have had a good meal and I am half-famished."

At first the doctor was persuaded that the story was true, so plausible did it sound, and his heart was filled with compassion for the old bonze. He listened carefully till the melancholy recital was finished.

Then something in the accent of speech struck his ear as being different to that of a human being, and he reflected.

"This may be the badger! I must not allow myself to be deceived! The crafty cunning animal is planning to palm off his customary tricks on me, but he shall see that I am as clever as he is."

The doctor pretended to believe in the old man's story, and answered:

"Indeed, I deeply sympathize with your misfortunes. You are quite welcome to share my meal – nay, I will give you with pleasure all that is left, and, moreover, I promise to bring you some more tomorrow. I will also inform my friends and acquaintances of your pious plan to restore the temple, and will give all the assistance in my power in your work of collecting subscriptions." He then pushed forward the untouched plate of food which contained poison, rose from the mats, and took his leave, promising to return the next evening.

All the friends of the doctor who had heard him boast that he would outwit the badger, arrived early next morning, curious to know what had befallen him. Many of them were very sceptical regarding the tale of the badger trickster, and ascribed the illusions of their friends to the sake bottle.

The doctor would give no answer to their many inquiries, but merely invited them to accompany him.

"Come and see for yourselves," he said, and guided them to the old temple, the scene of so many uncanny experiences.

First of all they searched the room where he had sat the evening before, but nothing was to be found except the empty basket in which he had carried the food for himself and the badger. They investigated the whole place thoroughly, and at last, in one of the dark corners of the temple-chamber, they came upon the dead body of an old, old badger. It was the size of a large dog, and its hair was grey with age. Everyone was convinced that it must be at least several hundred years old.

The doctor carried it home in triumph. For several days the people in the neighbourhood came in large numbers to gloat over the hoary carcase, and to listen in awe and wonder to the marvellous stories of the numbers of people that had been duped and befooled by the magic powers of the old goblin-badger.

The writer adds that he was told another badger story concerning the same temple. Many of the old people in the parish remember the incident, and one of them related the following story.

Years before, when the sacred building was still in a prosperous state, the priest in charge celebrated a great Buddhist festival, which lasted some days. Amongst the numerous devotees who attended the services he noticed a very handsome youth, who listened with profound reverence, unusual in one so young, to the sermons and litanies. When the festival was over and the other worshippers had gone, he lingered around the temple as though loth to leave the sacred spot. The head priest, who had conceived a liking for the lad, judged from his refined and dignified appearance that he must be the son of a high-class *samurai* family, probably desirous of entering the priesthood.

Gratified by the youth's apparent religious fervour, the holy man invited him to come to his study, and thereupon gave him some instruction in the Buddhist doctrines. He listened with the utmost attention for the whole afternoon to the bonze's learned discourse, and thanked him repeatedly for the condescension and trouble he had taken in instructing one so unworthy as himself.

The afternoon waned and the hour for the evening meal came round. The priest ordered a bowl of macaroni to be brought for the visitor, who proved to be the owner of a phenomenal appetite, and consumed three times as much as a full-grown man.

He then bowed most courteously and asked permission to return home. In bidding him good-bye, the priest, who felt a curious fascination for the youth, presented him with a gold-lacquered medicine-box (*inro*) as a parting souvenir.

The lad prostrated himself in gratitude, and then took his departure.

The next day the temple servant, sweeping the graveyard, came across a badger. He was quite dead, and was dressed in a straw-covering put on in such a way as to resemble the clothes of a human being. To his side was tied a gold-lacquered *inro*, and his paunch was much distended and as round as a large bowl. It was evident that the creature's gluttony had been the cause of his death, and the priest, on seeing the animal, identified the *inro* as the one which he had bestowed upon the good-looking lad the day before, and knew that he had been the victim of a badger's deceiving wiles.

It was thus certain that the temple had been haunted by a pair of goblin-badgers, and that when this one had died, its mate had continued to inhabit the same temple even after it had been abandoned. The creature had evidently taken a fantastic delight in bewitching wayfarers and travellers, or anyone who carried delectable food with them, and while mystifying them with his tricks and illusions, had deftly abstracted their baskets and bundles, and had lived comfortably upon his stolen booty.

Yotsuya Kwaidan: Chapter XIV
The Punishment

Tsuruya Namboku IV, Shunkintei Ryuō et al.,
adapted by James S. De Benneville

In this version of the story, O-Iwa has been ill-treated and facially disfigured by her husband Iémon Tamiya, who has then plotted for her to be sold into prostitution in the house of Toémon and his wife Okamisan. But O-Iwa refuses to work for them and is punished. It is in this chapter we first get a description of her transformation into the demon-like ghost-figure that she becomes – seemingly before her uncertain drowning – ahead of enacting revenge on all those who plotted against her.

O-Iwa did not move. The two women approached and laid hands on her. Her yielding made no difference in the roughness of their treatment. Dragged, hustled, shoved, with amplitude of blows, she was already much bruised on reaching the place of punishment – the *seméba*, to use the technical term of these establishments "for the good of the community." During a temporary absence of the mistress, a ray of kindliness seemed to touch the woman O-Kin. She pointed to the square of some six feet, to the rings fastened in the rafters. "Don't carry self-will to extremes. Here you are to be stripped, hauled up to those rings, and beaten until the bow breaks. Look at it and take warning. Kin is no weakling." She shoved back her sleeve, showing an arm as hard and brawny as that of a stevedore. With disapproval she observed O-Iwa. The latter stood unresisting, eyes on the ground. Only the lips twitched from time to time. As the only person in the house, male or female, not to fear the Okamisan, O-Kin could only put the courage down to ignorance. She shrugged her shoulders with contempt. "A man would cause you no pain. The same cannot be said of Kin. You shall have the proof." Perhaps severity would be more merciful, by quickly breaking down this obstinacy.

The wife returned with the instrument of torture, a bow of bamboo wound with rattan to strengthen it. O-Kin took it, ostentatiously bent and displayed its stinging flexibility before the eyes of O-Iwa. The latter closed them. She would cut off all temptation to weakness. At a sign O-Kin roughly tore off the *obi*. A twist, and the torn and disordered *kimono* of O-Iwa fell to her feet with the skirt. She had no shirt. Thus she was left completely naked. In modesty she sank crouching on the ground. The cold wind of the March night made her shiver as O-Kin roped her wrists. Again the woman whispered her counsel in her ear – "When you get enough, say 'Un! Un!'" Detecting no sign of consent she took a ladder, climbed up, and passed the ropes through the rings above. She descended, and the two women began to haul away. Gradually O-Iwa was raised from the sitting posture to her full height of extended arms, until by effort her toes could just reach the ground. In this painful position the slightest twist to relieve the strain on the wrists caused agonizing pains through the whole body. "Still obstinate – strike!" shouted the wife. O-Kin raised the bow and delivered the blow with full force across the buttocks. A red streak appeared. O-Iwa by a natural contortion raised her legs. The blows descended fast, followed at once by the raised welt of flesh, or the blood from the lacerated tissue. Across the shoulder blades, the small of the back, the buttocks, the belly, they descended with the full force of the robust arms and weight of O-Kin. Every time the legs were raised at the shock the suspended body spun round. Every time the toes rested on the ground the bow descended with merciless ferocity. The sight of the torture roused the fierce spirit in the tormentors. O-Kin redoubled the violence of her blows, seeking out the hams and the withers, the shoulders, the tenderest points to cause pain. The wife ran from side to side, gazing into the face and closed eyes of O-Iwa, trying to detect weakening under the torture, or result from some more agonizing blow. O-Iwa's body was striped and splashed with red. O-Kin's hands slipped on the wet surface of the rod. Suddenly she uttered an exclamation. Blood was now gushing from the nose, the eyes, the mouth of O-Iwa. "Okamisan! Okamisan! It won't do to kill her. Deign to give the order to cease. She must be lowered." The wife coolly examined the victim. "She has fainted. Lower her, and throw salt water over her. The sting will bring her to." O-Kin followed the instructions in the most literal sense. She dashed the bucket of water with great impetus right into O-Iwa's face. "Un!" was the latter's exclamation as she came to consciousness. "She consents! She consents!" cried O-Kin with delight. The wife was decidedly sceptical, but her aid plainly would go no further at this time. Said she – "Leave her as she is. There are other matters to attend to than the whims of an idle vicious jade. She would cheat this Matsu out of twenty *ryō*? Well: time will show the victor." She departed – "to drink her wine, pare her nails, and sing obscene songs to the accompaniment of the *samisen*."

Tied hand and foot O-Iwa lay semi-conscious in the cold shed of punishment. At midnight the girls returned to this 'home.' They gathered around the prostrate O-Iwa. From O-Kin they had an inkling of the courage displayed. They admired her, but none dared to touch her bonds. At last O-Haru San, unusually successful in her night's raid, ventured to approach the half drunk mistress of the house. "Haru makes report." She spread her returns before the gratified Okamisan. Timidly the girl added – "O-Iwa San repents. Deign to remit her punishment. She looks very ill and weak." – "Shut up!" was the fierce retort. Then as afterthought of sickness and possible loss came to mind: "She can be untied and sent to bed." – "And food?" – "She can earn it." The woman turned on O-Haru, who bowed humbly and slipped away. That night the girls contributed from their store to feed O-Iwa; as they did on the succeeding days and nights. The wife would have stopped the practice, but Toémon interfered. He meant to keep his dilapidated stock in as good repair as possible. He fed them pretty well. "The woman is not to be starved – at least too openly. The last case gave this Toémon trouble enough, and on the very day this epileptic came into the house, to bring confusion with her. Beat her if you will; but not enough to kill her." O-Matsu followed his words to the letter. One beating was followed by another; with interval enough between the torture to ensure recuperation and avoid danger to life. These scenes came to be regarded as a recreation of the house. The other inmates were allowed to attend, to witness the example and fascinate their attention. But at last the Okamisan despaired. Amusement was one thing; but her hatred of O-Iwa was tempered by the desire to find some use for her, to get a return for the twenty *ryō* out of which she had been swindled. Finally the advice of the *bantō* was followed. "The men of the house cannot be tempted to approach such an apparition. The other girls have not time to devote to making up O-Iwa as for the stage. They have not twenty *ryō* at stake, as had Chōbei. Let her wash the dishes." Thus was O-Iwa 'degraded' from her high estate as street-walker. Turned into a kitchen drudge she shed tears of joy. She almost forgot the matter of the pledge in this new and pleasant life. The time and the place, perhaps the drug she took, had done their work on the mind of O-Iwa. Iémon, the house of Samonchō, the *ihai* in the Butsudan, the pleasant garden – all were of the tissue of a dream amid a toil which deposited her on the straw wrappings of the charcoal and in a shed, thoroughly worn out at the end of her long day. The O-Iwa of Samonchō at this end of the lapsing year of service was dormant. But accidents will happen.

There was excitement in the house. Mobei, the dealer in toilet articles – combs, brushes, jewel strings – was at the grating. The women were clustered before the wares he exposed in his trays. This Mobei, as dealer in toilet articles (*koma-mono*) wandered all the wards of Edo, his little trays fitting neatly into each other, and wrapped in a *furoshiki* or bundle-handkerchief. His wares formed a marvellous collection of the precious and common place, ranging from true coral and tortoiseshell, antique jewellery and curious *netsuké* of great value, to their counterfeits in painted wood, horn, and coloured glass. "Mobei San, long has been the wait for you. Is there a bent comb in stock?" – "Truly this Mobei is vexing. He humbly makes apology, lady. Here is just the thing…. How much? Only a *bu*…. Too high? Nay! With women in the ordinary walks of life it is the wage of a month. To the honoured Oiran it is but a night's trifling." The other women tittered. O-Haru was a little nettled at the high sounding title of Oiran. She would not show her irritation. Mobei continued his attentions. He laid before her and the others several strings of jewels, their 'coral' made of cleverly tinted paste. "Deign to look; at but one *bu* two *shū*. If real they would cost twenty *ryō*." – "And Mobei has the real?" The dealer laughed. As in pity, and to give them a glimpse of the far off upper world, he raised the cover of a box in the lower tier. They gasped in admiration before the pink of the true coral. Hands were stretched through the grating to touch it. Mobei quickly replaced the cover. "For some great lady," sighed O-Haru – "Just so," replied Mobei, adjusting his boxes. He had sold two wooden painted combs and a string of horn beads in imitation of tortoiseshell. He pocketed the hundred 'cash,' those copper coins with a hole in the centre for stringing. Then briefly – "The necklace is for no other than the Kashiku of the Yamadaya, the loved one of Kibei Dono of Yotsuya. The comb (*kanzashi*) in tortoiseshell and gold is for the honoured lady wife of Iémon Dono, the go kenin. But Mobei supplies not only the secular world. This – for one who has left the world; for Myōzen Oshō of Myōgyōji, the gift of Itō Dono. For the custom of Mobei the Yotsuya stands first in order." He took a box from his sleeve and showed them the rosary of pure crystal beads. Even in the dull light of a lowering day the stones flashed and sparkled. The women showed little interest. A priest to them was not a man – ordinarily.

He shouldered his pack. "Mobei San – a comb with black spots, in imitation of tortoiseshell. Please don't fail me on the next visit." Mobei nodded agreement. Then he halted and turned. One of the women had called out in derision – "Here is O-Iwa San. Surely she wants to purchase. Mobei San! Mobei San! A customer with many customers and a full pocketbook." These women looked on O-Iwa's assignment to the kitchen as the fall to the lowest possible state. At sight of the newcomer Mobei gasped. O-Iwa on leaving the door of Toémon's house, *miso* strainers for repair in one hand, fifteen mon for *tōfu* tightly clasped in the other, came face to face with the toilet dealer, "The lady of Tamiya – here!" – "The lady of Tamiya!" echoed the astonished and curious women. Said O-Iwa quickly – "Mobei San is mistaken. This is Iwa; but lady of Tamiya...." Hastily she pulled her head towel over her face. In doing so the 'cash' slipped from her hand. A *mon* missing meant no *tōfu*; result, a visit to the *seméba*. In recovering the lost coin Mobei was left in no doubt. "'Tis indeed the lady of Tamiya. It cannot be denied." O-Iwa no longer attempted the impossible. She said – "It is Iwa of Tamiya. Mobei San, a word with you." The women were whispering to each other. "He called her '*shinzō*.'" Said O-Haru – "There always was something about her to arouse suspicion; so ugly, and with such grand airs. And how she endured the punishment! Truly she must be a *samurai* woman." The minds of all reverted to their master Toémon, and how he would take this news.

O-Iwa had drawn Mobei somewhat apart from the grating. With downcast face she spoke – "Deign, Mobei San, to say nothing in the ward of this meeting with Iwa." To Mobei's earnest gesture of comprehension – "Affairs had gone badly with Tamiya. Iémon San was misled into gambling by Natsumé Kyuzō and Imaizumi Jinzaémon. He was carried away by the passion. It was no longer possible to stay in Samonchō. Worse conduct followed. In the kindness and advice of Itō Dono, of Akiyama and Kondō Sama, this Iwa found support. But she disobeyed. She would not follow the advice given. However, gratitude is felt by Iwa. One cannot leave this place, or long since she would have paid the visit of acknowledgment. A matter of importance arose. Chōbei San came to Iwa's aid, and saved the situation. This place is terrible, but the consequences of not coming would have been more so. To Chōbei gratitude is felt. It was the opportunity offered the wife to show her faith and courage." Now she looked bravely in Mobei's face. It was the toilet dealer's turn to show confusion – "Honoured lady, is nothing known?" – "Known?" answered O-Iwa in some surprise. "What is there to know? When this Iwa left Samonchō to be sure the house was cracking apart everywhere. The light poured in as through a bamboo door.... Ah! Have matters gone badly with the Danna in Iwa's absence?" Mobei shook his head in dissent. "Alas! Itō Sama, Akiyama or Kondō San, has misfortune come to them, without a word of condolence from Iwa? Perhaps Chōbei San, in his precarious life...." The poor isolated world of the thoughts of this homely creature was limited to these friends in need.

Mobei had sunk to his knees before her. He raised eyes in which stood tears of pity and indignation. "The Ojōsan knows nothing of what has occurred in Yotsuya? This Mobei will not keep silent. With the affairs of Iémon Sama, of Itō Dono and Akiyama San nothing has gone wrong. The absence of the lady O-Iwa is otherwise related. She has abandoned house and husband to run away with a plebeian, the *bantō* at the greengrocer's on Shinjuku road. Such is the story circulated." O-Iwa drew away from him as from a snake – then: "Mobei, you lie! Why tell such a tale to this Iwa? Are not the words of Itō Dono, of Akiyama Sama, of Chōbei San still in Iwa's ears? What else has she had to console her during these bitter months but the thought of their kindness? This dress (a scantily wadded single garment), these bare feet in this snow, this degraded life – are not they evidences of Iwa's struggle for the honour of husband and House? Mobei, slander of honourable men brings one to evil. Mobei lies; lies!"

He seized her dress. The man now was weeping. "The lady of Tamiya is a saint. Alas! Nothing does she know of the wicked hearts of men. Too great has been the kindness of the Ojōsan to this Mobei for him to attempt deceit. Deign to listen. This day a week; was it not the day to a year of the Ojōsan's leaving the house in Yotsuya?" O-Iwa turned to him with a startled face. He continued – "A week ago Mobei visited Yotsuya. He has many customers there, not too curious about prices. Hence he brings the best of his wares. Coming to the house in Samonchō a feast was in progress. There were present Itō Dono, Akiyama Sama, Natsumé and Imaizumi Sama, Kondō Dono; O-Hana San, of course. All were exceedingly merry, Iémon Dono poured out a cup of wine. 'Mobei! Mobei! Come here! Drain this cup in honour of the occasion. We celebrate the anniversary of the expulsion of the *bakémono*. The demon is driven forth from the Paradise of Yotsuya. Namu Myōhō Renge Kyō! Namu Myōhō Renge Kyō!' This Mobei was amazed – 'The O-Baké…. What O-Baké?' – 'Why: O-Iwa San. A year since, with the aid of these good friends, and one not present here, Iémon freed himself from the clutches of the vengeful apparition. Our *Kumi-gashira* granted divorce in due form. The son of Takahashi Daihachirō – Yanagibara Kazuma – Tamiya Iémon no longer catches at sleep to wake in fear. Chief, deep is the gratitude of Iémon for the favour done by Itō Dono.' The Ojōsan a *bakémono*! At these outrageous words Mobei felt faint. Receiving the cup, as in modesty returned to the *rōka* to drink, the contents were spilled on the ground. Ah! Honoured lady, it is not only that the Ojōsan has been driven out. Her goods have been cleverly stolen by false messages of gambling losses. Stored with Kondō Sama they were brought back on the success of the wicked plot. The whole is a conspiracy of Iémon Dono with Itō Dono, with Akiyama, Chōbei, Kondō, and others. They bragged of it, and told the tale in full before this Mobei, laughing the while. Why, lady! On the word of Chōbei San the order of divorce was issued by Itō Dono. Within the month O-Hana San left the shelter of the house of Kondō Sama to enter the Tamiya as bride. Deign to look. Here is a jewelled comb reserved by Iémon Sama as present for O-Hana San his wife. Here is gift of Itō Dono to Myōzen Oshō for his efforts 'in the cause.'"

O-Iwa stood as one frozen. With Mobei's words the light was flooding into mind and soul. Step by step she now followed clearly the stages of this infamous conspiracy against her peace and honour. She had been fooled, cheated, degraded – and by Itō Kwaiba, the enemy of Matazaémon; by Iémon, son of the hereditary foe Takahashi Daihachirō. Mobei remained huddled at her feet, watching with fright the sudden and awful change in her face. The words came in a whisper. At first she brought out her speech with difficulty, then to rise to torrent force – "Cheated, gulled by the hereditary foe! And this Iwa lies bound and helpless! 'Tis understood! The end is at hand – Ah! The poison! The poison! Now it, too, rises; flowing upward to heart and head of Iwa. Accursed man! Accursed woman; who would play the rival and destroy the wife! The time is short; the crisis is at hand. Chōbei's dark words become light. Hana would poison Iwa through this treacherous leech. Iémon would kill her by the foul life of this brothel – Gods of Nippon! Buddhas of the Universe! All powerful Amida, the Protector! Kwannon, the Lady Merciful! Deign to hearken to the prayer of this Iwa. Emma Dai-ō, king of Hell, summon not the daughter of Tamiya before the dreaded throne for judgment – through the course of seven existences – until the vengeance of Iwa be sated with the miserable end of these her persecutors. May the sacred characters of the Daimoku, written on the heart of Iwa for her future salvation, be seared out as with hot iron. On Itō Kwaiba, Iémon, Akiyama Chōzaémon, Chōbei, all and every one engaged in this vile plot, rests the death curse of Iwa. Against these; against Natsumé, Imaizumi, Yoémon of Tamiya, lies the grudge of Iwa of Tamiya. Gods and Buddhas – grant this prayer!"

A violent hand was laid on the bosom of Mobei's robe. He screamed in terror at the fearful face bent over him. A broad round dead white swollen face, two sharp gleaming malignant dots darting flashes as from a sword between the puffed and swollen lids, froze him into a passive object. One of these lids drooped horribly down upon the cheek of the apparition. In the physical effort exerted, the slit of the mouth showed the broad black even teeth, which seemed about to clutch at his throat; as did the vigorous hand, the nails of which sank into his gullet. Framed in the mass of wild disordered hair Mobei was isolated as in a universe of space; left alone with this fearful vision. "Lady! Lady O-Iwa! Lady of Tamiya! This Mobei has done naught. Others have wronged O-Iwa San. Mobei is guiltless.... Ah! Ah!" With fright and pain he rolled over on the ground in a dead faint. Screaming and shouting the women Také and Kōta rushed around and out to his rescue. O-Iwa San was now under the full control of her disorder. Takézo staggered back, her hands to her face to hide the horrible sight, to wipe from eyes and cheeks the blood streaming from the deep tears made by O-Iwa's nails. Kōta from behind seized O-Iwa around the waist and shoulders.

Sharply up came the elbow shot, catching this interloper under the chin. Neck and jaw fairly cracked under the well-delivered blow. Kōta went down in a heap as one dead. A *chūgen* coming along the North Warigesui had reached the crossing. He thought it better to stand aside, rather than attempt to stop this maddened fiend tearing through space. At the canal bank there was a moment's pause. Then came a dull splash; as of some heavy body plunged in the water. With a cry the man hastened forward. Not a sign of anything could be seen. In this rural place no help was to be had, and he was little inclined to plunge at random into the foul stream. In haste he turned back to where a crowd was gathering around the prostrate Mobei, the groaning harlots to whom punishment had been meted out.

Ghost Story of the Flute's Tomb
Collected by Richard Gordon Smith

Long ago, at a small and out-of-the-way village called Kumedamura, about eight miles to the south-east of Sakai city, in Idsumo Province, there was made a tomb, the *Fuezuka* or Flute's Tomb, and to this day many people go thither to offer up prayer and to worship, bringing with them flowers and incense-sticks, which are deposited as offerings to the spirit of the man who was buried there. All the year round people flock to it. There is no season at which they pray more particularly than at another.

The *Fuezuka* tomb is situated on a large pond called Kumeda, some five miles in circumference, and all the places around this pond are known as of Kumeda Pond, from which the village of Kumeda took its name.

Whose tomb can it be that attracts such sympathy? The tomb itself is a simple stone pillar, with nothing artistic to recommend it. Neither is the surrounding scenery interesting; it is flat and ugly until the mountains of Kiushu are reached. I must tell, as well as I can, the story of whose tomb it is.

Between seventy and eighty years ago there lived near the pond in the village of Kumedamura a blind *amma* called Yoichi. Yoichi was extremely popular in the neighbourhood, being very honest and kind, besides being quite a professor in the art of massage – a treatment necessary to almost every Japanese. It would be difficult indeed to find a village that had not its *amma*.

Yoichi was blind, and, like all men of his calling, carried an iron wand or stick, also a flute or *'fuezuka'* – the stick to feel his way about with, and the flute to let people know he was ready for employment. So good an *amma* was Yoichi, he was nearly always employed, and, consequently, fairly well off, having a little house of his own and one servant, who cooked his food.

A little way from Yoichi's house was a small teahouse, placed upon the banks of the pond. One evening (April 5th; cherry-blossom season), just at dusk, Yoichi was on his way home, having been at work all day. His road led him by the pond. There he heard a girl crying piteously. He stopped and listened for a few moments, and gathered from what he heard that the girl was about to drown herself. Just as she entered the lake Yoichi caught her by the dress and dragged her out.

"Who are you, and why in such trouble as to wish to die?" he asked.

"I am Asayo, the teahouse girl," she answered. "You know me quite well. You must know, also, that it is not possible for me to support myself out of the small pittance which is paid by my master. I have eaten nothing for two days now, and am tired of my life."

"Come, come!" said the blind man. "Dry your tears. I will take you to my house, and do what I can to help you. You are only twenty-five years of age, and I am told still a fair-looking girl. Perhaps you will marry! In any case, I will take care of you, and you must not think of killing yourself. Come with me now; and I will see that you are well fed, and that dry clothes are given you."

So Yoichi led Asayo to his home.

A few months found them wedded to each other. Were they happy? Well, they should have been, for Yoichi treated his wife with the greatest kindness; but she was unlike her husband. She was selfish, bad-tempered, and unfaithful. In the eyes of Japanese infidelity is the worst of sins. How much more, then, is it against the country's spirit when advantage is taken of a husband who is blind?

Some three months after they had been married, and in the heat of August, there came to the village a company of actors. Among them was Sawamura Tamataro, of some repute in Asakusa.

Asayo, who was very fond of a play, spent much of her time and her husband's money in going to the theatre. In less than two days she had fallen violently in love with Tamataro. She sent him money, hardly earned by her blind husband. She wrote to him love-letters, begged him to allow her to come and visit him, and generally disgraced her sex.

Things went from bad to worse. The secret meetings of Asayo and the actor scandalized the neighbourhood. As in most such cases, the husband knew nothing about them. Frequently, when he went home, the actor was in his house, but kept quiet, and Asayo let him out secretly, even going with him sometimes.

Every one felt sorry for Yoichi; but none liked to tell him of his wife's infidelity.

One day Yoichi went to shampoo a customer, who told him of Asayo's conduct. Yoichi was incredulous.

"But yes: it is true," said the son of his customer. "Even now the actor Tamataro is with your wife. So soon as you left your house he slipped in. This he does every day, and many of us see it. We all feel sorry for you in your blindness, and should be glad to help you to punish her."

Yoichi was deeply grieved, for he knew that his friends were in earnest; but, though blind, he would accept no assistance to convict his wife. He trudged home as fast as his blindness would permit, making as little noise as possible with his staff.

On reaching home Yoichi found the front door fastened from the inside. He went to the back, and found the same thing there. There was no way of getting in without breaking a door and making a noise. Yoichi was much excited now; for he knew that his guilty wife and her lover were inside, and he would have liked to kill them both. Great strength came to him, and he raised himself bit by bit until he reached the top of the roof. He intended to enter the house by letting himself down through the 'tem-mado'. Unfortunately, the straw rope he used in doing this was rotten, and gave way, precipitating him below, where he fell on the *kinuta*. He fractured his skull, and died instantly.

Asayo and the actor, hearing the noise, went to see what had happened, and were rather pleased to find poor Yoichi dead. They did not report the death until next day, when they said that Yoichi had fallen downstairs and thus killed himself.

They buried him with indecent haste, and hardly with proper respect.

Yoichi having no children, his property, according to the Japanese law, went to his bad wife, and only a few months passed before Asayo and the actor were married. Apparently they were happy, though none in the village of Kumeda had any sympathy for them, all being disgusted at their behaviour to the poor blind shampooer Yoichi.

Months passed by without event of any interest in the village. No one bothered about Asayo and her husband; and they bothered about no one else, being sufficiently interested in themselves. The scandal-mongers had become tired, and, like all nine-day wonders, the history of the blind *amma*, Asayo, and Tamataro had passed into silence.

However, it does not do to be assured while the spirit of the injured dead goes unavenged.

Up in one of the western provinces, at a small village called Minato, lived one of Yoichi's friends, who was closely connected with him. This was Okuda Ichibei. He and Yoichi had been to school together. They had promised when Ichibei went up to the north-west always to remember each other, and to help each other in time of need, and when Yoichi had become blind Ichibei came down to Kumeda and helped to start Yoichi in his business of *amma*, which he did by giving him a house to live in – a house which had been bequeathed to Ichibei. Again fate decreed that it should be in Ichibei's power to help his friend. At that time news travelled very slowly, and Ichibei had not immediately heard of Yoichi's death or even of his marriage. Judge, then, of his surprise, one night on awaking, to find, standing near his pillow, the figure of a man whom by and by he recognized as Yoichi!

"Why, Yoichi! I am glad to see you," he said; "but how late at night you have arrived! Why did you not let me know you were coming? I should have been up to receive you, and there would have been a hot meal ready. But never mind. I will call a servant, and everything shall be ready as soon as possible. In the meantime be seated, and tell me about yourself, and how you travelled so far. To have come through the mountains and other wild country from Kumeda is hard enough at best; but for one who is blind it is wonderful."

"I am no longer a living man," answered the ghost of Yoichi (for such it was). "I am indeed your friend Yoichi's spirit, and I shall wander about until I can be avenged for a great ill which has been done me. I have come to beg of you to help me, that my spirit may go to rest. If you listen I will tell my story, and you can then do as you think best."

Ichibei was very much astonished (not to say a little nervous) to know that he was in the presence of a ghost; but he was a brave man, and Yoichi had been his friend. He was deeply grieved to hear of Yoichi's death, and realized that the restlessness of his spirit showed him to have been injured. Ichibei decided not only to listen to the story but also to revenge Yoichi, and said so.

The ghost then told all that had happened since he had been set up in the house at Kumedamura. He told of his success as a masseur; of how he had saved the life of Asayo, how he had taken her to his house and subsequently married her; of the arrival of the accursed acting company which contained the man who had ruined his life; of his own death and hasty burial; and of the marriage of Asayo and the actor. "I must be avenged. Will you help me to rest in peace?" he said in conclusion.

Ichibei promised. Then the spirit of Yoichi disappeared, and Ichibei slept again.

Next morning Ichibei thought he must have been dreaming; but he remembered the vision and the narrative so clearly that he perceived them to have been actual. Suddenly turning with the intention to get up, he caught sight of the shine of a metal flute close to his pillow. It was the flute of a blind *amma*. It was marked with Yoichi's name.

Ichibei resolved to start for Kumedamura and ascertain locally all about Yoichi.

In those times, when there was no railway and a rickshaw only here and there, travel was slow. Ichibei took ten days to reach Kumedamura. He immediately went to the house of his friend Yoichi, and was there told the whole history again, but naturally in another way. Asayo said:

"Yes: he saved my life. We were married, and I helped my blind husband in everything. One day, alas, he mistook the staircase for a door, falling down and killing himself. Now I am married to his great friend, an actor called Tamataro, whom you see here."

Ichibei knew that the ghost of Yoichi was not likely to tell him lies, and to ask for vengeance unjustly. Therefore he continued talking to Asayo and her husband, listening to their lies, and wondering what would be the fitting procedure.

Ten o'clock passed thus, and eleven. At twelve o'clock, when Asayo for the sixth or seventh time was assuring Ichibei that everything possible had been done for her blind husband, a wind storm suddenly arose, and in the midst of it was heard the sound of the *amma*'s flute, just as Yoichi played it; it was so unmistakably his that Asayo screamed with fear.

At first distant, nearer and nearer approached the sound, until at last it seemed to be in the room itself. At that moment a cold puff of air came down the *tem-mado*, and the ghost of Yoichi was seen standing beneath it, a cold, white, glimmering and sad-faced wraith.

Tamataro and his wife tried to get up and run out of the house; but they found that their legs would not support them, so full were they of fear.

Tamataro seized a lamp and flung it at the ghost; but the ghost was not to be moved. The lamp passed through him, and broke, setting fire to the house, which burned instantly, the wind fanning the flames.

Ichibei made his escape; but neither Asayo nor her husband could move, and the flames consumed them in the presence of Yoichi's ghost. Their cries were loud and piercing.

Ichibei had all the ashes swept up and placed in a tomb. He had buried in another grave the flute of the blind *amma*, and erected on the ground where the house had been a monument sacred to the memory of Yoichi.

It is known as *Fuezuka No Kwaidan* ('The Flute Ghost Tomb').

The Spirit of Yenoki
Collected by Richard Gordon Smith

There is a mountain in the province of Idsumi called Oki-yama
(or Oji Yam a); it is connected with the Mumaru-Yama mountains. I
will not vouch that I am accurate in spelling either. Suffice it to say
that the story was told to me by Fukuga Sei, and translated by Mr.
Ando, the Japanese translator of our Consulate at Kobe. Both of
these give the mountain's name as Okiyama, and say that on the
top of it from time immemorial there has been a shrine dedicated
to Fudo-myo-o (*Achala*, in Sanskrit, which means 'immovable',
and is the god always represented as surrounded by fire and sitting
uncomplainingly on as an example to others; he carries a sword in
one hand, and a rope in the other, as a warning that punishment
awaits those who are unable to overcome with honour the painful
struggles of life).

Well, at the top of Oki-yama (high or big mountain) is this very
old temple to Fudo, and many are the pilgrimages which are made
there annually. The mountain itself is covered with forest, and there
are some remarkable cryptomerias, camphor and pine trees.

Many years ago, in the days of which I speak, there were only a
few priests living up at this temple. Among them was a middle-aged

man, half-priest, half-caretaker, called Yenoki. For twenty years had Yenoki lived at the temple; yet during that time he had never cast eyes on the figure of Fudo, over which he was partly set to guard; it was kept shut in a shrine and never seen by any one but the head priest. One day Yenoki's curiosity got the better of him. Early in the morning the door of the shrine was not quite closed. Yenoki looked in, but saw nothing. On turning to the light again, he found that he had lost the use of the eye that had looked: he was stone-blind in the right eye.

Feeling that the divine punishment served him well, and that the gods must be angry, he set about purifying himself, and fasted for one hundred days. Yenoki was mistaken in his way of devotion and repentance, and did not pacify the gods; on the contrary, they turned him into a *tengu* (long-nosed devil who dwells in mountains, and is the great teacher of *jujitsu*).

But Yenoki continued to call himself a priest – 'Ichigan Hoshi', meaning the one-eyed priest – for a year, and then died; and it is said that his spirit passed into an enormous cryptomeria tree on the east side of the mountain. After that, when sailors passed the Chinu Sea (Osaka Bay), if there was a storm they used to pray to the one-eyed priest for help, and if a light was seen on the top of Oki-yama they had a sure sign that, no matter how rough the sea, their ship would not be lost.

It may be said, in fact, that after the death of the one-eyed priest more importance was attached to his spirit and to the tree into which it had taken refuge than to the temple itself. The tree was called the Lodging of the One-eyed Priest, and no one dared approach it – not even the woodcutters who were familiar with the mountains. It was a source of awe and an object of reverence.

At the foot of Oki-yama was a lonely village, separated from others by fully two *ri* (five miles), and there were only one hundred and thirty houses in it.

Every year the villagers used to celebrate the 'Bon' by engaging, after it was over, in the dance called 'Bon Odori'. Like most other things in Japan, the 'Bon' and the 'Bon Odori' were in extreme contrast. The 'Bon' was a ceremony arranged for the spirits of the dead, who are supposed to return to earth for three days annually, to visit their family shrines – something like our All Saints' Day, and in any case quite a serious religious performance. The 'Bon Odori' is a dance which varies considerably in different provinces. It is confined mostly to villages – for one cannot count the pretty *geisha* dances in Kyoto which are practically copies of it. It is a dance of boys and girls, one may say, and continues nearly all night on the village green. For the three or four nights that it lasts, opportunities for flirtations of the most violent kind are plentiful. There are no chaperons (so to speak), and (to put it vulgarly) every one 'goes on the bust'! Hitherto-virtuous maidens spend the night out as impromptu sweethearts; and, in the village of which this story is told, not only is it they who let themselves go, but even young brides also.

So it came to pass that the village at the foot of Oki-yama mountain – away so far from other villages – was a bad one morally. There was no restriction to what a girl might do or what she might not do during the nights of the 'Bon Odori'. Things went from bad to worse until, at the time of which I write, anarchy reigned during the festive days. At last it came to pass that after a particularly festive 'Bon', on a beautiful moonlight night in August, the well-beloved and charming daughter of Kurahashi Yozaemon, O Kimi, aged eighteen years, who had promised her lover Kurosuke that she would meet him secretly that evening, was on her way to do so. After passing the last house in her mountain village she came to a thick copse, and standing at the edge of it was a man whom O Kimi at first took to be her lover. On approaching she found that it was not Kurosuke, but a very handsome youth of twenty-three years. He did not speak to her; in fact, he kept a little away. If she advanced, he receded. So handsome was the youth, O Kimi felt that she loved him. "Oh how my heart beats for him!" said she. "After all, why should I not give up Kurosuke? He is not good-looking like this man, whom I love already before I have even spoken to him. I hate Kurosuke, now that I see this man."

As she said this she saw the figure smiling and beckoning, and, being a wicked girl, loose in her morals, she followed him and was seen no more. Her family were much exercised in their minds. A week passed, and O Kimi San did not return.

A few days later Tamae, the sixteen-year-old daughter of Kinsaku, who was secretly in love with the son of the village Headman, was awaiting him in the temple grounds, standing the while by the stone figure of Jizodo (Sanskrit, *Kshitigarbha*, Patron of Women and Children). Suddenly there stood near Tamae a handsome youth of twenty-three years, as in the case of O Kimi; she was greatly struck by the youth's beauty, so much so that when he took her by the hand and led her off she made no effort to resist, and she also disappeared.

And thus it was that nine girls of amorous nature disappeared from this small village. Everywhere for thirty miles round people talked and wondered, and said unkind things.

In Oki-yama village itself the elder people said:

"Yes: it must be that our children's immodesty since the 'Bon Odori' has angered Yenoki San: perhaps it is he himself who appears in the form of this handsome youth and carries off our daughters."

Nearly all agreed in a few days that they owed their losses to the Spirit of the Yenoki Tree; and as soon as this notion had taken root the whole of the villagers locked and barred themselves in their houses both day and night. Their farms became neglected; wood was not being cut on the mountain; business was at a standstill. The rumour of this state of affairs spread, and the Lord of Kishiwada, becoming uneasy, summoned Sonobé Hayama, the most celebrated swordsman in that part of Japan.

"Sonobé, you are the bravest man I know of, and the best fighter. It is for you to go and inspect the tree where lodges the spirit of Yenoki. You must use your own discretion. I cannot advise as to what it is best that you should do. I leave it to you to dispose of the mystery of the disappearances of the nine girls."

"My lord," said Sonobé, "my life is at your lordship's call. I shall either clear the mystery or die."

After this interview with his master Sonobé went home. He put himself through a course of cleansing. He fasted and bathed for a week, and then repaired to Oki-yama.

This was in the month of October, when to me things always look their best. Sonobé ascended the mountain, and went first to the temple, which he reached at three o'clock in the afternoon, after a hard climb. Here he said prayers before the god Fudo for fully half an hour. Then he set out to cross the short valley which led up to the Oki-yama mountain, and to the tree which held the spirit of the one-eyed priest, Yenoki.

It was a long and steep climb, with no paths, for the mountain was avoided as much as possible by even the most adventurous of woodcutters, none of whom ever dreamed of going up as far as the Yenoki tree. Sonobé was in good training and a bold warrior. The woods were dense; there was a chilling damp, which came from the spray of a high waterfall. The solitude was intense, and once or twice Sonobé put his hand on the hilt of his sword, thinking that he heard someone following in the gloom; but there was no one, and by five o'clock Sonobé had reached the tree and addressed it thus:

"Oh, honourable and aged tree, that has braved centuries of storm, thou hast become the home of Yenoki's spirit. In truth there is much honour in having so stately a lodging, and therefore he cannot have been so bad a man. I have come from the Lord of Kishiwada to upbraid him, however, and to ask what means it that Yenoki's spirit should appear as a handsome youth for the purpose of robbing poor people of their daughters. This must not continue; else you, as the lodging of Yenoki's spirit, will be cut down, so that it may escape to another part of the country."

At that moment a warm wind blew on the face of Sonobé, and dark clouds appeared overhead, rendering the forest dark; rain began to fall, and the rumblings of earthquake were heard.

Suddenly the figure of an old priest appeared in ghostly form, wrinkled and thin, transparent and clammy, nerve-shattering; but Sonobé had no fear.

"You have been sent by the Lord of Kishiwada," said the ghost. "I admire your courage for coming. So cowardly and sinful are most men, they fear to come near where my spirit has taken refuge. I can assure you that I do no evil to the good. So bad had morals become in the village, it was time to give a lesson. The villagers' customs defied the gods. It is true that I, hoping to improve these people and make them godly, assumed the form of a youth, and carried away nine of the worst of them. They are quite well. They deeply regret their sins, and will reform their village. Every day I have given them lectures. You will find them on the 'Mino toge', or second summit of this mountain, tied to trees. Go there and release them, and afterwards tell the Lord of Kishiwada what the spirit of Yenoki, the one-eyed priest, has done, and that it is always ready to help him to improve his people. Farewell!"

No sooner had the last word been spoken than the spirit vanished. Sonobé, who felt somewhat dazed by what the spirit had said, started off nevertheless to the 'Mino toge'; and there, sure enough, were the nine girls, tied each to a tree, as the spirit had said. He cut their bonds, gave them a lecture, took them back to the village, and reported to the Lord of Kishiwada.

Since then the people have feared more than ever the spirit of the one-eyed priest. They have become completely reformed, an example to the surrounding villages. The nine houses or families whose daughters behaved so badly contribute annually the rice eaten by the priests of Fudo-myo-o Temple. It is spoken of as 'the nine-families rice of Oki'.

A Haunted Temple in Inaba Province

Collected by Richard Gordon Smith

About the year 1680 there stood an old temple on a wild pine-clad mountain near the village of Kisaichi, in the Province of Inaba. The temple was far up in a rocky ravine. So high and thick were the trees, they kept out nearly all daylight, even when the sun was at its highest. As long as the old men of the village could remember the temple had been haunted by a shito dama and the skeleton ghost (they thought) of some former priestly occupant. Many priests had tried to live in the temple and make it their home but all had died. No one could spend a night there and live.

At last, in the winter of 1701, there arrived at the village of Kisaichi a priest who was on a pilgrimage. His name was Jogen, and he was a native of the Province of Kai.

Jogen had come to see the haunted temple. He was fond of studying such things. Though he believed in the shito dama form of spiritual return to earth, he did not believe in ghosts. As a matter of fact, he was anxious to see a shito dama, and, moreover, wished to have a temple of his own. In this wild mountain temple, with a history which fear and death prevented people from visiting or priests inhabiting, he thought that he had (to put it in vulgar English) 'a real good thing'. Thus he had found his way to the village on the evening of a cold December night, and had gone to the inn to eat his rice and to hear all he could about the temple.

Jogen was no coward; on the contrary, he was a brave man, and made all inquiries in the calmest manner.

"Sir," said the landlord, "your holiness must not think of going to this temple, for it means death. Many good priests have tried to stay the night there, and every one has been found next morning dead, or has died shortly after daybreak without coming to his senses. It is no use, sir, trying to defy such an evil spirit as comes to this temple. I beg you, sir, to give up the idea. Badly as we want a temple here, we wish for no more deaths, and often think of burning down this old haunted one and building a new."

Jogen, however, was firm in his resolve to find and see the ghost.

"Kind sir," he answered, "your wishes are for my preservation; but it is my ambition to see a shito dama, and, if prayers can quiet it, to reopen the temple, to read its legends from the old books that must lie hidden therein, and to be the head priest of it generally."

The innkeeper, seeing that the priest was not to be dissuaded, gave up the attempt, and promised that his son should accompany him as guide in the morning, and carry sufficient provisions for a day.

Next morning was one of brilliant sunshine, and Jogen was out of bed early, making preparations. Kosa, the innkeeper's twenty-year-old son, was tying up the priest's bedding and enough boiled rice to last him nearly two full days. It was decided that Kosa, after leaving the priest at the temple, should return to the village, for he as well as every other villager refused to spend a night at the weird place; but he and his father agreed to go and see Jogen on the morrow, or (as someone grimly put it) "to carry him down and give him an honourable funeral and decent burial."

Jogen entered fully into this joke, and shortly after left the village, with Kosa carrying his things and guiding the way.

The gorge in which the temple was situated was very steep and wild. Great moss-clad rocks lay strewn everywhere. When Jogen and his companion had got half-way up they sat down to rest and eat. Soon they heard voices of persons ascending, and ere long the innkeeper and some eight or nine of the village elders presented themselves.

"We have followed you," said the innkeeper, "to try once more to dissuade you from running to a sure death. True, we want the temple opened and the ghosts appeased; but we do not wish it at the cost of another life. Please consider!"

"I cannot change my mind," answered the priest. "Besides, this is the one chance of my life. Your village elders have promised me that if I am able to appease the spirit and reopen the temple I shall be the head priest of the temple, which must hereafter become celebrated."

Again Jogen refused to listen to advice, and laughed at the villagers' fears. Shouldering the packages that had been carried by Kosa, he said:

"Go back with the rest. I can find my own way now easily enough. I shall be glad if you return tomorrow with carpenters, for no doubt the temple is in sad want of repairs, both inside and out. Now, my friends, until tomorrow, farewell. Have no fear for me: I have none for myself."

The villagers made deep bows. They were greatly impressed by the bravery of Jogen, and hoped that he might be spared to become their priest. Jogen in his turn bowed, and then began to continue his ascent. The others watched him as long as he remained in view, and then retraced their steps to the village; Kosa thanking the good fortune that had not necessitated his having to go to the temple with the priest and return in the evening alone. With two or three people he felt brave enough; but to be here in the gloom of this wild forest and near the haunted temple alone – no: that was not in his line.

As Jogen climbed he came suddenly in sight of the temple, which seemed to be almost over his head, so precipitous were the sides of the mountain and the path. Filled with curiosity, the priest pressed on in spite of his heavy load, and some fifteen minutes later arrived panting on the temple platform, or terrace, which, like the temple itself, had been built on driven piles and scaffolding.

At first glance Jogen recognized that the temple was large; but lack of attention had caused it to fall into great dilapidation. Rank grasses grew high about its sides; fungi and creepers abounded upon the damp, sodden posts and supports; so rotten, in fact, did these appear, the priest mentioned in his written notes that evening that he feared the spirits less than the state of the posts which supported the building.

Cautiously Jogen entered the temple, and saw that there was a remarkably large and fine gilded figure of Buddha, besides figures of many saints. There were also fine bronzes and vases, drums from which the parchment had rotted off, incense-burners, or *koros*, and other valuable or holy things.

Behind the temple were the priests' living quarters; evidently, before the ghost's time, the temple must have had some five or six priests ever present to attend to it and to the people who came to pray.

The gloom was oppressive, and as the evening was already approaching Jogen bethought himself of light. Unpacking his bundle, he filled a lamp with oil, and found temple-sticks for the candles which he had brought with him. Having placed one of these on either side of the figure of Buddha, he prayed earnestly for two hours, by which time it was quite dark. Then he took his simple meal of rice, and settled himself to watch and listen. In order that he might see inside and outside the temple at the same time, he had chosen the gallery. Concealed behind an old column, he waited, in his heart disbelieving in ghosts, but anxious, as his notes said, to see a shito dama.

For some two hours he heard nothing. The wind – such little as there was – sighed round the temple and through the stems of the tall trees. An owl hooted from time to time. Bats flew in and out. A fungusy smell pervaded the air.

Suddenly, near midnight, Jogen heard a rustling in the bushes below him, as if somebody were pushing through. He thought it was a deer, or perhaps one of the large red-faced apes so fond of the neighbourhood of high and deserted temples; perhaps, even, it might be a fox or a badger.

The priest was soon undeceived. At the place whence the sound of the rustling leaves had come, he saw the clear and distinct shape of the well-known shito dama. It moved first one way and then another, in a hovering and jerky manner, and from it a voice as of distant buzzing proceeded; but – horror of horrors! – what was that standing among the bushes?

The priest's blood ran cold. There stood the luminous skeleton of a man in loose priest's clothes, with glaring eyes and a parchment skin! At first it remained still; but as the shito dama rose higher and higher the ghost moved after it – sometimes visible, sometimes not.

Higher and higher came the shito dama, until finally the ghost stood at the base of the great figure of Buddha, and was facing Jogen.

Cold beads of sweat stood out on the priest's forehead; the marrow seemed to have frozen in his bones; he shook so that he could hardly stand. Biting his tongue to prevent screaming, he dashed for the small room in which he had left his bedding, and, having bolted himself in, proceeded to look through a crack between the boards. Yes! there was the figure of the ghost, still seated near the Buddha; but the shito dama had disappeared.

None of Jogen's senses left him; but fear was paralysing his body, and he felt himself no longer capable of moving – no matter what should happen. He continued, in a lying position, to look through the hole.

The ghost sat on, turning only its head, sometimes to the right, sometimes to the left, and sometimes looking upwards.

For full an hour this went on. Then the buzzing sound began again, and the shito dama reappeared, circling and circling round the ghost's body, until the ghost vanished, apparently having turned into the shito dama; and after circling round the holy figures three or four times it suddenly shot out of sight.

Next morning Kosa and five men came up to the temple. They found the priest alive but paralysed. He could neither move nor speak. He was carried to the village, dying before he got there.

Much use was made of the priest's notes. No one else ever volunteered to live at the temple, which, two years later, was struck by lightning and burned to the ground. In digging among the remains, searching for bronzes and metal Buddhas, villagers came upon a skeleton buried, only a foot deep, near the bushes whence Jogen had first heard the sounds of rustling.

Undoubtedly the ghost and shito dama were those of a priest who had suffered a violent death and could not rest.

The bones were properly buried and masses said, and nothing has since been seen of the ghost.

All that remains of the temple are the moss-grown pedestals which formed the foundations.

The Secret of Iidamachi Pond

Collected by Richard Gordon Smith

In the first year of Bunkiu, 1861–1864, there lived a man called Yehara Keisuke in Kasumigaseki, in the district of Kojimachi. He was a *hatomoto* – that is, a feudatory vassal of the Shogun – and a man to whom some respect was due; but apart from that, Yehara was much liked for his kindness of heart and general fairness in dealing with people. In Iidamachi lived another *hatomoto*, Hayashi Hayato. He had been married to Yehara's sister for five years. They were exceedingly happy; their daughter, four years old now, was the delight of their hearts. Their cottage was rather dilapidated; but it was Hayashi's own, with the pond in front of it, and two farms, the whole property comprising some two hundred acres, of which nearly half was under cultivation. Thus Hayashi was able to live without working much. In the summer he fished for carp; in the winter he wrote much, and was considered a bit of a poet.

At the time of this story, Hayashi, having planted his rice and sweet potatoes (*sato-imo*), had but little to do, and spent most of his time with his wife, fishing in his ponds, one of which contained large *suppon* (terrapin turtles) as well as *koi* (carp). Suddenly things went wrong.

Yehara was surprised one morning to receive a visit from his sister O Komé.

"I have come, dear brother," she said, "to beg you to help me to obtain a divorce or separation from my husband."

"Divorce! Why should you want a divorce? Have you not always said you were happy with your husband, my dear friend Hayashi? For what sudden reason do you ask for a divorce? Remember you have been married for five years now, and that is sufficient to prove that your life has been happy, and that Hayashi has treated you well."

At first O Komé would not give any reason why she wished to be separated from her husband; but at last she said:

"Brother, think not that Hayashi has been unkind. He is all that can be called kind, and we deeply love each other; but, as you know, Hayashi's family have owned the land, the farms on one of which latter we live, for some three hundred years. Nothing would induce him to change his place of abode, and I should never have wished him to do so until some twelve days ago."

"What has happened within these twelve wonderful days?" asked Yehara.

"Dear brother, I can stand it no longer," was his sister's answer. "Up to twelve days ago all went well; but then a terrible thing happened. It was very dark and warm, and I was sitting outside our house looking at the clouds passing over the moon, and talking to my daughter. Suddenly there appeared, as if walking on the lilies of the pond, a white figure. Oh, so white, so wet, and so miserable to look at! It appeared to arise from the pond and float in the air, and then approached me slowly until it was within ten feet. As it came my child cried: "Why, mother, there comes O Sumi – do you know O Sumi?" I answered her that I did not, I think; but in truth I was so frightened I hardly know what I said. The figure was horrible to look at. It was that of a girl of eighteen or nineteen years, with hair dishevelled and hanging loose, over white and wet shoulders. 'Help me! help me!' cried the figure, and I was so frightened that I covered my eyes and screamed for my husband, who was inside. He came out and found me in a dead faint, with my child by my side, also in a state of terror. Hayashi had seen nothing. He carried us both in, shut the doors, and told me I must have been dreaming. 'Perhaps,' he sarcastically added, 'you saw the kappa which is said to dwell in the pond, but which none of my family have seen for over one hundred years.' That is all that my husband said on the subject. Next night, however, when in bed, my child seized me suddenly, crying in terror-stricken tones, 'O Sumi – here is O Sumi – how horrible she looks! Mother, mother, do you see her?' I did see her. She stood dripping wet within three feet of my bed, the whiteness and the wetness and the dishevelled hair being what gave her the awful look which she bore. 'Help me! Help me!' cried the figure, and then disappeared. After that I could not sleep; nor could I get my child to do so. On every night until now the ghost has come – O Sumi, as my child calls her. I should kill myself if I had to remain longer in that house, which has become a terror to myself and my child. My husband does not see the ghost, and only laughs at me; and that is why I see no way out of the difficulty but a separation."

Yehara told his sister that on the following day he would call on Hayashi, and sent his sister back to her husband that night.

Next day, when Yehara called, Hayashi, after hearing what the visitor had to say, answered:

"It is very strange. I was born in this house over twenty years ago; but I have never seen the ghost which my wife refers to, and have never heard about it. Not the slightest allusion to it was ever made by my father or mother. I will make inquiries of all my neighbours and servants, and ascertain if they ever heard of the ghost, or even of any one coming to a sudden and untimely end. There must be something: it is impossible that my little child should know the name 'Sumi', she never having known any one bearing it."

Inquiries were made; but nothing could be learned from the servants or from the neighbours. Hayashi reasoned that, the ghost being always wet, the mystery might be solved by drying up the pond – perhaps to find the remains of some murdered person, whose bones required decent burial and prayers said over them.

The pond was old and deep, covered with water plants, and had never been emptied within his memory. It was said to contain a kappa (mythical beast, half-turtle, half-man). In any case, there were many terrapin turtle, the capture of which would well repay the cost of the emptying. The bank of the pond was cut, and next day there remained only a pool in the deepest part; Hayashi decided to clear even this and dig into the mud below.

At this moment the grandmother of Hayashi arrived, an old woman of some eighty years, and said:

"You need go no farther. I can tell you all about the ghost. O Sumi does not rest, and it is quite true that her ghost appears. I am very sorry about it, now in my old age; for it is my fault – the sin is mine. Listen and I will tell you all."

Every one stood astonished at these words, feeling that some secret was about to be revealed.

The old woman continued:

"When Hayashi Hayato, your grandfather, was alive, we had a beautiful servant girl, seventeen years of age, called O Sumi. Your grandfather became enamoured of this girl, and she of him. I was about thirty at that time, and was jealous, for my better looks had passed away. One day when your grandfather was out I took Sumi to the pond and gave her a severe beating. During the struggle she fell into the water and got entangled in the weeds; and there I left her, fully believing the water to be shallow and that she could get out. She did not succeed, and was drowned. Your grandfather found her dead on his return. In those days the police were not very particular with their inquiries. The girl was buried; but nothing was said to me, and the matter soon blew over. Fourteen days ago was the fiftieth anniversary of this tragedy. Perhaps that is the reason of Sumi's ghost appearing; for appear she must, or your child could not have known of her name. It must be as your child says, and that the first time she appeared Sumi communicated her name."

The old woman was shaking with fear, and advised them all to say prayers at O Sumi's tomb. This was done, and the ghost has been seen no more. Hayashi said:

"Though I am a *samurai*, and have read many books, I never believed in ghosts; but now I do."

The Snow Tomb
Collected by Richard Gordon Smith

Many years ago there lived a young man of the *samurai* class who was much famed for his skill in fencing in what was called the style of *Yagyu*. So adept was he, he earned by teaching, under his master, no less than thirty barrels of rice and two 'rations' – which, I am told, vary from one to five *sho* – a month. As one *sho* is 0.666 feet square, our young *samurai*, Rokugo Yakeiji, was well off.

The seat of his success was at Minami-wari-gesui, Hongo Yedo. His teacher was Sudo Jirozaemon, and the school was at Ishiwaraku.

Rokugo was in no way proud of his skill. It was the modesty of the youth, coupled with cleverness, that had prompted the teacher to make his pupil an assistant-master. The school was one of the best in Tokio, and there were over one hundred pupils.

One January the pupils were assembled to celebrate the New Year, and on this the seventh day of it were drinking *nanakusa* – a kind of sloppy rice in which seven grasses and green vegetables are mixed, said to keep off all diseases for the year. The pupils were engaged in ghost stories, each trying to tell a more alarming one than his neighbour, until the hair of many was practically on end, and it was late in the evening. It was the custom to keep the 7th of

January in this way, and they took their turns by drawing numbers. One hundred candles were placed in a shed at the end of the garden, and each teller of a story took his turn at bringing one away, until they had all told a story; this was to upset, if possible, the bragging of the pupil who said he did not believe in ghosts and feared nothing.

At last it came to the turn of Rokugo. After fetching his candle from the end of the garden, he spoke as follows:

"My friends, listen to my story. It is not very dreadful; but it is true. Some three years ago, when I was seventeen, my father sent me to Gifu, in Mino Province. I reached on the way a place called Nakimura about ten o'clock in the evening. Outside the village, on some wild uncultivated land, I saw a curious fireball. It moved here and there without noise, came quite close to me and then went away again, moving generally as if looking for something; it went round and round over the same ground time after time. It was generally five feet off the ground; but sometimes it went lower. I will not say that I was frightened, because subsequently I went to the Miyoshiya inn, and to bed, without mentioning what I had seen to any one; but I can assure you all that I was very glad to be in the house. Next morning my curiosity got the better of me. I told the landlord what I had seen, and he recounted to me a story. He said: "About two hundred years ago a great battle was fought here, and the general who was defeated was himself killed. When his body was recovered, early in the action, it was found to be headless. The soldiers thought that the head must have been stolen by the enemy. One, more anxious than the rest to find his master's head, continued to search while the action went on. While searching he himself was killed. Since that evening, two hundred years ago, the fireball has been burning after ten o'clock. The people from that time till now have called it *'Kubi sagashi no hi*'. As the master of the inn finished relating this story, my friends, I felt an unpleasant sensation in the heart. It was the first thing of a ghostly kind that I had seen."

The pupils agreed that the story was strange. Rokugo pushed his toes into his '*geta*' (clogs), and started to fetch his candle from the end of the garden. He had not proceeded far into the garden before he heard the voice of a woman. It was not very dark, as there was snow on the ground; but Rokugo could see no woman. He had got as far as the candles when he heard the voice again, and, turning suddenly, saw a beautiful woman of some eighteen summers. Her clothes were fine. The *obi* (belt) was tied in the *tateyanojiri* (shape of the arrow standing erect, as an arrow in a quiver). The dress was all of the pine-and-bamboo pattern, and her hair was done in the *shimada* style. Rokugo stood looking at her with wonder and admiration. A minute's reflection showed him that it could be no girl, and that her beauty had almost made him forget that he was a *samurai*.

"No: it is no real woman: it is a ghost. What an opportunity for me to distinguish myself before all my friends!"

Saying which, he drew his sword, tempered by the famous Moriye Shinkai, and with one downward cut severed head, body, and all, into halves.

He ran, seized a candle, and took it back to the room where the pupils were awaiting him; there he told the story, and begged them to come and see the ghost. All the young men looked at one another, none of them being partial to ghosts in what you may call real life. None cared to venture; but by and by Yamamoto Jonosuke, with better courage than the rest, said, "I will go," and dashed off. As soon as the other pupils saw this, they also, gathering pluck, went forth into the garden.

When they came to the spot where the dead ghost was supposed to lie, they found only the remains of a snow man which they themselves had made during the day; and this was cut in half from head to foot, just as Rokugo had described. They all laughed. Several of the young *samurai* were angry, for they thought that Rokugo had been making fools of them; but when they returned to the house they soon saw that Rokugo had not been trifling. They found him sitting with an air of great haughtiness, and thinking that his pupils would now indeed see how able a swordsman he was.

However, they looked at Rokugo scornfully, and addressed him thus:

"Indeed, we have received remarkable evidence of your ability. Even the small boy who throws a stone at a dog would have had the courage to do what you did!"

Rokugo became angry, and called them insolent. He lost his temper to such an extent that for a moment his hand flew to his sword hilt, and he even threatened to kill one or two of them.

The *samurai* apologized for their rudeness, but added: "Your ghost was only the snow man we made ourselves this morning. That is why we tell you that a child need not fear to attack it."

At this information Rokugo was confounded, and he in his turn apologized for his temper; nevertheless, he said he could not understand how it was possible for him to mistake a snow man for a female ghost. Puzzled and ashamed, he begged his friends not to say any more about the matter, but keep it to themselves; thereupon he bade them farewell and left the house.

It was no longer snowing; but the snow lay thick upon the ground. Rokugo had had a good deal of sake, and his gait was not over-steady as he made his way home to Warigesui.

When he passed near the gates of the Korinji Temple he noticed a woman coming faster than he could understand through the temple grounds. He leaned against the fence to watch her. Her hair was dishevelled, and she was all out of order. Soon a man came running behind her with a butcher's knife in his hand, and shouted as he caught her:

"You wicked woman! You have been unfaithful to your poor husband, and I will kill you for it, for I am his friend."

Stabbing her five or six times, he did so, and then moved away. Rukugo, resuming his way homewards, thought what a good friend must be the man who had killed the unfaithful wife. A bad woman justly rewarded with death, thought he.

Rokugo had not gone very far, however, when, to his utter astonishment, he met face to face the woman whom he had just seen killed. She was looking at him with angry eyes, and she said:

"How can a brave *samurai* watch so cruel a murder as you have just seen, enjoying the sight?"

Rokugo was much astonished.

"Do not talk to me as if I were your husband," said he, "for I am not. I was pleased to see you killed for being unfaithful. Indeed, if you are the ghost of the woman I shall kill you myself!" Before he could draw his sword the ghost had vanished.

Rokugo continued his way, and on nearing his house he met a woman, who came up to him with horrible face and clenched teeth, as if in agony.

He had had enough troubles with women that evening. They must be foxes who had assumed the forms of women, thought he, as he continued to gaze at this last one.

At that moment he recollected that he had heard of a fact about fox-women. It was that fire coming from the bodies of foxes and badgers is always so bright that even on the darkest night you can tell the colour of their hair, or even the figures woven in the stuffs they wear, when assuming the forms of men or women; it is clearly visible at one *ken* (six feet). Remembering this, Rokugo approached a little closer to the woman; and, sure enough, he could see the pattern of her dress, shown up as if fire were underneath. The hair, too, seemed to have fire under it.

Knowing now that it was a fox he had to do with, Rokugo drew his best sword, the famous one made by Moriye, and proceeded to attack carefully, for he knew he should have to hit the fox and not the spirit of the fox in the woman's form. (It is said that whenever a fox or a badger transforms itself into human shape the real presence stands beside the apparition. If the apparition appears on the left side, the presence of the animal himself is on the right.)

Rokugo made his attack accordingly, killing the fox and consequently the apparition.

He ran to his house, and called up his relations, who came flocking out with lanterns. Near a myrtle tree which was almost two hundred years old, they found the body – not of fox or badger, but – of an otter. The animal was carried home. Next day invitations were issued to all the pupils at the fencing-school to come and see it, and a great feast was given. Rokugo had wiped away a great disgrace. The pupils erected a tomb for the beast; it is known as '*Yukidzuka*' (The Snow Tomb), and is still to be seen in the Korinji Temple at Warigesui Honjo, in Tokio.

The Kakemono Ghost of Aki Province

Collected by Richard Gordon Smith

Down the Inland Sea between Umedaichi and Kure (now a great naval port) and in the province of Aki, there is a small village called Yaiyama, in which lived a painter of some note, Abe Tenko. Abe Tenko taught more than he painted, and relied for his living mostly on the small means to which he had succeeded at his father's death and on the aspiring artists who boarded in the village for the purpose of taking daily lessons from him. The island and rock scenery in the neighbourhood afforded continual study, and Tenko was never short of pupils. Among them was one scarcely more than a boy, being only seventeen years of age. His name was Sawara Kameju, and a most promising pupil he was. He had been sent to Tenko over a year before, when scarce sixteen years of age, and, for the reason that Tenko had been a friend of his father, Sawara was taken under the roof of the artist and treated as if he had been his son.

Tenko had had a sister who went into the service of the Lord of Aki, by whom she had a daughter. Had the child been a son, it would have been adopted into the Aki family; but, being a daughter, it was, according to Japanese custom, sent back to its mother's family, with the result that Tenko took charge of the child, whose name was Kimi. The mother being dead, the child had lived with him for sixteen years. Our story opens with O Kimi grown into a pretty girl.

O Kimi was a most devoted adopted daughter to Tenko. She attended almost entirely to his household affairs, and Tenko looked upon her as if indeed she were his own daughter, instead of an illegitimate niece, trusting her in everything.

After the arrival of the young student O Kimi's heart gave her much trouble. She fell in love with him. Sawara admired O Kimi greatly; but of love he never said a word, being too much absorbed in his study. He looked upon Kimi as a sweet girl, taking his meals with her and enjoying her society. He would have fought for her, and he loved her; but he never gave himself time to think that she was not his sister, and that he might make love to her. So it came to pass at last that O Kimi one day, with the pains of love in her heart, availed herself of her guardian's absence at the temple, whither he had gone to paint something for the priests. O Kimi screwed up her courage and made love to Sawara. She told him that since he had come to the house her heart had known no peace. She loved him, and would like to marry him if he did not mind.

This simple and maidenlike request, accompanied by the offer of tea, was more than young Sawara was able to answer without acquiescence. After all, it did not much matter, thought he: "Kimi is a most beautiful and charming girl, and I like her very much, and must marry some day."

So Sawara told Kimi that he loved her and would be only too delighted to marry her when his studies were complete – say two or three years thence. Kimi was overjoyed, and on the return of the good Tenko from Korinji Temple informed her guardian of what had passed.

Sawara set to with renewed vigour, and worked diligently, improving very much in his style of painting; and after a year Tenko thought it would do him good to finish off his studies in Kyoto under an old friend of his own, a painter named Sumiyoshi Myokei. Thus it was that in the spring of the sixth year of Kioho – that is, in 1721 – Sawara bade farewell to Tenko and his pretty niece O Kimi, and started forth to the capital. It was a sad parting. Sawara had grown to love Kimi very deeply, and he vowed that as soon as his name was made he would return and marry her.

In the olden days the Japanese were even more shockingly poor correspondents than they are now, and even lovers or engaged couples did not write to each other, as several of my tales may show.

After Sawara had been away for a year, it seemed that he should write and say at all events how he was getting on; but he did not do so. A second year passed, and still there was no news. In the meantime there had been several admirers of O Kimi's who had proposed to Tenko for her hand; but Tenko had invariably said that Kimi San was already engaged – until one day he heard from Myokei, the painter in Kyoto, who told him that Sawara was making splendid progress, and that he was most anxious that the youth should marry his daughter. He felt that he must ask his old friend Tenko first, and before speaking to Sawara.

Tenko, on the other hand, had an application from a rich merchant for O Kimi's hand. What was Tenko to do? Sawara showed no signs of returning; on the contrary, it seemed that

Myokei was anxious to get him to marry into his family. That must be a good thing for Sawara, he thought. Myokei is a better teacher than I, and if Sawara marries his daughter he will take more interest than ever in my old pupil. Also, it is advisable that Kimi should marry that rich young merchant, if I can persuade her to do so; but it will be difficult, for she loves Sawara still. I am afraid he has forgotten her. A little strategy I will try, and tell her that Myokei has written to tell me that Sawara is going to marry his daughter; then, possibly, she may feel sufficiently vengeful to agree to marry the young merchant. Arguing thus to himself, he wrote to Myokei to say that he had his full consent to ask Sawara to be his son-in-law, and he wished him every success in the effort; and in the evening he spoke to Kimi.

"Kimi," he said, "today I have had news of Sawara through my friend Myokei."

"Oh, do tell me what!" cried the excited Kimi. "Is he coming back, and has he finished his education? How delighted I shall be to see him! We can be married in April, when the cherry blooms, and he can paint a picture of our first picnic."

"I fear, Kimi, the news which I have does not talk of his coming back. On the contrary, I am asked by Myokei to allow Sawara to marry his daughter, and, as I think such a request could not have been made had Sawara been faithful to you, I have answered that I have no objection to the union. And now, as for yourself, I deeply regret to tell you this; but as your uncle and guardian I again wish to impress upon you the advisability of marrying Yorozuya, the young merchant, who is deeply in love with you and in every way a most desirable husband; indeed, I must insist upon it, for I think it most desirable."

Poor O Kimi San broke into tears and deep sobs, and without answering a word went to her room, where Tenko thought it well to leave her alone for the night.

In the morning she had gone, none knew whither, there being no trace of her.

Up in Kyoto Sawara continued his studies, true and faithful to O Kimi. After receiving Tenko's letter approving of Myokei's asking Sawara to become his son-in-law, Myokei asked Sawara if he would so honour him. "When you marry my daughter, we shall be a family of painters, and I think you will be one of the most celebrated ones that Japan ever had."

"But, sir," cried Sawara, "I cannot do myself the honour of marrying your daughter, for I am already engaged – I have been for the last three years – to Kimi, Tenko's daughter. It is most strange that he should not have told you!"

There was nothing for Myokei to say to this; but there was much for Sawara to think about. Foolish, perhaps he then thought, were the ways of Japanese in not corresponding more freely. He wrote to Kimi twice, accordingly, but no answer came. Then Myokei fell ill of a chill and died: so Sawara returned to his village home in Aki, where he was welcomed by Tenko, who was now, without O Kimi, lonely in his old age.

When Sawara heard that Kimi had gone away leaving neither address nor letter he was very angry, for he had not been told the reason.

"An ungrateful and bad girl," said he to Tenko, "and I have been lucky indeed in not marrying her!"

"Yes, yes," said Tenko: "you have been lucky; but you must not be too angry. Women are queer things, and, as the saying goes, when you see water running uphill and hens laying square eggs you may expect to see a truly honest-minded woman. But come now – I want to tell you that, as I am growing old and feeble, I wish to make you the master of my house and property here. You must take my name and marry!"

Feeling disgusted at O Kimi's conduct, Sawara readily consented. A pretty young girl, the daughter of a wealthy farmer, was found – Kiku (the Chrysanthemum); – and she and Sawara lived happily with old Tenko, keeping his house and minding his estate. Sawara painted in his spare time. Little by little he became quite famous. One day the Lord of Aki sent for him and said it was his wish that Sawara should paint the seven beautiful scenes of the Islands of Kabakarijima (six, probably); the pictures were to be mounted on gold screens.

This was the first commission that Sawara had had from such a high official. He was very proud of it, and went off to the Upper and Lower Kabakari Islands, where he made rough sketches. He went also to the rocky islands of Shokokujima, and to the little uninhabited island of Daikokujima, where an adventure befell him.

Strolling along the shore, he met a girl, tanned by sun and wind. She wore only a red cotton cloth about her loins, and her hair fell upon her shoulders. She had been gathering shellfish, and had a basket of them under her arm. Sawara thought it strange that he should meet a single woman in so wild a place, and still more so when she addressed him, saying, "Surely you are Sawara Kameju – are you not?"

"Yes," answered Sawara: "I am; but it is very strange that you should know me. May I ask how you do so?"

"If you are Sawara, as I know you are, you should know me without asking, for I am no other than Kimi, to whom you were engaged!"

Sawara was astonished, and hardly knew what to say: so he asked her questions as to how she had come to this lonely island. O Kimi explained everything, and ended by saying, with a smile of happiness upon her face:

"And since, my dearest Sawara, I understand that what I was told is false, and that you did not marry Myokei's daughter, and that we have been faithful to each other, we can be married and happy after all. Oh, think how happy we shall be!"

"Alas, alas, my dearest Kimi, it cannot be! I was led to suppose that you had deserted our benefactor Tenko and given up all thought of me. Oh, the sadness of it all, the wickedness! I have been persuaded that you were faithless, and have been made to marry another!"

O Kimi made no answer, but began to run along the shore towards a little hut, which home she had made for herself. She ran fast, and Sawara ran after her, calling, "Kimi, Kimi, stop and speak to me"; but Kimi did not stop. She gained her hut, and, seizing a knife, plunged it into her throat, and fell back bleeding to death. Sawara, greatly grieved, burst into tears. It was horrible to see the girl who might have been his bride lying dead at his feet all covered with blood, and having suffered so horrible a death at her own hands. Greatly impressed, he drew paper from his pocket and made a sketch of the body. Then he and his boatman buried O Kimi above the tide-mark near the primitive hut. Afterwards, at home, with a mournful heart, he painted a picture of the dead girl, and hung it in his room.

On the first night that it was hung Sawara had a dreadful dream. On awakening he found the figure on the kakemono seemed to be alive: the ghost of O Kimi stepped out of it and stood near his bed. Night after night the ghost appeared, until sleep and rest for Sawara were no longer possible. There was nothing to be done, thought he, but to send his wife back to her parents, which he did; and the kakemono he presented to the Korinji Temple, where the priests kept it with great care and daily prayed for the spirit of O Kimi San. After that Sawara saw the ghost no more.

The kakemono is called the Ghost Picture of Tenko II., and is said to be still kept in the Korinji Temple, where it was placed some 230 to 240 years ago.

The Spirit of the Willow Tree
Collected by Richard Gordon Smith

About one thousand years ago (but according to the dates of the story 744 years ago) the temple of 'San-jū-san-gen Dō' was founded. That was in 1132. 'San-jū-san-gen Dō' means hall of thirty-three spaces; and there are said to be over 33,333 figures of the Goddess Kwannon, the Goddess of Mercy, in the temple today. Before the temple was built, in a village nearby stood a willow tree of great size. It marked the playing-ground of all the village children, who swung on its branches, and climbed on its limbs. It afforded shade to the aged in the heat of summer, and in the evenings, when work was done, many were the village lads and lasses who vowed eternal love under its branches. The tree seemed an influence for good to all. Even the weary traveller could sleep peacefully and almost dry under its branches. Alas, even in those times men were often ruthless with regard to trees. One day the villagers announced an intention to cut it down and use it to build a bridge across the river.

There lived in the village a young farmer named Heitaro, a great favourite, who had lived near the old tree all his days, as his forefathers had done; and he was greatly against cutting it down.

Such a tree should be respected, thought he. Had it not braved the storms of hundreds of years? In the heat of summer what pleasure it afforded the children! Did it not give to the weary shelter, and to the love-smitten a sense of romance? All these thoughts Heitaro impressed upon the villagers. "Sooner than approve your cutting it down," he said, "I will give you as many of my own trees as you require to build the bridge. You must leave this dear old willow alone for ever."

The villagers readily agreed. They also had a secret veneration for the old tree.

Heitaro was delighted, and readily found wood with which to build the bridge.

Some days later Heitaro, returning from his work, found standing by the willow a beautiful girl.

Instinctively he bowed to her. She returned the bow. They spoke together of the tree, its age and beauty. They seemed, in fact, to be drawn towards each other by a common sympathy. Heitaro was sorry when she said that she must be going, and bade him good day. That evening his mind was far from being fixed on the ordinary things of life. "Who was the lady under the willow tree? How I wish I could see her again!" thought he. There was no sleep for Heitaro that night. He had caught the fever of love.

Next day he was at his work early; and he remained at it all day, working doubly hard, so as to try and forget the lady of the willow tree; but on his way home in the evening, behold, there was the lady again! This time she came forward to greet him in the most friendly way.

"Welcome, good friend!" she said. "Come and rest under the branches of the willow you love so well, for you must be tired."

Heitaro readily accepted this invitation, and not only did he rest, but also he declared his love.

Day by day after this the mysterious girl (whom no others had seen) used to meet Heitaro, and at last she promised to marry him if he asked no questions as to her parents or friends. "I have none," she said. "I can only promise to be a good and faithful wife, and tell you that I love you with all my heart and soul. Call me, then, 'Higo,' and I will be your wife."

Next day Heitaro took Higo to his house, and they were married. A son was born to them in a little less than a year, and became their absorbing joy. There was not a moment of their spare time in which either Heitaro or his wife was not playing with the child, whom they called Chiyodō. It is doubtful if a more happy home could have been found in all Japan than the house of Heitaro, with his good wife Higo and their beautiful child.

Alas, where in this world has complete happiness ever been known to last? Even did the gods permit this, the laws of man would not.

When Chiyodō had reached the age of five years – the most beautiful boy in the neighbourhood – the ex-Emperor Toba decided to build in Kyoto an immense temple to Kwannon. He would contribute 1001 images of the Goddess of Mercy. (Now, in 1907, as we said at the beginning, this temple is known as 'San-jū-san-gen Dō,' and contains 33,333 images.)

The ex-Emperor Toba's wish having become known, orders were given by the authorities to collect timber for the building of the vast temple; and so it came to pass that the days of the big willow tree were numbered, for it would be wanted, with many others, to form the roof.

Heitaro tried to save the tree again by offering every other he had on his land for nothing; but that was in vain. Even the villagers became anxious to see their willow tree built into the temple. It would bring them good luck, they thought, and in any case be a handsome gift of theirs towards the great temple.

The fatal time arrived. One night, when Heitaro and his wife and child had retired to rest and were sleeping, Heitaro was awakened by the sound of axes chopping. To his astonishment, he found his beloved wife sitting up in her bed, gazing earnestly at him, while tears rolled down her cheeks and she was sobbing bitterly.

"My dearest husband," she said with choking voice, "pray listen to what I tell you now, and do not doubt me. This is, unhappily, not a dream. When we married I begged you not to ask me my history, and you have never done so; but I said I would tell you some day if there should be a real occasion to do so. Unhappily, that occasion has now arrived, my dear husband. I am no less a thing than the spirit of the willow tree you loved, and so generously saved six years ago. It was to repay you for this great kindness that I appeared to you in human form under the tree, hoping that I could live with you and make you happy for your whole life. Alas, it cannot be! They are cutting down the willow. How I feel every stroke of their axes! I must return to die, for I am part of it. My heart breaks to think also of leaving my darling child Chiyodō and of his great sorrow when he knows that his mother is no longer in the world. Comfort him, dearest husband! He is old enough and strong enough to be with you now without a mother and yet not suffer. I wish you both long lives of prosperity. Farewell, my dearest! I must be off to the willow, for I hear them striking with their axes harder and harder, and it weakens me each blow they give."

Heitaro awoke his child just as Higo disappeared, wondering to himself if it were not a dream. No: it was no dream. Chiyodō, awaking, stretched his arms in the direction his mother had gone, crying bitterly and imploring her to come back.

"My darling child," said Heitaro, "she has gone. She cannot come back. Come: let us dress, and go and see her funeral. Your mother was the spirit of the Great Willow."

A little later, at the break of day, Heitaro took Chiyodō by the hand and led him to the tree. On reaching it they found it down, and already lopped of its branches. The feelings of Heitaro may be well imagined.

Strange! In spite of united efforts, the men were unable to move the stem a single inch towards the river, in which it was to be floated to Kyoto.

On seeing this, Heitaro addressed the men.

"My friends," said he, "the dead trunk of the tree which you are trying to move contains the spirit of my wife. Perhaps, if you will allow my little son Chiyodō to help you, it will be more easy for you; and he would like to help in showing his last respects to his mother."

The woodcutters were fully agreeable, and, much to their astonishment, as Chiyodō came to the back end of the log and pushed it with his little hand, the timber glided easily towards the river, his father singing the while an 'Uta' [poetical song]. There is a well-known song or ballad in the 'Uta' style said to have sprung from this event; it is sung to the present day by men drawing heavy weights or doing hard labour: –

Muzan naru kana	*Is it not sad to see the little fellow,*
Motowa kumanono	*Who sprang from the dew of the*
yanagino tsuyu de	*Kumano Willow,*

Sodate-agetaru kono	*And is thus far budding well?*
midorigo wa	*Heave ho, heave ho, pull hard,*
Yoi, Yoi, Yoito na!	*my lads.*

In Wakanoura the labourers sing a working or hauling song, which also is said to have sprung from this story of the 'Yanagi no Sé': –

Wakano urani wa	*There are famous places in*
meishoga gozaru	*Wakanoura*
Ichini Gongen	*First Gongen*
Nini Tamatsushima	*Second Tamatsushima*
Sanni Sagari Matsu	*Third, the pine tree with its*
Shini Shiogama	*hanging branches*
Yoi, Yoi, yoi to na.	*Fourth comes Shiogama*
	Is it not good, good, good?

A third 'Uta' sprang from this story, and is often applied to small children helping.

The wagon could not be drawn when it came to the front of Heitaro's house, so his little five-year-old boy Chiyodō was obliged to help, and they sang: –

Muzan naru kana	*Is it not sad to see the little fellow,*
Motowa Kumanono	*Who sprang from the dew of the*
yanagino tsuyu de	*Kumano Willow,*
Sodate-agetaru kono	*And is thus far budding well?*
midorigo wa	*Heave ho, heave ho, pull hard,*
Yoi, yoi, yoito na.	*my lads.*

How the Lute Genjō was Snatched by an Oni

Translated by Marian Ury

At a time now past, during the reign of Emperor Murakami, the lute Genjō suddenly disappeared. It was an imperial treasure, handed down through reign upon reign. The Emperor lamented bitterly the fact that so venerable an heirloom had been lost while he was on the throne. Perhaps it had been stolen – but if that were the case it would not have stayed out of sight for so long. It was feared that some person with a grudge against the Emperor had taken it and destroyed it.

Now, among the courtiers of middle rank there was a man named Minamoto no Hiromasa. He knew all there was to know of the Way of musical instruments. While he was brooding mournfully over Genjō's disappearance, he happened to be in the Seiryōden at night after the noises of human activity were stilled, and he heard, from somewhere to the south, the sound of Genjō's strings. In his astonishment he wondered if he could have misheard. He listened carefully: it was none other than Genjō. There could be no mistake, and his wonder increased all the more. He told no one, but dressed informally as he was, he slipped on his shoes and went out past the palace guards' headquarters with only a page boy to attend him. He went southward; the sound seemed to be coming from somewhere ahead of him. It must be very near, he kept thinking – and soon he had come to Shujaku gate. It seemed to be yet farther ahead – and so he walked southward down Shujaku Avenue. He thought that whoever stole Genjō must be playing it in secret in a [certain] viewing pavilion. He hurried to the pavilion and listened: it sounded quite close by, and farther south. And thus he walked on toward the south until he was at Rashō gate.

He stood under the gate and heard Genjō sounding from the upper storey. "That's no human being playing the instrument," he thought in amazement. "It can only be an *oni* or some such being." The playing stopped and then resumed after a little while. "You there playing," said Hiromasa. "Who are you? Genjō was lost the other day; the Emperor's been searching everywhere. Tonight in the Seiryōden I heard it sound to the south, and so I've come after it."

At that moment the playing stopped and something came down from the ceiling. Hiromasa drew back in fear and saw that Genjō had been lowered at the end of a cord. Terrified though he was, he took the lute and carried it back to the palace, where he presented it to the Emperor with an account of what had happened. The Emperor was deeply moved. "So it was an *oni* that took it!" he exclaimed. All who heard of this praised Hiromasa.

The lute Genjō exists even today. It is in the palace, an imperial treasure handed down through reign upon reign. It is just like a living being. If it is played clumsily or incompletely, it becomes angry and won't resound. Also, if there is dust on it that isn't wiped away, it becomes angry and won't resound. You can tell its mood just by looking at it. Once there was a fire in the palace, and though no one carried it, it went out under its own power and was found in the courtyard.

An uncanny tale, isn't it! So the tale's been told, and so it's been handed down.

How a Woman Who Was Bearing a Child Went to South Yamashina, Encountered an Oni, and Escaped

Translated by Marian Ury

At a time now past, there was a young woman who was in service at a certain great house. She had neither parents nor relatives and no real friends, so that she had nowhere to turn in case of need. She never ventured from her chamber. Who would take care of her if she fell ill, she wondered anxiously; and then she found herself pregnant without a proper husband.

The more she pondered her fate, the more unrelieved was her misery. The first necessity was to find a place to give birth. She did not know what to do, and there was no one to advise her. She thought about speaking to her master, but she was ashamed to confess her condition.

She was an intelligent woman nonetheless, and an idea occurred to her. "When I feel the first signs of approaching birth, I will go away by myself, with only my serving girl as a companion. It doesn't matter where I go, so long as it is deep in the mountains. I'll find a tree and give birth under it. If I die, no one will ever know, and that will be the end of it. If I survive, I will return here and pretend that nothing has happened." The month gradually drew near. She was unspeakably wretched, but she behaved as though nothing were amiss. Secretly she made preparations, readying a small store of food and giving instructions to her young maid. Soon her time was at hand.

She felt the first signs before dawn. Anxious to be gone before it was light, she had the girl gather up the provisions and hurried with her from the house. The mountains must lie close by the eastern boundaries of the capital, she thought, and set out eastward; but daybreak found her no farther than the Kamo River bank. Where could she go now? But she summoned up her courage and, halting often to rest, walked on toward Awatayama and entered into the deep forest. She walked about looking for a suitable spot until she came to an area called North Yamashina. Nestled among the cliffs were the remains of an ancient mountain estate. The house itself had long since gone to ruin. There was no sign of human habitation. Here, she decided, she would give birth, and here she would abandon her child. There was a wall, but she managed to climb over it.

Here and there in the guest wing were places where the floor was still sound. She had sat down at the edge of the veranda to rest when she heard someone approaching from an inner room. "So someone lives here after all!" she thought in misery. A door slid open and a white-haired old woman came out. "Surely she'll scold me and order me away," she thought, but the old woman smiled benignly.

"Who is it that pays me this unexpected call?" said the old woman. Amidst tears the young woman told her her story. "You poor thing!" the old woman said, "you shall have your baby here," and called her in. The young woman was overjoyed. The Buddha had come to her aid, she thought. Within, a simple bed was prepared for her, and not long afterwards she had an easy delivery.

The old woman came to her and said, "My best congratulations! Old people like me who live in countrified places like this don't need to worry about taboos. Why don't you stay here for seven days, until your defilement is over." She had the serving girl heat water to wash the newborn. The mother was happy. The infant was a beautiful little boy; she could never abandon it now, and she lay there nursing it.

A few days later, as she was taking an afternoon nap with the infant beside her, she heard ever so faintly the old woman say, "Only a mouthful, but my how delicious!" She opened her eyes to see the old woman gazing at the child intently and was terrified. "She is an oni," the young woman thought, "and she will devour us." She knew that somehow or other she must steal away.

There came the time when the old woman took a long afternoon nap. The mother stealthily put the infant on the servant girl's back and, lightly dressed, left the house and ran back down the road she had come as fast as her legs would carry her. "Buddha save me!" she prayed. Soon they were at Awataguchi. From there she went to the Kamo River bank, where she stopped at a humble cottage and set her appearance to rights. After sundown she returned to the house of her master. It was her quick-wittedness that saved her. The child she entrusted to a nurse.

What became of the old woman after that no one knows. The young woman said nothing to anyone of what she had experienced. It was only after she herself had grown old that she told her story.

Now think: ancient places of that sort always have supernatural beings living in them. "Only a mouthful, but my how delicious!" Only an *oni* could have looked at an infant and said that.

This shows that you should never go into such places alone. So the tale's been told, and so it's been handed down.

How the Hunter's Mother Became an Oni and Tried to Devour Her Children

Translated by Marian Ury

At a time now past, in a district and province [the names of which are no longer known], there were two brothers who got their livelihood by killing deer and boar. They went into the mountains regularly to shoot deer, so that elder and younger brother went as a team.

They hunted by a technique called 'waiting.' They would lash pieces of wood high across the cleft of some great tree and sit down to wait; when deer passed underneath they would shoot. The brothers were sitting in the trees about fifty or sixty yards apart, facing each other. It was a moonless night toward the end of the ninth month, so dark that not a thing could be seen. They waited in hopes of hearing deer come, but night gradually deepened and there were none.

Now, as the elder brother was sitting in his tree the hand of some supernatural being reached down from above, seized his topknot, and began to draw him upward. Alarmed, he felt for the hand: it was the hand of a human being, emaciated and withered. "An *oni* has gotten hold of me and is pulling me upward in order to eat me – that must be the explanation," he thought. He would tell his brother sitting opposite, he decided. He shouted to him, and there was an answering shout.

The elder brother said, "Suppose just now some weird creature had taken hold of my topknot and were pulling me upwards: what would you do?"

"I'd figure out where it is and shoot it," the younger said.

The older said, "It's true. Something really has taken hold of my topknot just now and is pulling me upwards."

"I'll aim by your voice," the younger said.

"Well then, shoot," said the elder, and accordingly the younger let fly a forked arrow. He sensed that it had struck just above his brother's head. "It seems to me I've hit it," he said. The elder brother felt above his head and found that the hand that had seized him had been severed at the wrist and was dangling. He took it and said, "You've already cut off the hand that took hold of me; I have it here. Let's call it a night and go home."

"All right," said the younger. Both came down from their trees, and they went home together. It was well past midnight when they got back.

Now they had an aged mother, so infirm that she could scarcely get about. They had set up quarters for her in a tiny house of her own; their own houses stood on either side so they could keep an eye on her. Upon returning from the mountains they heard her moaning strangely. "Why are you moaning, Mother?" they asked, but she made no reply. They then lit torches and together examined the severed hand; it resembled their mother's hand. Horrified, they examined it closely: it could be no other. They opened the sliding door to their mother's room, and she rose to her feet. "You – you—" she said and started to lunge at them. "Is this your hand, madam?" they said, threw it inside, slid the door shut, and went away.

Not long afterwards she died. When her sons looked at her close up they saw that one of her hands was missing, severed at the wrist. So it had indeed been their mother's hand, they realized. Senile and demented, their mother had become an *oni* and followed her children into the mountains to devour them.

When parents become extremely old they always turn into *oni* and try to eat even their own children. But she was their mother and they buried her.

Now think: how fearsome it was! So the tale's been told, and so it's been handed down.

Shiramine
Ueda Akinari; translated by Wilfrid Whitehouse

I had once received permission to pass through the Ausaka Barrier, and had travelled widely in the East Land to view scenes famous in poetry; there, the autumn-clad mountains had compelled me to stop to admire – everywhere had there been scenes which had touched my heart – the shores of Narumi, haunt of plover – the smoke on the high Fuji peak – the plain of Ukijima – the barrier at Kiyomi – the coasts of Oiso and Koiso – the *murasaki* in full flower on the Musashi Plain – the early morning calm on Shiogama – the rush-thatched huts of the fishers at Kisagata – the bridge of boats at Sano – the hanging bridge at Kiso.

Still, I had a desire to see also the famed beauties of the West Land, and so in the autumn of the Third Year of the Nin-an Era (1168), I passed on through Naniwa along the coasts of Suma and Akashi, shivering in the cold blast, and in the forest of Mi-osaka in Sanuki, I laid aside my walking-staff for a while – although the hut there had no accomodation for resting after the fatigue of a long journey, being built to shelter those living a life of contemplation and asceticism.

Hearing that the mausoleum of the late ex-Emperor was on Shiramine near this spot, I decided to go there to worship and so ascended the mountain early in the Tenth Month. The mountain, behind which rises the precipitous peak of Chigadake, is densely covered with oaks and pines so that even when the day is bright and clear it seems as dark there as if a drizzle of rain were falling. On the day on which I climbed it, a thick mist was rising up from the bottoms of the ravines so that the road was uncertain even a little way ahead.

At last I saw in a little open space where the trees were not so densely intermingled that on a small mound of earth three stones were placed one on the other. With what sadness it was that I looked at this, the ex-Emperor's tomb, almost buried beneath brambles and creepers; the sight put me into such an agitation of heart that I could not tell whether it was in dream or in reality that I stood there; this then was the tomb of that Emperor whom I had last seen directing the affairs of State from his throne in the Shishin Hall or the Seiryô Hall of the Imperial Palace, the tomb of that lord formerly hailed by a hundred obedient courtiers as Great and Mighty Sovereign. Later, he had relinquished the throne in favour of the Emperor Konoe, but still in abdication he had continued to control the affairs of State. At that time who would have thought that he would pass to his rest deep in the bramble-clad mountains where none but deer pass by and where none would come and worship? When I thought with bitter sadness that even on the King of Hosts falls inevitable retribution for the deeds done in a former life, my tears gushed forth.

I thought to worship there the whole night through, and so seated myself on a flat stone before the tomb and chanted a sutra in a low voice. Then I composed this poem –

Matsuyama no	*This scene of the waves*
Nami no keshiki wa	*Rolling up near to the foot*
Kawaraji wo	*Of this pine-clad mount*
Katanaku kimi wa	*Is the same now as of old –*
Nari masari keri.	*Only you, my lord, have gone.*

Then with a fervent heart I continued my intercessions. How wet my sleeves – from the thick fog! Although the sun had not long set, the darkness in that remote spot among the mountains was most dismal. The stone floor and its coverlet of leaves were very cold. My senses were rendered so acute by the cold which froze me to the bones that my heart was filled with an unaccountable fear. The moon had by this time risen but the dense foliage totally intercepted all its light. I sat there in the pitch darkness feeling very desolate and gradually fell into a doze.

Suddenly I was awakened; I was certain that I had heard someone call me by name – "En-i, En-i, En-i." I opened my eyes and peered into the darkness. Before me stood a strange figure, a tall emaciated man, his features and the colour and pattern of his garments indistinguishable in the darkness. As becomes a priest, and one whose heart is converted, it was without fear that I asked him who he was. He answered that he had come to give me this answer to my poem –

Matsuyama no	*To this pine-clad mount*
Nami ni nagarete	*At the mercy of the waves,*
Koshi fune no	*My boat came drifting;*
Yagate munashiku	*And soon thereafter it was*
Nari ni keru kana.	*That I departed this life.*

Then from his saying that he was glad that I had come to visit him, I knew that it was the spirit of the ex-Emperor who stood before me. I bowed down to the ground before him, and my tears flowed forth.

"Why then do you not rest in peace?" I said to him, "It was because I envied you in your having been delivered out of this present filthy world that I came to worship here tonight in order that I might further my own progress along the Way of Buddha. For you to appear thus before me is very gracious, but it is also a source of sorrow to me. Since you have now left this world, cut yourself free from all the entanglements of this world also, and secure your soul a place in the Abode of the Blessed."

My counsel was from the depths of my heart, but the ex-Emperor only laughed loudly in answer. "Do you not know, Saigyô, that the present disturbances in the country are my work? Before my death, my heart inclined to evil; I caused the War of the Heiji Era (1159), to break out, and even in death I smote the land with a curse. Behold, I will cause even greater civil disturbances to break out in the not very distant future."

At these words, I controlled my emotion to say, "What evil intentions you express! You are reputed to have had great gifts of wisdom; you know well then the necessity of ruling in accordance with Ôdô, the Way of the Kings. But I will learn your views. When you brought about the Hôgen Insurrection, was it because you were convinced that your course of conduct was in accord with the dictates of the God of Heaven, or did you act from purely selfish motives? Answer me that fully."

The Emperor's face changed. "Listen!" he said. "The Imperial Throne stands high above men. Yet when the rule of the Emperor is unjust, we must censure him in accordance with the dictates of Heaven and the will of the people. In the Eiji Era (1141), when I obeyed the commands of the Emperor, my father, to relinquish the throne to the three year old Narihito, I acted with righteousness; you cannot accuse me of having acted for any selfish motive on that occasion. Narihito died young, and my son, Shigehito, was in my opinion as in that of everyone else the rightful successor. It was therefore a very bitter disappointment to me when, through the jealousy of Bifukumon-in, the throne was usurped by Prince Masahito, the fourth son. Shigehito had great gifts as a ruler; Masahito had none. On this occasion as at all times, the great fault of the Emperor my father was that he neglected the counsel of men of ability and ruled the country according to the advice of the Imperial Consorts. Still, while he lived, I acted in a sincerely filial manner and allowed no hint of discontent to appear. However, after his death I could endure it no longer and I acted as a man of valour should. We read in history how a subject took arms against his lord, and because he acted in harmony with the dictates of Heaven and the will of the people, laid the foundations of the Chou Dynasty which lasted for eight hundred years. His was not unrighteous conduct; still less was it a crime that I who had the right to the throne should abolish this reign of 'crowing hens.' You, Saigyô, are a priest; you are obsessed with following the Way of Buddha and with obtaining salvation in a future life. Because of that obsession, you distort the laws of ethics to bring them into conformity with the doctrine of religion, and so in your reasoning you confuse the Way of Buddha with Ôdô – the Way of the Kings – the example of Yao and Shun."

I answered him with no signs of fear. "In what you have related to me," I said, drawing closer to him, "you excuse yourself with reasons borrowed from the Moral Laws, yet your true motives are not higher than the desires of the senses. We will not go so far afield as ancient China for our examples; in Japan in ancient times Honda no Sumera-mikoto passed over Prince Ohosasagi and chose a younger son, Prince Uji, as his successor. On the death of the Emperor their father, each of the two sons wished to efface himself in favour of the other, and neither would ascend the throne. Three years passed, and still the matter of the succession was not settled, so Prince Uji in his grief believing that the fact that he was still alive was the only cause of the disturbed condition of the Empire, put an end to his life. There was then nothing to prevent the elder son ascending the throne. In their conduct on this occasion, the two brothers respected the traditional Way, they acted as true sons and affectionate brothers; their motives were sincere and above worldly and selfish desires. This is the true way of following Ôdô, the Way of the King, Yao and Shun. This Prince Uji was the first in the this country to reverence the teaching of Confucius and to take Ôdô, the Way of the Kings, as his guide, having studied these doctrines under Wani of Kudara. These princes were certainly true followers of those philosopher-kings of ancient China."

"Again, as you have said," I continued, "at the beginning of the Chou Dynasty, Wu Wang, indignant at the condition of the country, by force of arms brought the nation again to peace. The opinion of Mencius is that we must not consider that Wu Wang was guilty of regicide; his lord had acted against the laws of humanity and righteousness and might justly be called a man of evil – it was then a man of evil whom Wu Wang killed and not his lord. That is the opinion of Mencius. Now, all the Chinese books, the Classics, the Histories, the Anthologies, and the Essays, have all been brought to Japan, save only this book of Mencius. This book alone has not come into this country. Every ship without exception which bore a copy of this book encountered a storm and sank. And the reason for that is that the Eight Hundred Myriad Gods feared that if this clever sophism were introduced into this country where since the foundation of the State by Amaterasu Ô Mikami, the true succession has never been in doubt, there might in the future arise a disloyal subject to usurp the throne of the Imperial Line, and believe it no crime to do so. So, it is said, the Eight Hundred Myriad Gods with a Divine Wind sunk those ships which bore a copy of this book. From this it can be seen that the teachings of the philosophers of other countries are often not appropriate to this country.

"Again," I went on, "do we not read in the Chinese Anthologies, that though brothers quarrel among themselves, yet they should unite against an external enemy? But you forgot all the dictates of brotherly affection; before your father's dead body still lying in its temporary burial place in the Mogari no Miya was cold, you began a struggle for the throne with arrows and flying banners. There could not be a more unfilial deed.

"Moreover, the Imperial Power is in the gift of the gods. Even if through selfish motives the throne is usurped, the Imperial Power cannot be obtained. Although the people had wished Prince Shigehito to succeed, your unrighteous conduct brought disturbances to the State, and their love for you only as yesterday turned at once to hatred. So you were not able to attain your object, but instead received a punishment greater than has ever been inflicted since ancient times and finally passed to your rest in this remote spot. Now forget your former hatreds and return to the

Land of Paradise, I beseech you." So did I entreat him most heartily and sincerely.

The ex-Emperor heaved a deep sigh. "Your arguments are not without reason, and your reproof of my evil deeds is not unmerited," he said. "Still, how could I endure the long torment of exile on this island, confined in Takato's house on this pine-clad mountain, with no attendant but the man who three times a day brought me my food? When I heard from my pillow at night the cry of the wild geese flying across the sky, I longed for my home for I knew that they were on their way to the Capital. And when I heard the cry of the plover on the beach at dawn, my heart was like to burst with sorrow. My chances of being allowed to return to the Capital were as slender as those of a crow's head turning white; I resigned myself to death on this desolate shore, and earnestly desiring happiness in the next world, I copied out the five volumes of the Mahâyâna Sutra. I could not leave them here on this wave-beaten coast where stands no temple, where no sound of temple-gong or trumpet-shell is heard, and I therefore wrote to the priest of the Ninwa Temple in the Capital requesting that at least the Sutra which I had transcribed should be preserved there. With them, I sent this poem –

"Hama chidori	*These plover footprints*
"Ato wa miyako ni	*I send to the Capital;*
"Kayoedomo	*There may I not go,*
"Mi wa matsuyama ni	*But on this pine-clad mountain*
"Ne wo nomi zo naku.	*I must sit and mourn my lot.*

"However, Shônagon Shinzei believed that I had sent this Sutra in order to bring a curse on the country, and to my bitter sorrow, it was returned to me. Although from of old, fraternal struggles for sovereign power have not been rare both in our own country and in China, yet considering that in pursuing such a strife against my younger brother Masahito, I had sinned deeply, I had copied out this Sutra as a penance. In returning the Sutra to me, the Emperor had but acted on the advice of men who were evilly disposed towards me. Still, it was against Masahito especially that my hatred was renewed, for he had not pardoned me as he should have done according to the Laws, but had even refused to accept the Sutra that I had transcribed and sent. At last, I determined to turn this Sutra to an evil end and thus vent my hatred against him. I cut my finger and wrote a petition in blood, and sank it with the Sutra in the sea at Shido. Then I shut myself up away from the sight of all men and prayed earnestly that I might be changed into a devil.

"Soon," continued the ex-Emperor, "the Heiji Insurrection broke out as I had planned that it should. First, I tempted the haughty and ambitious Nobuyori and caused him to gain over to his side my greatest enemy Yoshitomo. In the Hôgen Insurrection, his father, Tameyoshi, and all the warriors among his kinsfolk had lost their lives fighting for me. At that time, he alone of all his kinsmen had opposed me. The bravery of Tametomo and the skilful tactics of Tameyoshi had on that occasion brought victory within our reach when Yoshitomo had set the Shirakawa Palace on fire when a southwest wind was blowing hard. I had managed to escape from the palace, but in my flight I had injured my leg on the steep slope of Nioigadake and had had to take shelter from the weather among some brushwood cut by a woodcutter. But at last I had been recaptured and exiled to this island. All my miseries from that time had thus been a result of the wicked plans of Yoshitomo.

Now in revenge I caused his heart to harden and made him join in Nobuyori's conspiracy. He rose in rebellion but was defeated as a rebel against the Emperor by Kiyomori, a much less skilful general than himself, and as a punishment for having caused the death of his own father, the punishment of the gods was that he should himself suffer death at the hands of his favoured retainer. Shonagon Shinzei had always had great pretensions to scholarship and had always hindered the promotion of others with great malevolence. Him also I tempted to turn traitor with Nobuyori and Yoshitomo. When the conspiracy was discovered, he was forced to flee; he hid in a cave on Mt. Uji but being at length discovered, he was executed and his head exposed on the river bank at Rokujo. Thus did I punish him for having counselled the Emperor to return the Sutra I had sent.

"Further, my anger caused Bifuku mon-in to die in the summer of the First Year of the Ôhô Era (1161). In the spring of the Second Year of the Chôkan Era (1164), I brought about the death of Tadamichi. I myself passed away in the autumn of the same year and being still burning with furious anger against my enemies, I then became a devil, the chief devil of three hundred devils. When I saw people happy, I turned their joy to sorrow; when I saw the country peaceful, I stirred up strife. At this moment, of all my enemies Kiyomori alone remains in high prosperity; his will is supreme throughout the whole of the country. I desire to bring him also to ruin, but as yet he is supported in his high position by the loyal counsels of Shigemori. But, behold, the rule of the Taira family will not last long now. I will bring retribution at last on Masahito for his cruel treatment of me." With the conclusion of his speech, the voice of the ex-Emperor grew fiercer and more terrifying.

"As you are in such close relations with the world of evil, and are myriads of leagues away from the Land of Paradise, I will not continue this fruitless converse with you further," I said, and sat facing him in silence.

At that moment the peaks and the valleys trembled, the wind blew as if it would throw down the trees of the forest, sand and pebbles whirled up into the sky. And while I looked, a corpse-candle blazed up below the knees of the ex-Emperor and lighted up the mountains and valleys as plainly as by day. By this light, I could now see clearly his dirty, yellowish-brown robes and his flushed face. His tangled hair hung loosely to his knees; the whites of his eyes were turned up; his breath came painfully and feverishly; the nails of his fingers and toes had grown as long as the claws of an animal; his appearance was most terrifying – the appearance of a devil. Looking up into the sky the ex-Emperor called out, "Sagami! Sagami!," and in answer a goblin-bird of the appearance of a hawk flew near, made obeisance and awaited his commands.

The ex-Emperor turned to the bird. "Why do you not quickly put an end to Shigemori so that we may proceed to torture Masahito and Kiyomori?" he asked.

"The term of the ex-Emperor Go Shirakawa's good fortune is not yet come to an end. And it is difficult to pervert the loyal heart of Shigemori – but the end of Shigemori's life will come in twelve years, and with his death the fortunes of the Heike will fade away," the goblin-bird answered.

The ex-Emperor clapped his hands with joy at this. "I will kill all the Heike my enemies in this very sea in front of me here," he said, and his voice echoed among the valleys and hills in a most dreadful manner.

At this fearful expression of his evil disposition, I could not withold my tears; and I recited this poem in order to try to bring him back to a right mind –

Yoshi ya kimi
Mukashi no tama no
Toko totemo
Kakaran nochi wa
Nani ni kawasen.

Although formerly
You dwelt in exalted splendour,
Now that you have died,
You must resign yourself – now
The end of your power has come.
The highest and the lowest are
equal in death.

This I recited in a loud voice, for I could not repress my horror.

These words seemed to have some effect on him; his face became calmer, the corpse-candle died out, and finally also his figure disappeared as though it had been a picture which had been wiped out. The goblin-bird had gone, I knew not where. The moon then nearly at its full sank down behind the peak. It was so dark beneath the trees that I seemed to be in the unreal world of dreams. Soon the morning dawned and the birds sang merrily in the sky. I chanted the whole of the Kongô Sutra and then descended the mountain to my hut. There, as I pondered calmly over the events of the night, I could not see any mistake in the slightest detail in the information which had been given me about people or about the dates of events from the time of the Heiji Insurrection, and I locked all these things in my heart.

Thirteen years later, in the autumn of the Third Year of the Jishô Era (1182), Taira no Shigemori fell ill and died. Then Kiyomori, the Heisôkoku Nyûdô, in his malice took prisoner the ex-Emperor

Go-Shirakawa and secluded him in the Palace, later taking him to the Kaya Palace at Fukuhara where he affiicted him with many sufferings. So Yoritomo rose in revolt and came down like a wind from the west, and Yoshinaka rose and fell on him like the snow from the North Land, and together they attacked the Heike who were swept towards the Western Sea. They were defeated at Shido in Yashima of Sanuki, and the corpses of many warriors were devoured by turtles and fishes. And when they were finally destroyed at Dan-no-ura in Akamagaseki, the infant Emperor, Antoku Tennô, jumped into the sea and so perished at the same time as the remnant of the Heike.

It was wonderful for me then to observe that everything which happened at that time was in exact accord with the prophecies of the spirit of the ex-Emperor Sutoku. From that time forward, the shrine of the ex-Emperor was adorned with jewels and coloured red and blue; his spirit was there worshipped and all who visit it offer *nusa* before him and adore him as *kami*.

The Blue Hood
Ueda Akinari; translated by Dale Saunders

Once there lived a saint by the name of Kai-an, master of Zen, who was endowed with great virtue. Even as a child he had grasped the intuitive principles of Zen doctrines, and now his life was that of a wandering pilgrim. He had completed his summer retreat in the Ryōtai temple in the province of Mino, and in the autumn of that year he set out to visit the northeastern provinces. In the course of his wanderings he entered the province of Shimotsuke.

At sundown in the village of Tonda, he went up to a large, prosperous-looking house and was on the point of requesting lodgings for the night when some men, returning from the fields, began to shout their fear at the sight of the monk standing in the evening dusk. "There's the demon from the mountain," they cried. "He's come! Get out, all of you!"

There was considerable stir within the house too. Women and children wept and screamed and scrambled about as they hid themselves in the corners. The master took a blunt stick and ran out. He looked around and saw the monk, a man about fifty, wearing a dark blue hood and a torn black robe and carrying a bundle on his back.

The monk beckoned with his stick and said, "Come, come, my son. Why do you take such precautions? Could a wandering monk expect to fall under such suspicion? I was only waiting here to ask for lodgings for a single night. Do not be afraid of a weakling monk, quite incapable of banditry."

The master tossed his stick aside and clapped his hands, laughing. "Imagine me threatening a monk who is requesting lodgings because of the silly phantasies of these stupid women! I will make up for my error by giving you a night as alms." And so saying he led the monk into the house with deference. He had a meal served and treated him hospitably.

And he spoke to the monk. "A little while ago, my servants were frightened when they saw you and cried out that the demon had come. The reasons for their behaviour make an interesting story, and although it may be strange, it has been passed on from one person to another." Thereupon he told the following tale.

"There is a monastery on the mountain, above this village, which was originally the family temple of the Oyama clan. Monks of great virtue have lived there from generation to generation and the present abbot is the nephew of a certain lord. He is especially well-known for his love of learning and his devotion to the religious life. The people of this province used to bring him incense and candles and they placed great faith in him. He often did me the honour of visiting my house, and we were very friendly. But last spring he spent over a hundred days in the province of Koshi, where he had been called to preside over a ceremony of anointment. He brought back a boy of twelve or thirteen whom he kept with him at all times. Deeply infatuated by the lad's beauty he tended, unfeelingly as it seemed, to neglect the religious practices he had engaged in for so many years.

"Then about the fourth month of this year, the boy took to his bed with a slight illness. But day to day his condition worsened, and the abbot was deeply troubled. He consulted the most reputable doctors in the province, but his efforts were futile, and the boy finally died. The abbot felt that his most beloved possession had been torn from him, that the flowers of his hair ornaments had been scattered by the wind. He had no more tears to weep, no more voice with which to lament, and so great was his sorrow he did not have the boy cremated or buried. Instead, he kept the boy's body with him and spent days with his cheek against the dead cheek, his fingers intwined with the lifeless fingers. Finally, his mind became deranged and he began to play with the body as he had when the boy was alive. In his despair at seeing the flesh decay and rot, he sucked at the body and licked at the bones until he had quite completely devoured it.

"The temple people believed that the abbot must certainly have turned into a demon and they lost no time in getting out.

"And now, he comes down to the village every night and frightens everyone. Or he eats fresh bodies from the graves he violates. Of course, I have heard of what they call demons in the tales of olden times, but I actually saw the abbot turn into such a thing. Since such is the case, how can we stop him? The story has now spread throughout the province; each family boards itself up at nightfall, and people have come to the point of not going out at all. That is the real reason why we mistook you, a travelling priest, for him."

"Strange things do occur in this world," said Kai-an when he had heard the story. "Usually beings who are born in human form do not realize the magnificence of the teachings of the Buddhas and the bodhisattvas; they spend their whole life in stupidity and perverseness and are held back by passions and evil, which obstruct the way to becoming a Buddha. Sometimes, they appear in the form they had in a previous existence and avenge the cause of their fury. Sometimes they turn into demons or horrible snakes and cast their evil spells. There are countless examples since olden times.

"Some also change into demons during their lives as humans. A lady-in-waiting of the King of Ch'ou changed into a snake, Wang Han's mother became a she-devil, and Wu Cheng's wife turned into a moth. There is the case too, of a certain monk who stopped in his travels for a night in a poor hut. The wind was howling and the rain falling in the night. Not even a lamp shown, and he was unable to sleep for his unbearable sense of loneliness. Late in the night he heard the baaing of a sheep, and after a while something sniffed at him several times as if to see if he were asleep.

"The monk was suspicious and struck out forcefully with the meditation switch that he had placed at his pillow. The thing gave out a great cry and collapsed on the spot. Hearing the noise, the lady of the house came with a lighted lamp, and they saw that a young woman lay prostrate on the floor. The old woman tearfully implored him to spare the girl's life, and what could he do but leave them and quit the house?

"Sometime later he had occasion to pass through the village again. A great number of people were gathered in the fields staring at something. The monk approached and asked what had happened and was informed by the villagers that they had captured a woman who had changed into a demon and were at that moment burying her.

"In any case, it is always a question of women, and I have never heard of a like case concerning a man. It is usually because of the stubbornness of their nature that women turn into such disgusting creatures. However, there was indeed a man, a certain Ma Chou-mou, a vassal of Emperor Yang of Sui. He had a fondness for the tender flesh of children and secretly he abducted the very young of the community, had them steamed, and devoured them. But that was disgusting barbarism, very different from what you told me. Now if this monk turned into a demon, doubtless it must be the result of causes from a previous existence.

"Anyway, he was always serious about his ascetic practices and devoted in his service of the Buddhas. Had it not been for the boy he took into his life he could have become a good monk. Once he had capitulated to error and the weakness of his passions he changed into a demon. This was because of his character which was excessively singleminded. That too is the way of a very obstinate nature. There is a saying that applies to this monk's case: 'He who gives in to his passions becomes a demon; by controlling them he obtains the Fruit of Buddhahood.' If I bring this demon back to its original self through exhortation I shall certainly have returned this night's hospitality." It was with the words he had spoken to his host that the monk set forth his worthy intent.

The host touched his head to the matting. "If the revered monk were to do that for the people of this province it would be as if they were reborn in paradise," he exclaimed, shedding tears of joy.

Around the dwellings of this mountain village neither conch nor bell could be heard. The moon, which had passed its twentieth day, had risen. The host realized it was late in the night by the moonlight which filtered in through the holes in the old door. "Come, please go to bed," he said, and himself withdrew to his room.

The temple on the mountain was uninhabited and brambles pressed against the two-storeyed gate. The pavilion where the sutras were kept was empty, and a dank moss had grown on it. Spiders had cast their webs from one statue to the other, swallow droppings spotted the *homa* altar; and the monk's quarters, as well as the corridors, had fallen into a dreadfully dilapidated state.

At the hour when the rays of the sun were bending toward the direction of the Monkey, the Zen master Kai-an went into the temple and sounded his alarm staff. "I am a wandering monk. Please give me lodgings for a single night." He repeated this call many times, but there was no answer.

Finally a withered old monk came hobbling out of the sleeping room. "Where are you bound for that you should pass here, Reverend monk?" he said in a cracked voice. "There is a definite reason why this temple has fallen into such a state of disrepair. The moors are no longer inhabited by humans, and I do not have the least bit of food. There is no way I can offer you lodgings even for a night. Hurry back to the village."

"I left the province of Mino," replied the Zen master, "and I am on my way to Michinoku. As I was passing through the village at the foot of this mountain, I was delighted with the beauty of these heights and by the sound of the flowing water. So I came this far without quite realizing it. The sun is low, and it is a long way back to the village. I beg you most urgently to give me lodging for the night."

"Evil things sometimes happen in such an abandoned place as this," said the monk who was master of the place. "I cannot forcibly detain you, nor force you to leave. Do as you will," and he said no more.

The visitor did not question him further but sat down beside him. The sun had set before their eyes. In the deep shadow of the moonless night, not a lamp shone and they could not even see what lay immediately before them. They could hear only the murmur of a stream in some nearby valley. Then the host monk retired to his room. Not a sound could be heard.

The moon appeared late in the night. Its light was bright and translucent, and there was not a corner it did not seek out. It must have been near the hour of the Rat when the host monk left his room and restlessly began to search for something. Unable to find it he cried out in a loud voice, "Where could the old baldpate be hiding? He was around here someplace." He passed right in front of the Zen master several times as he said this, but without seeing him. It looked as though he was going to run toward the main building when instead he tore around the garden like a madman. At last, exhausted, he fell with his face against the ground and did not rise again.

It was at daybreak, as the morning sun was casting its first light, that he awakened as someone emerging from a bout with *sake*, and he saw that the Zen master was still in the same spot. Dumbfounded, he leaned against a pillar, gave a long sigh and stood there silent.

"Abbot, what is your trouble?" said the Zen master going up to him. "If you are hungry, fill your belly with the flesh of this humble monk."

"Did you stay here all last night?" questioned the host monk.

"I was here, and I did not go to sleep," replied the Zen master. "It is true I have unfortunately taken a liking for human flesh," said the host monk. "However, I have not yet known the taste of the flesh of a Buddha. You are truly a Buddha! With my dim, bestial eyes, even if I had tried to see the coming of a living Buddha, he would have quite naturally been invisible to me. Oh, how powerful you are!" And as he said this he lowered his head and became quiet.

"According to what the villagers say," replied the Zen master, "you have been deranged by a temporary passion, and have suddenly taken to committing the crimes of wild animals. However horrible and pitiful that may be, it is an unparalleled case of evil causes bringing about evil results. Night after night you go down to the village and inflict injuries on the people, and in the neighbouring villages no one ever has peace.

"When I heard about this I could not bear to abandon them to such a fate, and I came here with the express purpose of making you see the light and so to bring you back to your real self. But will you or not heed my teaching?"

"You are truly a Buddha," said the host monk. "Please teach me those principles by which I can at once wipe out such dreadful evil deeds."

"If you wish to hear me, come here," said the Zen master, and he made him sit on a flat stone in front of the bamboo grating placed by the veranda. Then he took off the dark blue hood he was wearing on his own head and put it on the monk's. He then gave him two lines of a poem from the *Shōdō*, on which the monk was to meditate.

> *'The moon shines on the river; the wind blows in the pines.*
> *The night is long; the night is pure. Why?'*

"You must quietly seek the meaning of these two lines without leaving this spot. When you perceive their importance you will have found your original Buddha nature." Thus he carefully instructed the monk and then went back down the mountain.

From that day on, the villagers were free, it is said, of this terrible curse. But as they did not know whether the monk was dead or alive, they were afraid and avoided climbing the mountain.

A year went by rapidly. In the winter of the following year during the first days of the tenth month, the virtuous Kai-an returned from the northern provinces. He passed through this place again and stopped at the house of his former host and questioned him about the monk's condition.

"Thanks to your great power, the demon has never again come down from the mountain," said the host, joyfully welcoming him. "And so everyone here feels as if he had been reborn in paradise. Yet we are frightened to go up the mountain, and not a person has. So no one knows about him, but surely he has not remained alive this long. Please pray for his salvation during your stay here tonight, and we will all join our prayers to yours."

"If he has entered the other world through the fruit of his good deeds," said the Zen master, "I can say that he is my senior on the way to Enlightenment. On the other hand, as long as he is alive he is my disciple. In either case, I must see what has become of him." When he had said this, he climbed the mountain for the second time.

People did indeed appear to have stopped frequenting the place, and it was difficult to believe that it was the same path he had taken the year before.

Going into the temple, he saw that reeds and grasses had grown profusely, higher than a man. The dew was falling like an autumn storm. It was not possible to distinguish the three paths. The doors of all the buildings had broken loose. The corridor that went around the monks' quarters and the kitchens were covered with moss, and rainwater stood in the rotten planks.

He looked around the outer veranda where he had bidden the monk sit. A wraith of a man was seated there, his hair and beard so tangled in the writhing vines that it was scarcely possible to tell whether it was a monk or a layman. Midst the reeds and grasses bent beneath him, the figure was chanting indistinctly and spasmodically in a faint voice, like that of a mosquito and Kai-an heard:

> *'The moon shines on the river, the wind blows in the pines.*
> *The night is long; the night is pure. Why?'*

The Zen master looked at him and then, grasping his meditation switch more firmly, he said: "Well, what is the reason?" and shouted: "*Katsu!*" and struck him on the head. Then suddenly the figure dissolved like ice in the morning sun, leaving in the grass only the blue hood and some bones. Truly, his evil attachment must have disintegrated at just that instant. This is indeed a worthy teaching!

Henceforth the fame of the Zen master's great power spread beyond the clouds and over the seas, and people cried in admiration, "The founder's flesh is not yet dried out." The villagers gathered together, cleaned the temple, and took it upon themselves to restore it. Then they prevailed upon the Zen master to establish himself there, and he reformed the former Shingon monastery and founded the Sōtō Zen temple which still exists today, respected and prosperous.

The Cottage in the Wilderness
Ueda Akinari; translated by Wilfrid Whitehouse

In the village of Mama, Katsushika-gori, in the province of Shimofusa, there lived a man named Katsushiro, whose ancestors had long lived in that neighbourhood in great prosperity; he himself had once owned many fields but hating farm-work and being by nature very unpractical, he had been reduced to destitution. On account of this, all his kinsfolk had ceased to be friendly towards him, and he was desirous of seizing any opportunity of retrieving his fortunes. Now a man from the Capital named Sasabe Soji was in the habit of visiting the village every year to buy silk, staying on these occasions with his own kinsfolk in the village. He had always been friendly with Katsushiro who therefore asked to be allowed to go with him to the Capital to sell silk. Sasabe readily agreed and they made all their arrangements for travelling together. Katsushiro was very glad for he knew Sasabe to be a man on whom he could rely. Then with the money from the sale of what fields still remained in his possession, he bought a quantity of white silk and made his preparations for departure.

Katsushiro's wife, Miyagi, was a strikingly beautiful and intelligent woman. She did not wish her husband to leave her to go up to the

Capital as a silk merchant and tried her utmost to dissuade him. However, Katsushiro was firm in his determination to go and she could not move him from his purpose. So in spite of her dread of her future loneliness, she did her best to prepare for his departure.

The night before their parting, they spent in consoling one another. "You leave me behind to wander forlorn over mountain and moor," she said. "There cannot be a life of greater anguish than that you leave me to. Night and day keep me in your thoughts all the while, and come back to me quickly. If we live long enough, we shall meet again. Still, it is said that we never know whether we shall die before the morrow. Therefore, though you must keep a brave heart, have pity on me."

"I am very troubled myself at the thought that I must go to live in a strange land – a life as unsettled as a seat on a drifting log. However, I will return in the autumn, when the leaves of the arrowroot turn in the wind. Be brave and wait for me till then," he said attempting to console her.

Then at dawn he turned his back on the east and hurried away in the direction of the Capital.

In the summer of this same year, the first year of the Kyotoku Era (1452), a conflict arose between the Governor of Kamakura, Ashikaga Shigeuji, and the Uesugi family for supremacy in the Eastern Provinces. The palace at Kamakura was set on fire by the enemy and Shigeuji fled into Shimofusa to his allies. The whole country east of the Hakone Barrier was thrown into turmoil; the old fled to hide in the mountains, the young were conscripted as soldiers. In every village, rumours were rife that one of the antagonists would burn down the village or that the other party would enter the village on the following day. Women and children ran from place to place crying bitterly. Katsushiro's wife considered whether she should fly with the others, but in the end decided to stay, relying on her husband's promise to return in the autumn. Many days of anxiety passed; autumn came but he did not return; autumn drew to its close and still no tidings of him came. She was alone, forlorn and filled with sadness; she lamented that the mind of man was as changable as was the state of the country.

> *I cannot tell him my bitter sorrow now,*
> *But would you tell him, cock at Ausaka,*
> *That autumn is at its close!*

She composed this poem, but she had no way of sending it to her husband, so far away in the Capital.

In this turmoil, general throughout the country, the hearts of men degenerated. Sometimes visitors to the house, struck by Miyagi's great beauty, tried to seduce her, but she preserved her honour as carefully as the Three Famous Women of Virtue of ancient China and she rejected these temptations with scorn. After this she bolted her doors to all comers. The maid servant returned to her own home; finally her store of money ran out. Thus the old year ended. The new year came, but the disorder continued. Moreover, in the autumn of the year before, by order of the Shogunate, Tsuneyori, To no Shimozuke no Kami, the lord of the castle of Gujo in the province of Mino, had advanced against Shigeuji and had made his headquarters in Shimozuke, and co-operating with Chiba Sanetane, his kinsman, was attempting to bring all the eastern provinces into subjection. However, Shigeuji had decisively repelled him, and the end of all these disturbances was not yet in sight. Taking advantage of the troubles, bandits made stockades here and there, and looted and set fire to property. All the eight provinces east of the Barrier were in a state of great unrest; all the land was laid waste.

Katsushiro having arrived at the Capital with Sasabe had sold all his silk at a great profit, for the citizens of the metropolis at that time were great lovers of splendid attire. He planned to return to the East, but just then he heard a rumour that the forces of the Uesugi family had captured Kamakura and had pursued their foes into Shimofusa, thus bringing the horrors of war into the neighbourhood of his old home, which had indeed become the field of battle for the opposing forces. Rumour is prone to exaggerate even what is near at hand, so all the more so did it exaggerate the disturbances in that distant eastern province. It was therefore with a fearful heart that at the beginning of the Eighth Month, Katsushiro left the Capital. Passing Misaka in Kiso at nightfall, he was stopped by robbers and stripped of all he possessed. There also he heard that all were barred from going on to the east by barriers newly erected. He could send no message to his wife; he did not know what had happened in his old home, whether the house had been burnt down by the soldiers, whether his wife had been killed, whether his native village was now the haunt only of goblins. So he returned to the Capital. While passing through the province of Omi, he fell sick of a fever. Sasabe's father-in-law, a rich man named Kodama Kahei, lived in this province at the village of Musa, and Katsushiro begged to be allowed to stay with him for a while. Kodama consented and cared for him devotedly, obtaining a doctor and medicine for him. Katsushiro, when he had recovered somewhat, was full of gratitude to him for all his kindness and stayed with him till spring, as he was still unable to walk well. During his stay he became very friendly with the people of this village who for their part admired him for his honesty and treated him with great friendliness. At last Katsushiro was able to continue his journey to the Capital to see Sasabe, but immediately after this, he returned to the village where he had been treated so kindly and lived with Kodama. There he remained for seven years; years that passed away like a dream.

In the second year of the Kansho Era (1461), the struggle in Kawachi between the two factions of the Hatakeyama family was involving the Capital and the vicinity in turmoil. In addition, an epidemic had been raging since the spring. Corpses lay about the street; men's hearts failed them at this instance of the transitoriness of life; they felt that the end of the world must be near at hand.

Katsushiro was pondering over the depths to which he had fallen and on the impossibility of making a livelihood. He did not wish to remain any longer in that distant land, dependent on the charity of a stranger. He had never had any tidings of his wife and felt that he had not been true to her, living so long in the wilderness overgrown with *wasuregusa*, the Herb of Forgetfulness. If she were dead, he ought at least to go to erect a tomb over her grave.

He told Kodama what he intended to do, and in an interval of fine weather during the rainy season of the Fifth Month, he set out. At the end of ten days, he arrived in his native province. It was after sunset and the rainclouds hung low. Still, he thought it impossible to get lost in the place where he had lived so long. He wandered across the summer fields and came to a place where the bridge over a river had fallen down; no clatter of horses' hoofs crossing it was now to be heard. The fields lay desolate; the road had completely disappeared. The houses that had stood there formerly had gone; rarely was there an inhabited house to be seen; and those which still stood looked very different from what they had been of old. He could not even tell which was his own house. However, by the light of the stars which shone through the rents in the clouds, he made out a blasted pine at a distance of twenty paces. By this landmark, he recognized his old home, and with a joyful heart went up to it. It appeared to be unchanged and to be inhabited, for through the cracks in the old door the light of a lamp shone. Who was living there – his wife? – or a stranger? – he wondered in great agitation. He stood at the gate and coughed. Someone inside heard it and at once asked, "Who is there?" He recognized his wife's voice, now grown harsh with age. He feared lest it should prove to be a dream; his heart throbbed painfully as he replied, "It is I who have returned. How marvellous it is that you are still living here thus in this miscanthus-overgrown wilderness!"

His wife recognized his voice and presently she opened the door and appeared before him. She looked black and filthy; her eyes were sunken, her dishevelled hair hung down her back. When she saw that it was her husband, she began to weep silently and bitterly and could not utter a word.

Katsushiro was touched to the heart; he also was unable to speak, but after a while he said, "Had I thought that you were still alive, I would not have stayed so long away from you. When I arrived in the Capital, I heard of the battle of Kamakura and learnt of the defeat of the Governor and of the retirement of his troops into Shimofusa, hotly pursued by the enemy. The next day I bade farewell to Sasabe and started on my return journey. I left the Capital at the beginning of the Eighth Month, and on the Kiso Highway, I was attacked by robbers who stripped me of all I possessed; clothes and money were all stolen, and I barely escaped with my life. Moreover, I learnt from the villagers there that no one could pass the barriers newly erected on the Tokaido and the Tosando, and that the Commander-in-Chief had just been sent from the Capital to help the Uesugi against the troops which had retired into Shimofusa. I also heard that this place had been destroyed by fire and every foot of the ground trodden under the feet of warhorses. I thought, therefore, that you had either perished in the fire or had been drowned in the sea. So I abandoned my intention of returning here and went back to the Capital, where I had lived for seven years on charity. However, as I yearned more and more to return to this my old home, at last I decided to make my way here, if only to see your grave, for I never dreamt of finding you alive. I cannot but feel that you are some deceiving vision like the cloud of Mt. Wushan which appeared to King Hsiang Wang in the form of a woman, or like the wraith of the consort of the Han Emperor?" And then he burst into tears.

His wife controlled her tears to say, "Soon after you left me, and long before the autumn when you had promised to return, conditions here became horrible. The villagers all deserted their homes and fled by sea or hid themselves in the mountains. The few who were left were like wild beasts; seeing my widowed and lonely condition, they tempted me with cunning words, but I preferred an end like a jewel which is smashed to pieces rather than remain like a tile which is whole. What torments I had to bear with patience all this long time! The clear sparkle of the Milky Way showed that autumn had come, but you did not return. I waited on through the winter and through the spring, but still no tidings of you came. Then I decided to go myself to the Capital, but I found that it was impossible for a woman to cross the barrier through which even men were not permitted to go. Therefore I remained here to pine for you, but without hope, in this house beneath the pine, living among the foxes and owls. Now I am glad that the vexation of my spirit has melted away with your coming; how pitiful it must be to die of yearning for one's beloved!"

She began to weep again, but with "The night is short," and such words of soothing, they lay down to sleep.

The wind sucked at the paper of the windows with a noise like that of the wind whispering through the pine-trees. It was rather cold during the night but worn out by his long journey, Katsushiro slept soundly. Just before morning he woke up feeling cold, and put out his hand in his sleep to pull the coverlet over him, touching something which rustled under his hand, and something fell on his face which he took to be raindrops. He looked up and saw that the roof seemed to have been blown off by the wind, and from where he lay, he could see the moon, wan in the morning light. There were no doors to the house; reeds and miscanthus grew through the mouldering bamboo fences; his sleeves were wet with the dew that fell from their leaves. Ivy and vines covered the walls; the garden was buried in weeds: it was not yet autumn, but the place was a picure of autumn desolation. His wife who had lain by his side had gone, and from this fact he began to suspect that he had been bewitched by a fox. However, when he looked around him, he saw that it was really his own home, though now long deserted. He recognized this large room, and that granary in the corner of the yard, constructed according to his own plans. Bewildered, he tottered as he stood and looked around. He realized that his wife must have died long before, and that since then the only occupants of the house had been foxes and wolves. The house had fallen to ruin, and some goblin had appeared to him in the guise of his wife, or perhaps it was that her yearning spirit had returned to greet him. He saw that his former fears were real; she was actually dead. His feelings then were too deep for words to describe. Thinking of that old line, 'I alone remain unchanged,' he wandered sorrowfully about the grounds. The verandah had been removed from what had formerly been their bedroom, and instead there was a mound with a roof over it as a protection against the weather. He felt a great sorrow, succeeded by a feeling of horror when he realized that this was her grave, out of which her spirit had come the night before. Among the offerings in front of it he found a tablet of plain wood on which was pasted a strip of Nasuno paper. On this he could decipher a poem in his wife's handwriting, though it was defaced and in parts almost unreadable. It was evidently a poem that she had written when very near her death; it was full of a reproachful yearning.

In sorrow thinking –
'Will he not come back again?'
How sad it has been
To live till now deceived by
The vain hope of his return!

Then, for the first time, did he fully realize that his wife was dead, and he flung himself on the ground weeping. It was sad, he thought, that still he did not know the day or even the year in which she had died, so he checked his grief and went out to try to find someone who could tell him. The sun had by this time risen high in the sky.

First he went to the nearest house, where he saw the master, a man whom he had not known of old, who asked him where he was from.

Katsushiro bowed in answer. "I am the owner of the next house," he replied, "but I have been in the Capital for the last seven years trying to earn a living. I returned last night to find my home in ruins and uninhabited. My wife has died; her grave is there: but the date of her death is not written upon it. It grieves me sore that I do not know the date of her death. If you know, tell me."

"Your story is a very sad one," answered the man. "Your wife must have died long before I came here – that was only a year ago. I do not know anything about anyone who used to live there. All the people fled from this village at the outbreak of the war, and most of the people who now live here came from other parts of the country. However, one old man does still remain here who must be one of the former inhabitants. He sometimes goes to your house to offer intercessions for the dead. He is, I think, the only one who will be able to tell you the date of your wife's death."

"Where does he live?" asked Katsushiro.

"He is the owner of the hemp field a hundred paces towards the beach, and he lives in a small hut in the field."

Full of joy, Katsushiro made his way to the hut and found an old bent man of about seventy years of age, sitting on a round seat in front of an outdoor fireplace, drinking tea.

"Why is it that you have been so long in coming back?" he asked as soon as he saw Katsushiro.

Katsushiro then recognized him as an old man named Uruma, one of the old inhabitants of the village. He first congratulated the old man on having lived to such a great age and then related his own story fully, beginning at his going up to the Capital, of his long unwilling sojourn there, and concluding with the strange events of the preceding night. And as he thanked the old man for his kindness in having made a grave for his wife and offering intercessions there, he could not prevent his tears falling afresh.

"Soon after you went away," the old man then began, "in the summer, war broke out. The villagers fled in all directions, and the young men were conscripted as soldiers. Soon the fields were overgrown with dense thickets inhabited by foxes and hares. However, your wife, relying on your promise to return in the autumn, would not leave her home. And as it was impossible for me to walk more than a hundred paces on account of my paralysed legs, I also shut myself up in my house. Your home became for a while the haunt of a fearful goblin, but your wife bravely remained there even then. Her story is the most pitiful I have ever heard. Autumn passed and spring also, and on the Tenth Day of the Eighth Month she died. In compassion I carried soil and buried her coffin in a mound. And I put the poem she had written on her deathbed as the inscription over her grave and made my poor offerings before it. As I cannot write, I was unable to put on it the date of her death, and as the temple is so far away, I could not obtain a posthumous name for her. Since then five years have passed away. And from your story of what happened last night, I am convinced that it was the spirit of your wife that returned to reproach you for your conduct towards her. Let us return then to her grave and hold intercessions for the repose of her soul." Leaning heavily on his staff, the old man led the way back to the house. There they bowed down before the grave and chanted prayers and wept till dawn.

During the night, as they were keeping vigil, the old man told Katsushiro this story: "Long, long ago, when as yet the grandfather of my grandfather had not been born, a beautiful maiden named Mama no Tekona lived in this village. Her family was poor – she wore but a hempen dress with a blue collar; her hair was unkempt, her feet were bare: but her face was as beautiful as the full moon, and when she smiled, she was like a flower in bloom. She was famed as being fairer than any of the splendidly attired high-born ladies of the Capital. She was loved not only by men of the village but also by the government officials who came down from the Capital and even by men of the neighbouring provinces. Filled with anguish at the thought that she must leave the love of all these unrequited, Tekona at last threw herself into the sea. Many poets have written of this sad story, and it has been handed down as a tradition in this place. When as a boy my mother told me this interesting story, I felt a great pity for her; yet I feel now that the fate of your wife was even sadder than that of Tekona of old." He wept as he told the story and now his tears overcame him, for the old easily lose control of their feelings. It is impossible to describe the feelings of Katsushiro on hearing this story, but he tried then to express them in his poor, rustic way –

> *Dear to the heart*
> *Of these men of ancient time*
> *Was Mana no Tekona;*
> *And as dearly beloved*
> *Was this wife of mine to me.*

He could not well express the feelings of his heart, yet his poem excites our sympathies more than many of the poems of those who are far greater masters of expression.

This story was told by those merchants who visited this village from time to time, and through them it has been handed down to us.

The Kibitsu Cauldron
Ueda Akinari; translated by Wilfrid Whitehouse

Who was it, I wonder, who said, and so truly, "To have to live with a jealous wife is most irksome, but old age makes manifest her virtues"? Jealousy brings evil results in its train; even when it does not bring disaster, by it the performance of duties is obstructed and scandal caused among the neighbours while the greater disasters of jealousy are loss of home and country and being made an object of ridicule to the world. Who can tell the number of those who from ancient times until now have come to disaster and ruin through this poison of jealousy! If the wife's jealousy is strong, after her death she becomes a serpent or a thunderbolt to perfect her revenge. And there is but little satisfaction then in attempting to punish her by putting her flesh in salt. Still, such metamorphoses are exceedingly rare and can always be avoided by the husband correcting his conduct and leading his wife into a better way of thought. So, as has been rightly said, must women be firmly controlled by their husbands and tamed as birds are tamed.

In the village of Niwase, Kaya-gôri, in the province of Kibi, there lived a man named Izawa Shôdayû. His grandfather had been in the service of the Akamatsu family in the Province of Harima but during the War of the First Year of the Kakitsu Era (1441), he had left the Akamatsu mansion and had come to live in this village. In the three generations to the time of his grandson, Shôdayû, the family had become prosperous through hard work – in spring ploughing and in autumn reaping. However, his only son, Shôtarô, hated the work of farmer and gave himself up to the pleasures of wine and women, paying no heed to the admonitions of his father. In their sorrow at his conduct, his father and mother decided that their best plan would be to marry him to some beautiful girl of good family so that he might be reformed. While with this object in view they were looking around for a suitable girl, a man recommended to them as an excellent wife for him the daughter of Kasada Miki, the priest of the Kibitsu Shrine, as being an exceptionally dutiful, as well as beautiful, girl who was also very accomplished in playing the *koto*, further recommending the marriage as being especially advantageous as she was of good lineage, the family being descended from Kamowake of Kibi.

Shôdayû was pleased with the proposal. "Thank you very much," he answered. "I should esteem it a great honour to become connected in marriage with such a family. However, Kasada is of noble birth, while I am a nameless peasant. I am afraid that he will not listen to the proposal on account of this inequality of rank."

"You think too humbly of yourself," the go-between said with a smile. "I will proceed to arrange the marriage."

He then went to Kasada who agreed to this proposal with delight, as did also his wife. "Our daughter is now seventeen years of age," she said, "and I cannot feel at ease until she is happily married. Choose a Lucky Day as soon as possible and send us the betrothal presents." She urged the marriage on her husband so earnestly that arrangements for it were made at once; the betrothal gifts were sent and the marriage ceremony was fixed for a convenient Lucky Day.

In order to pray for their happiness, Kasada gathered together diviners and priests and offered hot water to the *kami*. Those who pray at this shrine make offerings and then boil water to tell what the future holds in store for them. When the diviner has finished his prayers and the water is boiled, it is a sign of good fortune if the water in the cauldron boils up with a noise like that of the bellowing of a bull, whereas as a sign of ill luck, no sound whatever is heard. This is called the *mikamabarai* ceremony of Kibitsu. No doubt the *kami* did not approve of the marriage of Kasada's daughter; for when he performed the ceremony for her, there was not a sound to be heard, not even so much as the chirping of an insect in the autumn field. This discouraged Kasada and he told his wife of the evil omen.

His wife had no such fears. "It was probably because the priests were not ceremonially pure that no sound was heard from the cauldron," she answered. "Now that the betrothal gifts have been exchanged, we could not break off the engagement, even if it were with an enemy or a foreigner. And as Izawa is from a military family, and one very strict in such matters, he would not consent. Also our daughter has heard that her bridegroom is very handsome and she is counting the days until her marriage. So if we told her now that the marriage was to be broken off, we cannot tell what the consequences would be. And, if any evil results were to follow the breach of the marriage contract, it would be of no use then for us to feel remorse."

As the marriage was agreeable to Kasada's wishes, he was not altogether discouraged from the marriage by the evil omen; he took heed of his wife's counsel and went on with the preparations. And on the appointed day, all the kinsfolk of both families assembled to celebrate the wedding, praying that the young couple might 'live for ever like the crane and the tortoise'.

Isora, Kasada's daughter, from the time when she went to the house of the Izawa family, rose early in the morning and retired to bed late at night and was continuous in her service of her husband's parents. Also, making allowances for her husband's disposition, she served him with devotion, so that his parents were touched and delighted. Shôtarô himself admired his wife's character and loved her, and they lived together in all harmony for a time. But he could not control his fickle nature. In a very short time he was deeply attached to a prostitute named Sode of the port of Torno, and finally he ransomed her and installed her in a house which he bought for her near the village, and there he stayed with her day after day and would not return home. Isora was deeply hurt by his conduct and reasoned with him, sometimes pleading with him, taking as her excuse the anger of his parents, and sometimes rebuking him for the wicked fickleness of his conduct. Her words had no effect at all on him; after this he did not return home for several months. When at last he did so, his father shut him up in a room, feeling that his conduct towards Isora was not to be endured. Isora was very sorry for him and served him humbly and faithfully from morning till night, besides sending money to Sode. Thus faithfully did she do her duty to her husband.

Then one day when his father was absent from home, Shôtarô spoke to Isora. "Seeing your virtue and your fidelity," he said, "I have repented of all my past misdeeds. I wish now to send that woman back to her home at Inamino in the Province of Harima and so bring back peace to my father's heart. I pitied her and took compassion on her because she is an orphan. If I deserted her now, she would have to return to her former life of a port prostitute. So I should like to take her up to the Capital to put her in the service of some noble, for in the Capital she would receive better treatment than at a port, even though she was forced to lead the same kind of life there. As I am shut up here, she is most probably in want. From whom can she obtain money for clothes and for her travelling expenses? I hope you will understand and provide her with these." Thus he deceived her by his appearance of sincerity.

Isora was highly delighted at these words and assured her husband that he need not have any anxiety about these matters. She sold some of her clothes in secret and obtained money from her mother with lying excuses and gave it all to Shôtarô. And when he had the money, he escaped from the house and took Sode up to the Capital.

Isora was grieved to find how greatly she had been deceived by her husband and in the end she fell dangerously ill. Both the Izawa family and the Kasadas were full of anger against Shôtarô and filled with compassion for her. They called in a doctor; they nursed her devotedly; but she became so ill that she was unable to take any nourishment at all and appeared to be on the point of death.

Meanwhile Sode and Shôtarô had gone to the house of one of her cousins named Hikoroku who lived in the village of Arai, Inami-gôri in the Province of Harima, where they intended to rest for a few days.

"You will not find the citizens of the Capital very hospitable," said Hikoroku to Shôtarô. "Stay with me here, and we will share our bowl of rice together and find some way of making a living for you."

Shôtarô was greatly pleased with the suggestion and decided to stay. Hikoroku, delighted to have found a new friend, rented the house next to his own for Shôtarô to live in.

Then Sode fell ill. It seemed at first to be nothing more dangerous than a cold, but soon she appeared to be in great pain and became as deranged as though she were possessed by an evil wraith. Shôtarô was greatly grieved that they had met with such a misfortune so soon after coming to the village and nursed her with devotion, often forgetting the time for his own meals. But she lay every night weeping bitterly and feeling as if an unbearable weight were pressing on her chest, though each morning she felt again as if nothing were wrong with her. Shôtarô's fear was that she was being tormented by the wraith of the wife that he had deserted and left behind at home.

Hikoroku consoled him in this fear. "Such a thing is impossible," he said. "I have seen people suffer so with fevers before. When the fever abates a little, she will forget her present sufferings as completely as if it had all been a bad dream."

Shôtarô was convinced by his words and trusted that she would recover. He continued to nurse her devotedly, but all his care proved useless; seven days later she died. Looking up to heaven and beating the ground with his hands, he lamented loudly, he wept bitterly and he prayed madly that he might die with her. Hikoroku tried all means of comforting him, and persuading him that he could not keep her body with him for ever, they cremated her corpse, collected her ashes, erected a tomb, set up a stone, called in a priest and offered earnest intercessions for the repose of her soul.

Shôtarô bowing low yearned after his beloved now in the Lower World, but there was no way to summon her spirit back to him. As he looked up to heaven, he thought of his old home, but it now seemed more distant from him than was the Kingdom of the Lower World. There was no road for him to advance; no way now, he felt, to retrace his steps. He slept by day, and the nights he spent in vigil at her tomb.

The grass grew denser and denser; the sad chirp of insects was to be heard. Shôtarô had thought that the autumn had brought sorrow only to him, but then he found erected at the side of Sode's grave a new tombstone; the same sorrow had come also to someone else. To this tomb he saw a woman stricken with great grief come to pray and offer food and water.

"How sad it is to see so young a person wandering thus in this lonely wilderness!" he said to her at last.

The woman turned to look at him. "Each night when I come here to pray, I find you always here before me. You have no doubt lost a beloved wife. When I think of what you must be feeling, I am overcome with grief," she said and wept bitterly.

"It is as you say," answered Shôtarô. "Ten days ago my beloved wife died. Left alone in this world, I come here to turn my mind from contemplation of my loneliness. I think that is the reason also for your presence here."

"The grave which I visit is that of my master. Ever since his burial, my mistress has grieved so sorely that she has fallen dangerously ill and I come here in her stead to offer flowers and incense."

"It is quite understandable that she has fallen ill. Who was your master? And where did he live?"

"My master was a noble of this Province, but, falsely accused, he was found guilty of a crime and lost his fief. And now his wife lives here in this lonesome spot! My mistress is well known for her great beauty even in the neighbouring provinces; it was through her beauty that he lost his fief and his house."

It was not because he was tempted by what the servant had said of her mistress and her beauty that he continued, "Is the place near here where she is living so forlorn? I would like to visit her and comfort her by the recital of my story as sad as her own. Please take me to her."

"Her house stands a little apart from the road along which you came. She is very lonely; visit her now and then. She will be looking forward to seeing you," the woman answered and led the way to the house.

They walked on a few hundred yards and came to a narrow path along which they went for a distance of about one hundred yards. Here she entered a thatched cottage set in a dark grove. The seven days old moon shone on a wretched bamboo door and by its light a small wild garden could be seen. Through the rents in the paper windows the dim, desolate light of a lamp shone. "Wait here a little while," the woman said and went in. The sliding doors were partly open and he could see the flickering light and the gleam of elegant bookshelves.

The woman came out to him again. "When I told my mistress that you had come," she said, "she told me to ask you in so that you could converse with one another across a screen. She will come forward to the edge of the verandah. Come in this way." She led him through the front garden round to the rear to the parlour, a fairly large room, the door of which was open just sufficiently for a person to pass through, the opening being covered by a low screen. He could see by the shabby bedclothes protruding that the Lady was lying there behind it.

Shôtarô faced in that direction. "I am very sorry to hear that in addition to your great loss you have been ill," he said. "As I have just lost my beloved wife, I have come, though it is rude of me to do so without waiting for an invitation, thinking that we might talk to each other of the loss we both have suffered."

The Lady pushed aside the screen a little way. "It seems strange to see you again," she said. "I warn you of a heavy retribution to come."

He looked at her in amazement and saw that it was his wife Isora whom he had left behind at home. Her face was very pale, her lifeless eyes were dreadful to see and the hand she held out towards him was white and thin.

He cried out in a loud voice and fell as if dead.

When he returned to his senses, he saw through half-opened eyes that the house was really an ancient oratory in the wilderness and that the only occupant was a black image of Buddha that stood there solitary. Guided by the barking of dogs in the distant village, he hastened home and related all that had happened to Hikoroku.

"Impossible!" exclaimed Hikoroku when he had heard all the story. "You must have been bewitched by a fox. When one's heart is filled with dread, then one is liable to attack by those deceiving *kami*, the fox and the badger. When a man of your feeble spirit is overwhelmed with sorrow, he must pray to Buddha and the *kami* that his heart may be brought to peace. Having purified yourself by bathing in cold water, go to the honoured necromancer who dwells in the village of Toda and ask him to give you a charm against them."

Thus persuaded, Shôtarô went to the necromancer and related the whole of his story so that he might have his future foretold.

"Calamity pursues you still," the necromancer then said. "It will not be easy to avert it. Even though the evil thing has already caused the death of your beloved, the curse has not yet been dispelled and your own days are numbered. The one who is working this evil left this world seven days ago; you will therefore be in danger for forty-two days more. You must seclude yourself within doors and fast and abstain from all things unclean for that space of time. If you obey my commands, then it is possible for you to escape the death which encircles you, but if you make even the slightest deviation from them, you cannot escape the calamity."

So the necromancer gave him strict instructions and taking a brush he wrote characters in the ancient seal pattern all over Shôtarô's body even to his hands and feet and wrote many charms on paper in red. "Paste these charms on every door in the house," he said, "and offer earnest prayers to Buddha and the *kami*. Do not err lest you bring about your own death."

With mingled joy and dread, Shôtarô returned to his house, and on every window and door he pasted these charms and then began his period of abstinence and seclusion.

At midnight that night a whispering and yet dreadful voice was heard to curse and to say, "He has pasted a holy charm here," and no further sound was heard.

How long the night seemed then to Shôtarô in his terror at hearing this voice! As soon as morning dawned, with a feeling as of one returned from the dead, he knocked on the dividing wall between his own house and Hikoroku's and related to him through the wall all the events of the night. Now for the first time did Hikoroku consider the commands of the necromancer worthy of obedience, and that night he himself also sat up and waited for midnight. The wind blew through the pine trees as though it would overthrow them. Rain fell heavily also, and the night was so dreadful above all others that they began to call to each other through the dividing wall. Then about two o'clock, a red light shone through the paper window of the kitchen, and a voice cursed and cried, "He has pasted a charm on this window too." Hearing this dreadful voice at dead of night made Shôtarô's hair stand on end with fright, and for a while he lay as if dead.

Thus they spent the days and nights. When the day dawned, they talked over the events of the night; when night fell again, they longed for the dawn. The days seemed to them as long in passing as a thousand years. Every night the goblin that had been Isora went round the house or shrieked from the roof-ridge, and every night its angry voice grew more and more dreadful.

At last the forty-second night came. This being the last night, Shôtarô was even more careful than on the preceding nights. Then at last towards four o'clock, day began to break and Shôtarô felt as relieved as if he were waking from a long, evil dream. He called to Hikoroku who bent over to the wall and asked what was the matter.

"My period of purification and abstinence is now at an end," Shôtarô said. "I have not seen you for so long a time that I feel I must see you now and talk to you of all the sorrows and the dreadful experiences that I have undergone during this long time, so that my heart may be comforted. Please rise from your bed that I may come in to you."

Hikoroku was not over-circumspect. "There is nothing to fear now that dawn has come," he said. "Please come in."

Shôtarô's door was yet but half-open when from the neighbouring eaves a bloodcurdling cry arose. Hikoroku heard it and fell over backwards to the ground. Then, feeling that something very dreadful must have happened to Shôtarô, he rushed out into the road with an axe in his hand. They had been mistaken in thinking that the dawn had come; it was the pale and hazy light of the moon in mid heaven that shone around. A cold wind blew. Hikoroku could see that Shôtarô's door was wide open; he himself was not to be seen. He rushed to see whether Shôtarô had fled back into the house. He was not there; there was no place there where he could be hiding. Hikoroku then thought that perhaps he had fallen outside in the road and searched for him here and there in amazement and dread with the help of a lantern. The wall by the side of the open door was smeared with fresh blood which was trickling down to the ground. But neither Shôtarô's corpse nor even his bones were to be seen anywhere. By the light of the moon he could see something hanging on the edge of the eaves, and when he lifted up his lantern, he could see by its light that it was a man's queue. Nothing else was to be seen. His horror then was beyond the power of pen to describe.

When morning dawned, he searched the neighbouring moors and hills but he could find no further trace of him. He sent word of what had occurred to the Izawa family, who with bitter lamentation informed the Kasadas.

Thus wonderfully were both the prediction of the necromancer and the evil omen of the Kibitsu cauldron realized.

The Ghost Who Bought Candy
Retold by Hiroko Yoda

The city of Matsue, in far Western Japan, is a storied place, famed for its history and beauty. The placid Ohashi River flows through the heart of the city before emptying into grand Lake Shinji, a mirror-like expanse of grey ringed by low peaks. But once the sun sets and the moon wheels up into the night sky, strange things can happen, and sometimes do.

Not far from the banks of Lake Shinji, there is a Buddhist temple called Daio-ji. Of the cemetery there a strange story is told. Once there was a little penny-candy shop selling *mizu-ame*, a sugar-syrup with rich golden-amber hue, made of sweet malt. This was a common and popular treat in those times of old, especially among children, who loved to scoop the sticky substance out of small bowls with a wooden chopstick.

Very late one evening, far after normal hours, came a rapping at the shop's door. The shopkeeper, an elderly man who had served the community for many years, was surprised to have a visitor. This was the hour known in traditional Japanese timekeeping as *ushimitsu-doki*, 'the time when even plants and trees sleep.'

He was even more surprised by the figure darkening his door. His normal customers were children. But this was a grown woman, frail and wan. Even stranger was her kimono, bone white, of the sort used only for the deceased in funerals.

While her dress was unusual, her presence at a candy shop was not. In those days, it wasn't uncommon for mothers to use *mizu-ame* syrup to quiet their babies when their milk wasn't available. *Poor thing*, he thought. *Her baby must be keeping her up. Poor things both.*

The woman apologized for bothering the old shopkeeper after hours, and requested a little *mizu-ame*. From a sleeve she produced a single *rin*, the smallest denomination of coin, only enough to afford the tiniest amount of the sweet stuff. He agreed, of course, pouring a measure of syrup into a little bowl, which he let her take along with the candy. The woman thanked him in the faintest of voices, then bowed like withered grass. Holding the little bowl close to her breast, she turned and left, disappearing into the darkness.

Night after night this scene repeated. The woman would arrive at a late hour, always purchasing just one *rin* worth of syrup. The shopkeeper never complained; the poor lady was so thin and drawn, he could hardly refuse. As this went on, he began to wonder if she needed help. One night, he kindly asked after her health. But she didn't reply, only thanking him again before turning and vanishing into the shadows.

This time, however, the old man decided to follow the strange woman. He kept his footsteps quiet and his distance enough so as not to be noticed. Down the road he followed her, then around a corner. The path took her away from the area where the townsfolk lived. She seemed to be heading towards the local temple. Sure enough, she ducked in through a side entrance at the temple's gate. The shopkeeper scurried to catch up and slipped through just behind.

But the woman in white didn't head for the temple proper. Her path led straight to the cemetery. The night closed in around her like black ink. The old man was terrified. He turned and ran, practically sprinting back down the path, through town, and to the safety of his home and store.

The next night the woman came again. But this time, she didn't ask for syrup. Rather, she beckoned to the man to join her. He followed her, and along the way called upon some friends and neighbours to join. Before long a small group had formed. They ended up at the same temple that the shopkeeper had visited the night before: Daio-ji. The woman in white led them through the gate and into the darkness of the cemetery. And then, upon reaching a certain grave, she vanished into thin air.

The group was too stunned to react. But then a cry broke the silence. It sounded like a baby, but muffled, as though issuing from the ground beneath their feet. The men hurried for shovels and excavated the grave. Inside they found a coffin that looked almost new. They pried off the top and peered inside. The flicker of lantern-light illuminated the face of a baby, smiling and laughing. It was being held tightly in the arms of a corpse dressed in funeral white. Beside the pair they spotted a little cup of *mizu-ame* – the same the shopkeeper had given the woman in white.

It transpired that the mother had been declared dead and prematurely buried. Her child was born inside the coffin. She died inside and could not feed her newborn. Yet her soul could not bear to see her baby die in darkness and hunger. So it came forth as a ghost. In times of old, it was customary to bury the dead with a few coins: the fare to pay the ferryman across the river to the realm of the dead.

But instead of leaving the mortal plane, the woman spent her fare on sustenance for the baby, keeping it alive long enough to be discovered. What happened to the woman's soul after that, none can say. But one thing is certain. A mother's love never fades – even in death.

Biographies
& Sources

Ueda Akinari

Shiramine; The Blue Hood; The Cottage in the Wilderness; The Kibitsu Cauldron

(Originally published in English in *Monumenta Nipponica*, 1938/41/66. *See* Dale Saunders *and* Wilfrid Whitehouse.)

Ueda Akinari (1734–1809) is widely regarded as one of the most influential Japanese writers of all time. Adopted at the age of four by a wealthy merchant, Akinari would follow in the footsteps of his late father after inheriting the family business, although he would prove to be a rather ineffective businessman. It was during this unhappy period that Akinari began publishing his first literary works under the pseudonym Wa Yakutaro, writing in the *ukiyo-zōshi* style that was popular at the time. After a fire destroyed his business, Akinari began studying medicine, and it was around this time that he also published the work for which he is mostly widely known: *Ugetsu Monogatari*, a collection of tales written in the *yomihon* style and focusing on the supernatural – a subject he had been fascinated by since childhood. Towards the end of his life, Akinari wrote a second collection of *yomihon* tales, *Harusame Monogatari*, which was published almost a century after his death at the age of 76.

Lafcadio Hearn

Furisodé to *Mujina*

(Originally published variously in *Glimpses of Unfamiliar Japan*, 1894; *In Ghostly Japan*, 1899; *Shadowings*, 1900; *Kottō: Being Japanese Curios, with Sundry Cobwebs*, 1902, *Kwaidan: Stories and Studies of Strange Things*, 1903)

After being abandoned by both of his parents, Lafcadio Hearn (1850–1904) was sent from Greece to Ireland and later to the United States where he became a newspaper reporter in Cincinnati and later New Orleans where he contributed translations of French authors to the *Times Democrat*. His wandering life led him eventually to Japan where he spent the rest of his life finding inspiration from the country and, especially, its legends and ghost stories. Hearn published many books in his lifetime, informative on aspects of Japanese custom, culture and religion and which would have great influence on future folklorists and writers. Standout examples of Hearn's output include *Glimpses of Unfamiliar Japan* (1894), *Kokoro: Hints and Echoes of Japanese Inner Life* (1896), *Japanese Fairy Tales* (1898, and sequels), *Shadowings* (1900), *Kottō: Being Japanese Curios, with Sundry Cobwebs* (1902) and *Kwaidan: Stories and Studies of Strange Things* (1903). In 1891 Hearn married and had four children but later died of heart failure in Tokyo in 1904.

Grace James

The Strange Story of the Golden Comb

(Originally published in *Japanese Fairy Tales*, 1910)

Grace James (1882–1965) was born in Tokyo to English parents. Growing up in Japan until the age of twelve when her family moved back to England, James was fascinated with Japanese culture and became a Japanese folklorist. She published retellings of traditional stories in her collection *Japanese Fairy Tales* (1910) and wrote about her experiences of Japan in her memoir *Japan: Recollections and Impressions* (1936). James was also an author of children's fiction including the *John and Mary* series.

Tsuruya Namboku IV

Yotsuya Kaidan ('*Kwaidan*' in Benneville's version)

(Benneville's adaptation used here, originally published in English in *The Yotsuya Kwaidan, or O-Iwa Inari*, 1917)

Born Ebiya Genzō in Nihonbashi (now Tokyo), the playwright later to be known as Tsuruya Namboku IV (1755–1829) was renowned for his work in the field of *kabuki*, with a particular focus on plays featuring supernatural elements. After studying for many years under the dramatist Sakurade Jisuke I, he would take the role of chief playwright for the Kawarazaki Theatre in 1801, and assume the professional name Tsuruya Namboku IV ten years later in 1811. Over the course of his lifetime, Namboku would write more than 120 plays, including *Sakurahime Azuma No Bunshō* and *Yotsuya Kwaidan*, the latter of which remains one of the most influential works of fiction to emerge from Japan.

Yei Theodora Ozaki

The Spirit of the Lantern, The Badger-Haunted Temple

(Originally published in *Romances of Old Japan*, 1920; *Japanese Fairy Tales*, 1908)

The translations of Japanese stories and fairy tales by Yei Theodora Ozaki (1871–1932) were, by her own admission, fairly liberal ('I have followed my fancy in adding such touches of local colour or description as they seemed to need or as pleased me'), and yet proved popular. They include *Japanese Fairy Tales* (1908), 'translated from the modern version written by Sadanami Sanjin', and *Warriors of Old Japan, and Other Stories* (1909).

Dale Saunders

The Blue Hood

(Originally published in English in *"Ugetsu Monogatari", Or Tales of Moonlight and Rain*, by Ueda Akinari, translated by Dale Saunders, *Monumenta Nipponica*, vol. 21, no. 1/2, 1966, pp. 171–202. Reprinted courtesy of *Monumenta Nipponica*, Sophia University, Tokyo.)

Dale Saunders (1919–95) was an American scholar of Japanese Studies, Romance Languages and Literature, and East Asian civilization. After earning degrees from Western Reserve University, Harvard and University of Paris, he went on to teach at Harvard, Boston University, University of Paris, International Christian University in Tokyo and University of Pennsylvania. In addition to his teaching and scholarship, he is known for his translations such as that featured here, as well as of modern Japanese literature by authors such as Abe Kōbō and Mishima Yukio, and works into French, such as *A History of Japanese Literature: From the Manyoshu to Modern Times* by Shūichi Katō.

Richard Gordon Smith

Ghost Story of the Flute's Tomb to *The Spirit of the Willow Tree*

(Originally published in *Ancient Tales and Folklore of Japan*, 1908)

Richard Gordon Smith (1858–1918) was a British naturalist and sportsman. He travelled widely throughout East and Southeast Asia, spending considerable time in Japan. Living in Kyoto for many years, Smith recorded Japanese folk tales and detailed observations of nature and life in Japan. His collection *Ancient*

Tales and Folklore of Japan was published in 1908. Smith also collected animal and plant species, many of which had been previously unknown to science. His diaries were posthumously published as *Travels in the Land of the Gods: The Japan Diaries of Richard Gordon Smith* (1986).

Marian Ury

How the Lute Genjō Was Snatched by an Oni; How a Woman Who Was Bearing a Child Went to South Yamashina, Encountered an Oni, and Escaped; How the Hunters' Mother Became an Oni and Tried to Devour Her Children

(Originally published in English in: Ury, Marian. *Tales of Times Now Past: Sixty-Two Stories From a Medieval Japanese Collection.* Ann Arbor, MI: University of Michigan Center for Japanese Studies, 1993. Reprinted courtesy of the University of Michigan Press.)

Born in Chicago, USA, Marion Ury (1932–95) was a professor of comparative literature at the University of California, specializing in medieval Japanese works. Ury held a doctorate in Oriental Languages and was the author of numerous articles on the subject, along with volumes of classic poetry and stories she had translated, such as *Poems of the Five Mountains* and *Tales of Times Now Past*.

Wilfrid Whitehouse

Shiramine; The Cottage in the Wilderness; The Kibitsu Cauldron
(Originally published in English in *"Ugetsu Monogatari", Or Tales of a Clouded Moon*, by Ueda Akinari (1739–1809), translated by Wilfrid Whitehouse, *Monumenta Nipponica*, vol. 1, no. 1, 1938,

pp. 256–54, vol. 1, no. 2, 1938, pp. 549–57 and vol. 4, no. 1, 1941, pp. 184–91. Reprinted courtesy of *Monumenta Nipponica*, Sophia University, Tokyo.)

Wilfrid Whitehouse is best known for his translations of Japanese literature. Among his most famous works was the first English translation of Uedo Akinari's *Ugetsu Monogatari*, which was published in an academic journal titled *Monumenta Nipponica* in 1938 and 1941. Other works translated by Whitehouse include *Lady Nijo's Own Story* and *The Tale of the Lady Ochikibo*.

Hiroko Yoda

Introduction and *The Ghost Who Bought Candy*

A native of Tokyo, Japan, Hiroko Yoda is a translator, writer, folklorist, and president of AltJapan Co., Ltd., which specializes in bringing Japanese entertainment to the wider world. She is the co-author of the popular trilogy *Yokai Attack! The Japanese Monster Survival Guide*, *Ninja Attack! True Tales of Assassins, Samurai, and Outlaws*, and *Yurei Attack! The Japanese Ghost Survival Guide* (Tuttle, 2011). She is also the author of the upcoming *Eight Million Ways to Happiness* (Tiny Reparations, 2025). 'The Ghost Who Bought Candy' is her own adaptation of a classic Japanese folktale, once summarized briefly by Lafcadio Hearn but also told by many people throughout Japan.

A Selection of Fantastic Reads

A range of Gothic novels, horror, crime,
mystery, fantasy, adventure, dystopia, utopia,
science fiction, myth, folklore and more:
available and forthcoming from Flame Tree 451

Categories: Bio = Biographical, BL = Black Literature, C = Crime,
F = Fantasy, FL = Feminist Literature, G = Gothic, H = Horror, L = Literary,
M = Mystery, MF = Myth & Folklore, P = Political, SF = Science Fiction,
TH = Thriller. Organized by year of first publication.

1764	*The Castle of Otranto*, Horace Walpole	G
1786	*The History of the Caliph Vathek*, William Beckford	G
1768	*Barford Abbey*, Susannah Minifie Gunning	G
1783	*The Recess Or, a Tale of Other Times*, Sophia Lee	G
1791	*Tancred: A Tale of Ancient Times*, Joseph Fox	G
1872	*In a Glass Darkly*, Sheridan Le Fanu	C, M
1794	*Caleb Williams*, William Godwin	C, M
1794	*The Banished Man*, Charlotte Smith	G
1794	*The Mysteries of Udolpho*, Ann Radcliffe	G
1795	*The Abbey of Clugny*, Mary Meeke	G
1796	*The Monk*, Matthew Lewis	G
1798	*Wieland*, Charles Brockden Brown	G
1799	*St. Leon*, William Godwin	H, M
1799	*Ormond, or The Secret Witness*, Charles Brockden Brown	H, M
1801	*The Magus,* Francis Barrett	H, M
1807	*The Demon of Sicily*, Edward Montague	G
1811	*Undine*, Friedrich de la Motte Fouqué	G
1814	*Sintram and His Companions*, Friedrich de la Motte Fouqué	G
1818	*Northanger Abbey*, Jane Austen	G
1818	*Frankenstein*, Mary Shelley	H, G
1820	*Melmoth the Wanderer*, Charles Maturin	G
1826	*The Last Man*, Mary Shelley	SF

1828	*Pelham*, Edward Bulwer-Lytton	C, M
1831	*Short Stories & Poetry*, Edgar Allan Poe (to 1949)	C, M
1838	*The Amber Witch*, Wilhelm Meinhold	H, M
1842	*Zanoni*, Edward Bulwer-Lytton	H, M
1845	*Varney the Vampyre*, Thomas Preskett Prest	H, M
1846	*Wagner, the Wehr-wolf*, George W.M. Reynolds	H, M
1847	*Wuthering Heights*, Emily Brontë	G
1850	*The Scarlet Letter*, Nathaniel Hawthorne	H, M
1851	*The House of the Seven Gables*, Nathaniel Hawthorne	H, M
1852	*Bleak House*, Charles Dickens	C, M
1853	*Twelve Years a Slave*, Solomon Northup	Bio, BL
1859	*The Woman in White*, Wilkie Collins	C, M
1859	*Blake, or the Huts of America*, Martin R. Delany	BL
1860	*The Marble Faun*, Nathaniel Hawthorne	H, M
1861	*East Lynne*, Ellen Wood	C, M
1861	*Elsie Venner*, Oliver Wendell Holmes	H, M
1862	*A Strange Story*, Edward Bulwer-Lytton	H, M
1862	*Lady Audley's Secret*, Mary Elizabeth Braddon	C, M
1864	*Journey to the Centre of the Earth*, Jules Verne	SF
1868	*The Huge Hunter*, Edward Sylvester Ellis	SF
1868	*The Moonstone*, Wilkie Collins	C, M
1870	*Twenty Thousand Leagues Under the Sea*, Jules Verne	SF
1872	*Erewhon*, Samuel Butler	SF
1874	*The Temptation of St. Anthony*, Gustave Flaubert	H, M
1874	*The Expressman and the Detective*, Allan Pinkerton	C, M

1876	*The Man-Wolf and Other Tales*, Erckmann-Chatrian	H, M
1878	*The Haunted Hotel*, Wilkie Collins	C, M
1878	*The Leavenworth Case*, Anna Katharine Green	C, M
1886	*The Mystery of a Hansom Cab*, Fergus Hume	C, M
1886	*Robur the Conqueror*, Jules Verne	SF
1886	*The Strange Case of Dr Jekyll & Mr Hyde*, R.L. Stevenson	SF
1887	*She*, H. Rider Haggard	F
1887	*A Study in Scarlet*, Arthur Conan Doyle	C, M
1890	*The Sign of Four*, Arthur Conan Doyle	C, M
1891	*The Picture of Dorian Gray*, Oscar Wilde	G
1892	*The Big Bow Mystery*, Israel Zangwill	C, M
1894	*Martin Hewitt, Investigator*, Arthur Morrison	C, M
1895	*The Time Machine*, H.G. Wells	SF
1895	*The Three Imposters*, Arthur Machen	H, M
1897	*The Beetle*, Richard Marsh	G
1897	*The Invisible Man*, H.G. Wells	SF
1897	*Dracula*, Bram Stoker	H
1898	*The War of the Worlds*, H.G. Wells	SF
1898	*The Turn of the Screw*, Henry James	H, M
1899	*Imperium in Imperio*, Sutton E. Griggs	BL, SF
1899	*The Awakening*, Kate Chopin	FL
1899	*The Conjure Woman*, Charles W. Chesnutt	H
1902	*The Hound of the Baskervilles*, Arthur Conan Doyle	C, M
1902	*Of One Blood: Or, The Hidden Self*, Pauline Hopkins	FL, BL
1903	*The Jewel of Seven Stars*, Bram Stoker	H, M

1904	*Master of the World*, Jules Verne	SF
1905	*A Thief in the Night*, E.W. Hornung	C, M
1906	*The Empty House & Other Ghost Stories*, Algernon Blackwood	G
1906	*The House of Souls*, Arthur Machen	H, M
1907	*Lord of the World*, R.H. Benson	SF
1907	*The Red Thumb Mark*, R. Austin Freeman	C, M
1907	*The Boats of the 'Glen Carrig'*, William Hope Hodgson	H, M
1907	*The Exploits of Arsène Lupin*, Maurice Leblanc	C, M
1907	*The Mystery of the Yellow Room*, Gaston Leroux	C, M
1908	*The Mystery of the Four Fingers*, Fred M. White	SF
1908	*The Ghost Kings*, H. Rider Haggard	F
1908	*The Circular Staircase*, Mary Roberts Rinehart	C, M
1908	*The House on the Borderland*, William Hope Hodgson	H, M
1909	*The Ghost Pirates*, William Hope Hodgson	H, M
1909	*Jimbo: A Fantasy*, Algernon Blackwood	G
1909	*The Necromancers*, R.H. Benson	SF
1909	*Black Magic*, Marjorie Bowen	H, M
1910	*The Return*, Walter de la Mare	H, M
1911	*The Lair of the White Worm*, Bram Stoker	H
1911	*The Innocence of Father Brown*, G.K. Chesterton	C, M
1911	*The Centaur*, Algernon Blackwood	G
1912	*Tarzan of the Apes*, Edgar Rice Burroughs	F
1912	*The Lost World*, Arthur Conan Doyle	SF
1913	*The Return of Tarzan*, Edgar Rice Burroughs	F
1913	*Trent's Last Case*, E.C. Bentley	C, M

1913	*The Poison Belt*, Arthur Conan Doyle	SF
1915	*The Valley of Fear*, Arthur Conan Doyle	C, M
1915	*Herland*, Charlotte Perkins Gilman	SF, FL
1915	*The Thirty-Nine Steps*, John Buchan	TH
1917	*John Carter: A Princess of Mars*, Edgar Rice Burroughs	F
1917	*The Terror*, Arthur Machen	H, M
1917	*The Job*, Sinclair Lewis	L
1917	*The Sturdy Oak*, Ed. Elizabeth Jordan	FL
1918	*When I Was a Witch & Other Stories,* Charlotte Perkins Gilman	FL
1918	*Brood of the Witch-Queen*, Sax Rohmer	H, M
1918	*The Land That Time Forgot*, Edgar Rice Burroughs	F
1918	*The Citadel of Fear*, Gertrude Barrows Bennett (as Francis Stevens)	FL, TH
1919	*John Carter: A Warlord of Mars*, Edgar Rice Burroughs	F
1919	*The Door of the Unreal*, Gerald Biss	H
1919	*The Moon Pool*, Abraham Merritt	SF
1919	*The Three Eyes*, Maurice Leblanc	SF
1920	*A Voyage to Arcturus*, David Lindsay	SF
1920	*The Metal Monster*, Abraham Merritt	SF
1920	*Darkwater*, W.E.B. Du Bois	BL
1922	*The Undying Monster*, Jessie Douglas Kerruish	H
1925	*The Avenger*, Edgar Wallace	C
1925	*The Red Hawk*, Edgar Rice Burroughs	SF
1926	*The Moon Maid*, Edgar Rice Burroughs	SF
1927	*Witch Wood,* John Buchan	H, M
1927	*The Colour Out of Space*, H.P. Lovecraft	SF

1927	*The Dark Chamber*, Leonard Lanson Cline	H, M
1928	*When the World Screamed*, Arthur Conan Doyle	F
1928	*The Skylark of Space*, E.E. Smith	SF
1930	*Last and First Men*, Olaf Stapledon	SF
1930	*Belshazzar*, H. Rider Haggard	F
1934	*The Murder Monster*, Brant House (Emile C. Tepperman)	H
1934	*The People of the Black Circle*, Robert E. Howard	F
1935	*Odd John*, Olaf Stapledon	SF
1935	*The Hour of the Dragon*, Robert E. Howard	F
1935	*Short Stories Selection 1*, Robert E. Howard	F
1935	*Short Stories Selection 2*, Robert E. Howard	F
1936	*The War-Makers*, Nick Carter	C, M
1937	*Star Maker*, Olaf Stapledon	SF
1936	*Red Nails*, Robert E. Howard	F
1936	*The Shadow Out of Time*, H.P. Lovecraft	SF
1936	*At the Mountains of Madness*, H.P. Lovecraft	SF
1938	*Power*, C.K.M. Scanlon writing in *G-Men*	C, M
1939	*Almuric*, Robert E. Howard	SF
1940	*The Ghost Strikes Back*, George Chance	SF
1937	*The Road to Wigan Pier*, George Orwell	P, Bio
1938	*Homage to Catalonia*, George Orwell	P, Bio
1945	*Animal Farm*, George Orwell	P, F
1949	*Nineteen Eighty-Four*, George Orwell	P, F
1953	*The Black Star Passes*, John W. Campbell	SF
1959	*The Galaxy Primes*, E.E. Smith	SF

New Collections of Ancient Myths, Folklore and Early Literature

2014	*Celtic Myths*, J.K. Jackson (ed.)	MF
2014	*Greek & Roman Myths*, J.K. Jackson (ed.)	MF
2014	*Native American Myths*, J.K. Jackson (ed.)	MF
2014	*Norse Myths*, J.K. Jackson (ed.)	MF
2018	*Chinese Myths*, J.K. Jackson (ed.)	MF
2018	*Egyptian Myths*, J.K. Jackson (ed.)	MF
2018	*Indian Myths*, J.K. Jackson (ed.)	MF
2018	*Myths of Babylon*, J.K. Jackson (ed.)	MF
2019	*African Myths*, J.K. Jackson (ed.)	MF
2019	*Aztec Myths*, J.K. Jackson (ed.)	MF
2019	*Japanese Myths*, J.K. Jackson (ed.)	MF
2020	*Arthurian Myths*, J.K. Jackson (ed.)	MF
2020	*Irish Fairy Tales*, J.K. Jackson (ed.)	MF
2020	*Polynesian Myths*, J.K. Jackson (ed.)	MF
2020	*Scottish Myths*, J.K. Jackson (ed.)	MF
2021	*Viking Folktales*, J.K. Jackson (ed.)	MF
2021	*West African Folktales*, J.K. Jackson (ed.)	MF
2022	*East African Folktales*, J.K. Jackson (ed.)	MF
2022	*Persian Myths*, J.K. Jackson (ed.)	MF
2022	*The Tale of Beowulf*, Dr Victoria Symons (Intro.)	MF
2022	*The Four Branches of the Mabinogi*, Shân Morgain (Intro.)	MF
2023	*Slavic Myths*, Ema Lakinska (Intro.)	MF
2023	*Turkish Folktales*, Nathan Young (Intro.)	MF
2023	*Gawain and the Green Knight*, Alan Lupack (Intro.)	MF

2023	*Hungarian Folktales*, Boglárka Klitsie-Szabad (Intro.)	MF
2023	*Korean Folktales*, Dr Perry Miller (Intro.)	MF
2023	*Southern African Folktales*, Prof. Enongene Mirabeau Sone (Intro.)	MF

New Collections of Ancient, Folkloric and Classic Ghost Stories

2022	*American Ghost Stories*, Brett Riley (Intro.)	H, G
2022	*Irish Ghost Stories*, Maura McHugh (Intro.)	H, G
2022	*Scottish Ghost Stories*, Helen McClory (Intro.)	H, G
2022	*Victorian Ghost Stories*, Reggie Oliver (Intro.)	H, G
2023	*Ancient Ghost Stories*, Camilla Grudova (Intro.)	H, G
2023	*Haunted House Stories*, Hester Fox (Intro.)	H, G
2023	*Indian Ghost Stories*, Dr Mithuraaj Dusiya (Intro.)	H, G
2023	*Japanese Ghost Stories*, Hiroko Yoda (Intro.)	H, G

A TASTE FOR THE FANTASTIC

FLAME TREE offers several series with stories from the distant past to the far future, covering the entire range of imaginative literature and great works that shaped our world.

From the fireside tradition of oral storytelling, early written versions of mythology (such as Norse, African, Egyptian and Aztec) emerge in the majestic works of literature of the Middle Ages (Dante, Chaucer, Boccaccio), the Early Modern period (Shakespeare, Milton, Cervantes) and the classic speculative tales by way of Shelley, Stoker, Lovecraft and H.G. Wells.

You'll find too, early Feminist adventure fiction, and the foundations of Black proto-science fiction literature from the 1900s.

Our short story collections also gather new tales by modern writers to bring together the sensibilities of humankind from the past, the present and the future.

Find us in all good bookshops, and at *flametreepublishing.com*